LOYALTIES

LOYALTIES

—Book II—

SCRUPLES ON THE LINE:
A Fictional Series Set During the American Civil War

Evie Yoder Miller

RESOURCE *Publications* • Eugene, Oregon

LOYALTIES
Book II

Scruples on the Line: A Fictional Series Set During the American Civil War

Resource Publications
An Imprint of Wipf and Stock Publishers
199 W. 8th Ave., Suite 3
Eugene, OR 97401

www.wipfandstock.com

PAPERBACK ISBN: 978-1-7252-8235-3
HARDCOVER ISBN: 978-1-7252-8236-0
EBOOK ISBN: 978-1-7252-8237-7

Manufactured in the U.S.A.   SEPTEMBER 17, 2020

Contents

List of Illustrations

Maps

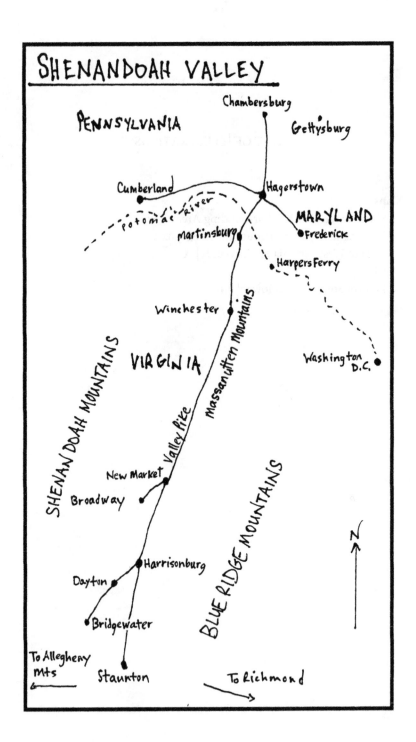

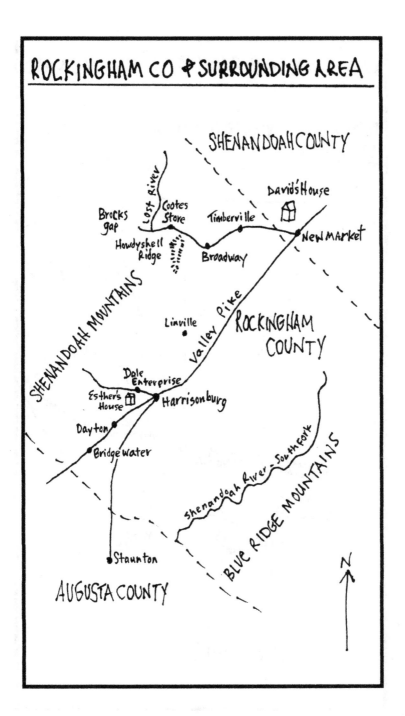

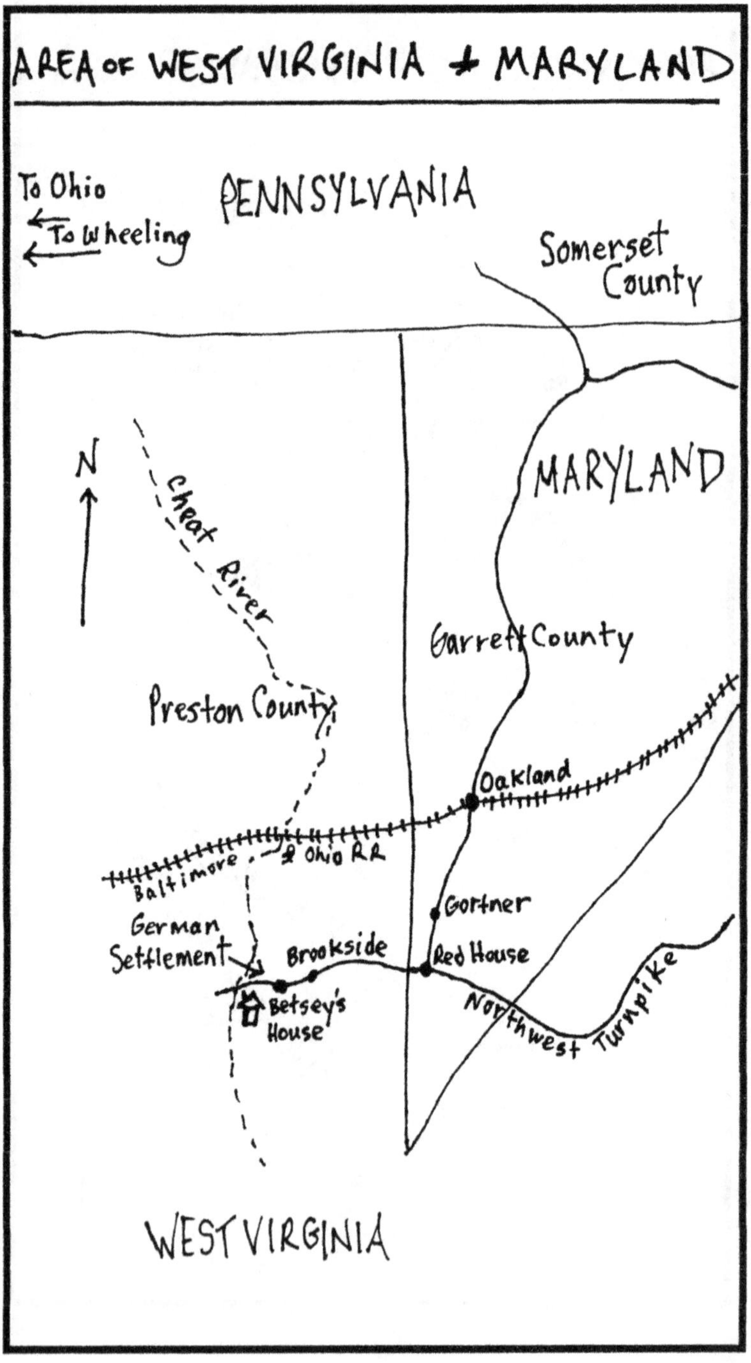

AREA OF WEST VIRGINIA & MARYLAND

To Ohio
To Wheeling

PENNSYLVANIA

Somerset County

N

Cheat River

MARYLAND

Garrett County

Preston County

Oakland

Baltimore & Ohio R.R.

German Settlement

Brookside

Gortner

Red House

Betsey's House

Northwest Turnpike

WEST VIRGINIA

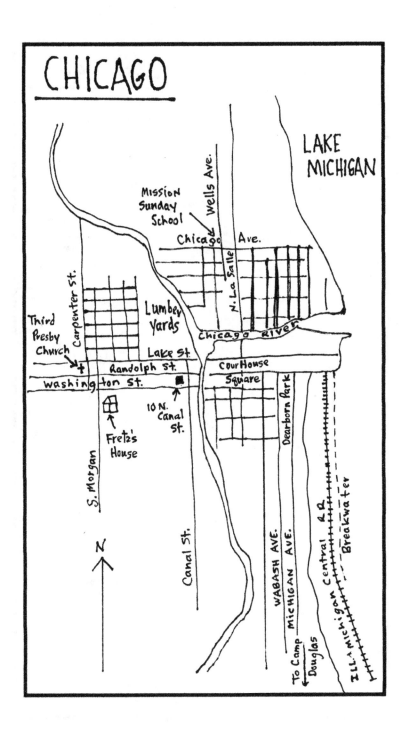

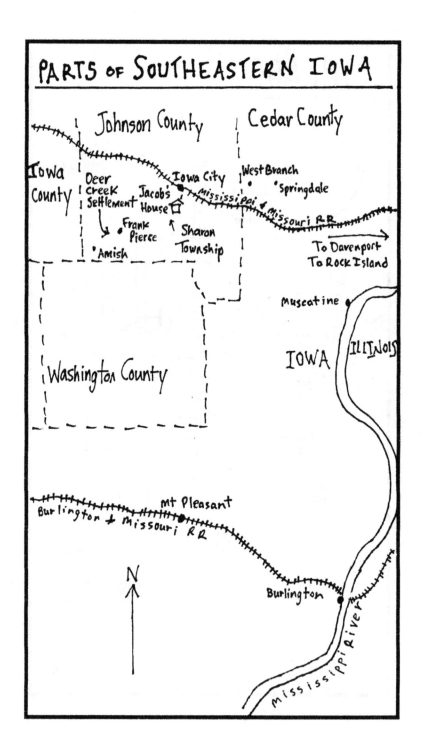

PARTS OF SOUTHEASTERN IOWA

Jacob Schwartzendruber Family
(Select characters in novel)

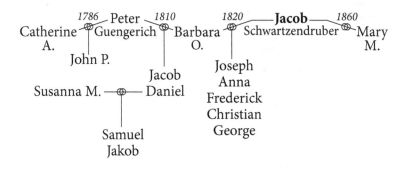

Catherine A. — *1786* Peter Guengerich — *1810* Barbara O. — *1820* **Jacob** Schwartzendruber — *1860* Mary M.

John P.

Susanna M. —⊕— Jacob Daniel

Joseph
Anna
Frederick
Christian
George

Samuel
Jakob

Fretz (John) Funk Family

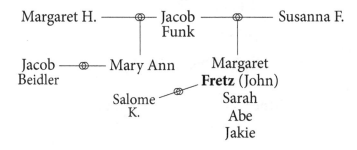

Margaret H. —⊕— Jacob Funk —⊕— Susanna F.

Jacob Beidler —⊕— Mary Ann

Salome K.

Margaret
Fretz (John)
Sarah
Abe
Jakie

Betsey Petersheim Family

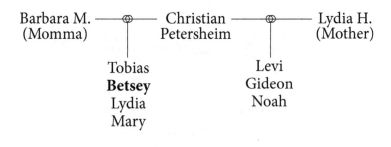

Barbara M. ——⊕—— Christian ——⊕—— Lydia H.
(Momma) | Petersheim | (Mother)

Tobias   Levi
Betsey   Gideon
Lydia   Noah
Mary

David Bowman Family

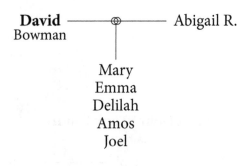

David ————⊕———— Abigail R.
Bowman |

Mary
Emma
Delilah
Amos
Joel

Esther Shank Family

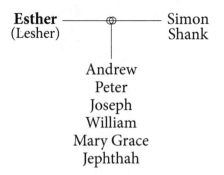

Esther ————⊕———— Simon
(Lesher) | Shank

Andrew
Peter
Joseph
William
Mary Grace
Jephthah

dedicated
to all who struggle with competing demands,
whether caught somewhere
between sharing bread or stones,
risking or retreating,
condemning or blessing

The name – of it – is "Autumn" –
The hue – of it – is Blood –
An Artery – upon the Hill –
A Vein – along the Road –

Great Globules – in the Alleys –
And Oh, the Shower of Stain –
When Winds – upset the Basin –
And spill the Scarlet Rain –

It sprinkles Bonnets – far below –
It gathers ruddy Pools –
Then – eddies like a Rose – away –
Upon Vermillion Wheels –

—EMILY DICKINSON
written in 1862

J. Fretz Funk — Chicago, August 1862

I'm no fool. A fork in the road requires a choice. A tug on a chicken wishbone means someone gets the bigger part. Two weights on a scale rarely balance.

Some of my best friends are volunteering. Phil! He signed up at the same time President Lincoln made this a total war on soldiers *and* citizens, calling for 300,000 more men. Six months ago, when Phil and I visited Camp Douglas on that cold sunny day, I thought I knew where he stood; I took his silence to mean the same as mine. Instead, we've moved in opposite directions. When we went to see the circus and menagerie late in May (what humbug!) he was already near to signing up. I'd been oblivious!

When Andy and Phil enlisted, I tagged along to the Chicago Board of Trade. I support them, as much as I can. Last month I spent a night at Camp Stokes with them. Ever since, I've been numb. I met all the boys—I can't remember nearly all their names—and slept on the ground in a tent with Phil and others.

Some of their horses hadn't been properly groomed. That afternoon I showed a city fellow named Ben Forswell how to run a hand down a horse's leg to get him to pick up his foot and lift a hoof to the back. Father taught me—the only sure way to clean out dirt. They'll get cuts and bruises, even abscesses, if not cared for. My knife with the stone hook impressed Ben, the way I could remove lodged pebbles. The men don't have time to do everything well, but I repeated: horses must be kept properly rasped.

Andy was on guard duty later that night, but before total darkness set in, we sat around a campfire—stoked to keep bugs away—and jawed awhile before prayers were said. In the flickering light I studied the faces of the men—all of them acknowledged Christians. Recruits obeying the call of the government and choosing a battery with others, determined to stay sober and use intelligent means on the battlefield.

It wasn't long before Ben, the man who has a wife and children in Chicago, put questions to me. "So what stops you?"

Phil jumped in. "Give him time, man."

1

He knows I don't lack for time. Most of the time when I'm away from the lumberyard, I wrestle. What should I do? For that matter, I have extra time at work because business is slower. Farmers are caught up in making money; city people are restless, waiting to see if the Illinois militia will initiate a draft.

But Ben persisted, as shrill as the insects: "Father Abraham's call didn't get through yet?"

I didn't want to sound like a coward; I don't think I am. "I'm not convinced—the use of violent measures. Not that I don't support you, if you feel this is what you're to do." I'm sure Ben's a good man. He probably doesn't know I gave Andy and Phil five dollars each to buy rubber blankets so they wouldn't need to feel wet ground underneath when sleeping.

A man with his front teeth missing spoke up. "Can't let the Rebels make progress. Why our men can't get to Richmond—" His unfinished sentence hung in the drifting smoke.

"McClellan." Ben spat the name. "The man's a dithering fool, talking back to his commander."

"Yeah, said he didn't have enough men; then didn't use all he had," Andy said.

"When Lincoln gets rid of him," another man said, tipping back on his camp stool, "we'll be in Richmond in no time. Knock those fool Rebs off."

"I've heard McClellan keeps to the West Point Code: honorable victory with minimal casualties," I said.

"You think war can be carried out with 'highest principles?'" Ben asked. "No pillaging or stealing, I suppose."

"By definition it's not a *just* war when it extends to unarmed persons," I said quietly.

Ben got up to tap embers and throw on another log. Flames leaped up in a quick blaze of heat. We'd worked well with horses, but now the stakes were raised.

"Abe's gonna take care of us," a high-pitched voice piped up, off to the right. "Not let guerrillas sneak up on our men. Can't let civilians whip us; have to be just as fierce. Make 'em fear what *we'll* do to *them*."

"That's been missing," another voice said. "No reason to be scared of us."

"My understanding—guerillas are armed," I said. "I meant innocent folks. Farmers and such, trying to carry on with their lives."

"No such thing." Ben's voice rose. "Your *innocent*. Farmers feed Rebels, right? Makes 'em the enemy, too."

A man across the way said, "Over 30,000 is a lot of lives."

I looked up quickly and nodded. "The Seven Days' Battles." I stopped. I didn't dare mention that a Confederate general had referred to the last battle there as murder, not war. Frontal assault.

Another man crowed. "Two-thirds of 'em, Rebels, though."

"All they care about is their capitol," a deep voice boomed to my left. The man idly tapped a stick in front of him.

I couldn't say the word *slaughter*. That word's been in the press ever since Seven Days'. Nor could I mention the rumor: President Lincoln's read a draft of an Emancipation Proclamation to his cabinet. I'm left waiting to see if his commitment follows.

"No way the South'll make it to Washington," Phil said. "Not set foot in *our* capitol." He kept pushing his curly hair—more unruly than I remembered—off his forehead.

"Bloody right," the man with the missing teeth said.

Didn't the men know the North's General Banks had been driven back in the Shenandoah Valley? Sent back to Harper's Ferry, crossing the river, and back to Williamsburg?

"Nine months to serve my country," Ben said. "That's how I look at it. Short time, when you think about it. Sure, I'll miss out—my children's birthdays. But this war won't take much longer. They can't keep losing men the way they have."

The high-pitched voice came again. "My wife understands—got me a good one. 'A righteous cause,' she says."

"Another place Fretz gets hung up," Phil said.

"My wife?" the same man asked.

We all laughed, but I didn't like Phil speaking for me again. Did he think me a voiceless lout? "Far too many have died without the nobler purpose," I said quietly.

"Slavery?" Ben asked. He said it the same way he might have spoken of a whorehouse.

"Unjust, the way the black man is treated like a beast." My voice stayed steady. "Lower than lower class." I didn't want to upset the boys. Some might believe there are only two kinds of men: loyal and disloyal.

"Well . . ." Ben took his time lighting his pipe. "Old Abe's smart. Let that take its course, not force things." Sweet tobacco aroma mingled with smoke. "Good things come with time."

"Got to admit, we know how to get things done," the deep-voiced stick-tapper said.

"Yeah. Be civilized about it," the high-pitched voice answered. "Don't have to enslave dark ones to keep them in their place. No need to make this more than it is."

I shuddered. What actions might he consider civilized?

It sounded like my old friend Randolph Smith, writing from eastern Pennsylvania, sending his picture. What a handsome fellow in army gear! Standing there with his belt and sash, his blue eyes smiling, one hand resolute on a pillar, the other hand behind his back. The uniform transformed him.

But his words sickened me. I couldn't repeat his slurs against a race of people. I wrote back: what did he mean about an infernal question? His answer: dark-skinned people are "a plagued sight better off in slavery than if they were free." I'd written also that Negroes should be able to enlist if they so desired. But he wrote, "If we have not men enough, *white* men, to uphold the starry flag, why then, let the country go to ruin." In the same letter he said he wouldn't give up on me: "the *nobility* of fighting for the rights of freedom."

I spend fitful nights in bed. Part of me says courage, generosity, and honor arise on the battlefield. But I can't balance those qualities with that other word—*slaughter.* Our hogs back home—lesser beasts—killed for food. But humans massacred for a righteous cause? Sacrificed to bring unity? All while keeping one group *in their place!* What has happened to our promising country? If I'm asked to live as people did of old—*an eye for an eye*—no honor in it.

I can't sleep. My half-sister Mary Ann apologizes the next morning. She tries to soothe baby Augustus, but his crying spells at night add to my disordered mind. What are we here for? What is the meaning of life, *my* life? My friends have a right to make their choices; I must make mine. We write letters back and forth; we won't turn from each other. Phil urges, "Go to the evening meetings as often as you can. Pray for us."

People understand what enlisting means; they're not blind. Plenty of sadness mixed with our repeated singing of "The Star-Spangled Banner." That reality came closer last night when I went to Joe's house. His family tried to manage their tears along with their pride. On the very last day Joe could volunteer for bounty, he signed up.

"Duty," he said. Joe, the last of my close Chicago friends.

I felt grief, but I couldn't argue. Phil, Andy, now Joe. I lifted my stein of lager beer. All the good times we've had together—the German Pleasure Gardens, the harmless wagers, the ladies. If anyone helped me adapt to Chicago, Joe did. But now, any morning, I could be sitting, eating my breakfast, and Phil could be bleeding to death, his legs lost to an artillery shell. I could be balancing the books at work—my own business: McMullen, Funk and Co.—not knowing Andy is feverish, dying of an infection in some poorly-staffed hospital.

Sure, I keep going to nighttime war meetings with their stirring speeches and calls to enlist. The Young Men's Christian Association meets in churches on Sunday evenings. At the close there's always the muster roll. Anyone can sign up, right there in the house of the Lord. My stomach churns. Religion and warfare rolled into one.

Out on the streets little boys play at war. I stop to talk. They're forming companies; they have banners and drums, just like their fathers and older brothers. Little more than a year ago, I regularly put on my black cape and marched with the Wide Awakes. Now I rarely go. My mind's awhirl. I can't blindly nod as thousands die. It's my country, but I can't support this action of my government.

Since my night at Camp Stokes, I've read of McClellan being replaced by General John Pope. He comes from the West with a reputation for cruelty. Maybe that's the fierceness the high-pitched fellow in camp is looking for. And General Grant, now the overall commander of the Federal armies; I don't trust him either. His pictures make him look like a cattleman, like he sleeps in his uniform. Another rumor circulates again: General Lee is nearing Washington with 250,000 men. Surrounded by uncertainty and outrageous numbers, how can anyone know what's true?

It's not a matter of fear, nor of failed duty. I see my mother standing quietly, surrounded by her Mennonite piety. What's going to happen? I'm twenty-seven. Will I stick around and push numbers on paper? I can't leave my partner, Jim, in the lurch. No, that's not it. It's my conscience. I can't get past: *Do harm to no one.* More important than not having a clearly stated goal of fighting to end slavery.

My new friend from back home, John Oberholtzer, still edits *Das Christliche Volksblatt*; we've never met, but we keep up correspondence. One of his ideas sears me: the individual conscience is the greatest source of authority. If so— If my government compelled me as a citizen—it has the right to do so—I'd have to take another look. But I'd likely ask for equivalency, not exemption from military demands.

One thing I won't do: flee to Canada. Not even with relatives there. People are crossing the border at great risk. The War Department put out an order earlier this month to arrest anyone trying to escape a possible draft. No one dare leave Chicago without proper papers. There's a tug with a six-pound cannon sitting at the harbor entrance; they search every vessel that goes out. Sixty were arrested one night at the Michigan Central Depot. Another time, a large steamer carrying stowaways was ordered back by telegraph to Milwaukee. If you're arrested, you're sent to Camp Douglas.

This thing called freedom—what is it? Elusive, never wholly pure. Everyone's restricted. Different degrees, of course; consequences. Will I get to choose?

That first time I came to Chicago, a Saturday morning in early April—how can it be only five years ago? I was all eyes. Leftover snow on the ground; eight tracks of rail, laid on timbers. The world's third largest railroad depot, platforms on both sides covering almost two acres. My first glimpse of waves from the big lake, sweeping up twenty feet high against the breakwater. And then a blast of biting wind from the northeast. Fierce, even in April.

Later when the dirty snow disappeared, the city looked like it was sitting in a swamp with planks forming streets and sidewalks. Mud everywhere. Like someone threw a wet rag in my face. Twenty-two years old when I left my home, parents, dearest girlfriend. So confident—and scared. Leaving home was only the beginning. I had to let Salome go, what with time and distance. All that had been trumpeted—wonderful opportunity—faded to a veneer, barely covering slime.

Now I understand: no promising situation comes without muck and cold. Dirt, even mud, is only matter out of place. But those irritants are minor, compared with the loathsome possibility that looms. If Lincoln's call for 300,000 isn't met by the fifteenth of this month, the numbers will be filled with a draft. Even Ross looks grim at work; he and his family have a new baby.

And Teddy, a fellow Sunday school teacher, has joined the army and sent a message for his boys. I passed along the first part: "Live as you know the Lord Jesus wishes all little boys to live." But I couldn't read the rest aloud: "If we don't meet again here on earth, we'll meet to sing praises in God's heaven." I could be brushing my horse while Teddy languishes, alone.

BETSEY PETERSHEIM — western Virginia, September 1862

Der Paep is fatt! The work team and wagon, gone too! Tobias said a strange man came to the woods and gave orders. "Go in, boy," the man said. Of a sudden, Poppa was somewhere, far away. We live on top of a mountain, but we could no longer see him anywhere. That was Thursday; this is Saturday. No one goes by on the road for us to "halloo" to. We are all alone, whilst the wind whistles. A big old pine tree went *whomp* in the woods behind our house.

We seven children huddle with Mother. She is beside herself. But not double, I have to explain to Mary. The little ones dare not go outside unless they tag with Tobias or me. We feed and brush Frank and Tom extra and hurry the cows. Tobias whispers, "It might be like what happened; they fetched Peter Schrock to work a week." If I ask more, Tobias acts sour. What if Poppa has to hide a long time, or run to Ohio like Mack and Muck?

Sometimes Mother sends Gideon to help me gather eggs. I do not need help—I am a big nine—but Gideon pesters Noah when cooped up inside. We hunt fast. The hens do not like Gideon; they squawk and flap about. We look both ways from the hen house before we make a dash back. If we see anyone, we are to scream. And be loud about it. Inside, Gideon chases Mary like a clucking hen and pulls her braids.

Tobias and I go together to empty chamber pots. One of us dumps and the other keeps watch. One time at dusk I saw a black bear staring from the bushes, but it turned and wobbled away. We ran back to the house fast. We have to empty more than usual, for we all have the runs. Levi has it bad and cannot hold himself. I do not know what will happen next, and no one can ask Poppa. One day takes forever.

Mother mumbles, "*En dunkler, finschderer Weg.*" She will not let Tobias ride Tom to Auntie Mommie's. "What good would it do to lose you, too?" Yesterday she sent us to the garden to yank onions and dig more potatoes. We did it lickety-split, but we did not clean the fork when done. Poppa's eyes would be sad; we know better how to do.

The first night Mother tried to sit up and keep watch. The lamp flickered. But when I peeked down from the loft again, I spied her head dropping. I tiptoed down the ladder and took her hand. She did not put on her nightgown; she did not fix her hair in a long braid but went straight to the rope bed. I waited, shivering in my nightgown; her long finger beckoned. I climbed in and she gripped my hand. It was winter ice. I let go and stayed stiff on Poppa's side. The lamp still flickered. The next night Lydia was allowed to sleep with Mother. Tonight will be Mary's turn.

"Will Levi and Gideon get turns?" I ask.

"It cannot go that long," Mother says. "Poppa will be back."

"Today?" Mary asks. Mother looks cross.

Noah has to keep to the cradle, except when he sucks. But he bangs on the sides, and Lydia is the only one who can quiet him. He pays no heed when I try to soothe. Tobias has slept on a pallet under the kitchen table both nights. Last night when I was in charge in the loft, Levi smelled bad. Mary had dropped right off. I listened for *schpuckich* noises and touched myself a little bit.

We did not hear drums all day yesterday. Not once. I patted Mother's shoulder and said, "*Sell is en Sege!*" She looked at me like she could not see me. I took my hand away quick. I am not a blessing. She sewed yarn around scraggly walnuts that had dropped. The little boys were allowed to roll the balls back and forth. But they do not roll straight and Gideon misbehaved. He threw a ball overhanded and knocked the tin pitcher to the floor. I sopped up the floor while Gideon had to sit on the wood box. He finally curled up and fell asleep with his thumb in his mouth. Mother said not to disturb.

Today she put us to doing double the Saturday work; it was worse than Auntie Mommie's bossing. We girls had to take everything out of the pantry, except the heavy bags. Mother did not call it fall cleaning, but I was to wipe the shelves clean, especially up high. I stood on a chair like at Auntie Mommie's and stretched to reach the corners. Lydia remembered how to put everything back exactly right, but Mother never came to check.

Then I had to scrub the floor again, because Levi let loose and his cloth could not contain him. I do not like scratchy floor boards on my bare knees. I went dragging to gather wet rags, but Tobias fetched clean water for me. Mother whistled her words: "The mare that does double work should be best fed." I stayed a slowpoke.

When we finished all the extras, I pretended to be the teacher of numbers. But the little boys would not sit still as they do for Poppa. Mother begged Tobias to think of something to do besides tussle and tear around the table. Levi cries if he does not win at I Spy. I asked Mother if we could have geography class and make a map with spoons and forks. She said "no!"

She sweeps and sweeps the floor. Sometimes she mumbles, "Higgle-dy-piggledy." Other times I hear "Wilderness, boogery vale." She has not combed her hair once. This noon when we held hands to say our prayer, Mother's eyes got extra red and Mary burst out crying.

Tomorrow is not a Sunday for our Amish church. We would not go anyway, because we have no way but on foot. We are to pray that Uncle Christian might come to protect us. "All you young'ns, think hard on him, that he might hear," Mother said.

"We need Jack to bark," Lydia said.

"Pfft!" Mother said. "That poor stray."

"Daniel Beachy could come to borrow a rake," I said. But it has not been so. There is no one to prevail against the coons in the corn. We will never make do without Poppa.

When Tobias and I did the milking again, I said, "I want Johnny Kline to come."

"That preacher man lives far away."

I did not tell Tobias, but I thought hard on Mack or Muck, our other surprise visitors, too. They would know what to do if they were here. But they might have walked into trouble with their secret talk. Even Mister— Poppa now calls him a runaway—would help, too, if his dark feet were not bad and the coast was clear.

Last night turned cool early, so Tobias and I had to fetch more wood before it was completely dark. We could not run with our loads, but neither did we dawdle. He is better than me at stacking on the porch. One time things went a-tumble. Noah cried out and Mother came to the door. Her lips stayed tight and her hair fell in *schtruwwelich* strands. She looked like a witch.

My friend Sarah told me about such; her big sister Mary had told her never to get on the wrong side of one. A wild one can put a hex on a horse or cow. Maybe a chicken or child, too.

"How do you know for certain," I asked, "whether a witch?"

"Throw a broom on the floor of a doorsill. A witch cannot step over."

Jacob Schwartzendruber — Iowa, September 1862

So much is contrary. I have seen too much in my life. At times I think I cannot go on. The war, the women. Emanuel! Even Caspar's distress with blockage. My deepest concern, though: ruptures in our Amish church. So often I must labor alone, misunderstood, while pouring out my heart and soul. My body falters, awakened at times by a too-rapid heartbeat. Over sixty years and now extra burdens.

We Amish have had to divide into two districts here in southeastern Iowa. The wagon load tilts. My son Frederick convinced me we had grown too large to meet in one home. In the summer we could gather in members' barns for adequate space, but that is not possible with the onset of cold weather. "Face it," he said, albeit kindly. So it is, our division runs between those of us who live in Sharon Township and those residing in the Deer Creek area of Washington Township. One week we meet here; the next, over there. I will go every Sunday, so long as health and weather permit. Too much hangs in the balance, for it to be left to the poisonous winds that blow.

Not only here in Iowa—my church fears go beyond. Back in June, the first week after Pentecost, they had a big to-do in a barn in Wayne County, Ohio, for four days. They wanted all ministers of Amish persuasion to attend. But the ones who planned this shindig did not consult with their brothers in Holmes County, their next-door neighbors! Only half—around seventy ministers I am told—attended. I spared myself the clatter of voices, but my letter was read.

Joseph Goldschmidt, our bishop from Henry County, made the trip; long ago he helped us organize our church here. After sending me the official written report, he came to talk last month and found me pulling weeds where Frederick wants more fencing.

Without delay I asked, "What was decided? Is there unity?"

Brother Goldschmidt hemmed and hawed. "A multitude of questions: whether to allow insurance, whether permissible to make likenesses."

"We must never innovate if the works and fruit thereof falsify the Word of God. Surely all could agree."

He spoke slowly. "Matters were kept orderly—a goodly show of Christian moderation and brotherly love. Just as the secretary has written up in the report."

"But was there agreement? One accord to remove all hindrances? We cannot have half-hearted weeding." I reached down to demonstrate—a firm, two-handed pull at the base of a horse weed. I steadied my breathing. "You know as well as I: to destroy a problem, you pull it up by the roots, not yank off part, cover it with dirt, and call that unity."

Joseph wiped at his brow. "Brethren were free to express disagreement. Everyone was listened to."

"But was there agreement—one heart and mind? Do not hedge."

"It is hard to put everything into words." Joseph tilted his head back and scratched under his bushy beard. "We stand firm on believer's baptism."

"Nor seek to spare! Those who push for division have not stopped. Am I right?"

He never said yes; he never said no. Nor was it clear whether forgiveness took place between the Elkhart and LaGrange congregations in Indiana—at odds already some seven years. Joseph digressed instead. "The ones who called this *Dieners-Versammlung* insist it is good to hold such a meeting every year. They mentioned the German Baptists holding their annual meeting for some time now. In response, our Amish brothers in Mifflin County, Pennsylvania have called for a gathering in their area next year."

Not once did the Brother show one iota of impatience about the proceedings. He seemed stumped, though, about how to explain the irregularity of referring to certain brethren as president and vice-president, even though such titles elevate. Only when I asked regarding guidance on the national emergency, could Joseph assure me, "Much unity, offering prayers for the suppression of the Rebellion."

If only that would help me be at peace about Emanuel. Our young man is gone, my failure on display. Last month he enlisted with the 22nd Volunteer Infantry of Union Forces. I do not know that members of his family blame me—his mother continues her disregard, ever since I made visit—but I hold myself responsible. He is the lost coin the woman in the Bible sweeps and sweeps the floor in search of. I could not reach him. It is not that we needed to ban him; he never joined.

Word is, he received a twenty-five dollar bounty for enlisting, plus a two dollar premium. Why? Why would he sign up? No one can explain. Not Frederick. Not my grandson Jakob. No military draft puts pressure here in Iowa; Emanuel was not forced. At age twenty-eight he is fully old enough to have counted the cost. It is what I feared already last fall—gravitating to false gods. Trifling with the commandment to love, not hate. Furthermore, his blood brother has gone back to Pennsylvania and enlisted there. How can the father, *der alter Henner,* allow such laxness!

Jakob knows some of what transpires among the young, but he has little to report about Emanuel; they ran with different friends. No explanation how a Captain Hall and a Captain John T. Jones from this area could dip into our own. This group in Iowa City that Emanuel joined is said to number twenty-six—Jakob called it a regiment—including four of the Fry boys, their father well-known, for he owns much land. They met at a place called Camp Pope, not far from here; folks are said to have flocked there every day to watch the boys drill with their wooden bayonets.

Now Emanuel and his friends are on their way to Missouri. They left Iowa City after midnight—even at that hour, hundreds reportedly saw them off—traveling on an assortment of boxcars, cattle cars, even open coal cars. They headed first for Davenport and from there took riverboats, although some say they proceeded by train. The mode of travel matters not. I cannot bear to think on Emanuel and these others. Exposed to evil, even committing with their own hands. Willingly looking death in the face at such a young age!

Everyone remembers what happened to the Coppoc brothers from these parts. First Edwin; then Barclay. All from being mixed up with that John Brown. Two young men, lost. Yes, it is not right for people with dark skin to be enslaved. But God will mete out punishment in His own good time. We are not to take killing into our own hands.

Mary asks again, "Why does this one lad trouble so much?"

I am dumbfounded—my woman's lapses. "Never neglect the one."

"Because of family?" she pesters.

I shake my head. "It is more than my Christian being married to Emanuel's sister. It is like unto *seeking* the hangman's hood. Joining scores of other misguided ones. Lost."

Mary's forehead wrinkles. "Are we not all lost souls?"

I shrink from her quick jab. "We can never know for certain, but we always seek cleansing." Her dark eyes stay fixed on me. "Have I not preached 'Whoso sheddeth man's blood, by man shall his blood be shed'? What could be clearer than the book of Genesis, chapter nine? Nothing good can come for this young man!"

"You will wear yourself out," she says.

I return her stare.

"Taking responsibility for all."

"I—surely you know, this task has been given. The call to shepherd."

She gets up, clicking her teeth.

I refrain from saying more. This woman given to me, my second wife. Barbara would never have . . . But the young, we have not instructed as we ought. Too busy clearing land, building bigger houses. Hoodwinked by an extended time of peace—fifty years, since 1812. Too many of our youth do not hear the German language at home anymore; they do not understand what is being preached against warfare.

Not only Emanuel! Brother Goldschmidt said young Amish men in Somerset County—where my grandson Samuel wants to go!—entered the Union army last spring. Others—fathers in the East with sufficient wealth— bought substitutes for their sons.

I asked Joseph, "Does that money not allow someone else to kill in our stead? Have we become dulled?"

His eyes widened. "It did not come up."

Yes, of course, that is the pattern begun among us in Europe: pay a tax to be excused from military involvement. But in this country, it has become a much larger tax, though for the same benefit. Too much money! That might be the true meaning of my dream with the wagon tilting. We will become poor, appeasing a government bent on evil methods. I fear far more than monetary poverty.

When I bring up my concerns to Samuel, Jakob's brother, he says the members back East in Elklick Township keep more to our nonresistant stand than do those at the Glades. How does he know for certain? Yes, there was always a hard element at the Glades back in Somerset—no regard for the Indian or the Negro. But Samuel cannot know fully what awaits him. He must postpone this search for a suitable woman. If only I could convince him to stay. If only everything were in order with our church here.

I am reduced—one upheaval after another. Not only our dividing into two meeting groups. Some say I am too strict; others, like Joseph Keim, say I am too loose. How can both be true? Some say we should tolerate new things; others object and say not to rush to achieve peace at any price. Contrary winds! How am I to hold the reins loosely, when I have been called to hold tight? I dare not seek the middle way; only the right way will do.

Lately, this Keim brought charges to my door. Colored dishes! I knew Mary's pieces might cause trouble. I had warned her. She does not know how word got out; nor has she been charitable. Her dark eyes flashed, as she brought a pan of apples and sat near me. "He should look to his own mote! What difference, pottery or plain glass?"

"He reminds us not to be puffed up. Not to count ourselves better than others."

"I have not fallen prey. Have you?" She made no pause in her apple peeling; I would cut myself if I wielded a knife as fast as she. "Are we to retrieve your tin dishes from the woodshed?"

"It is a matter of the heart. How you count your brother."

"So it is." But she threw more sparks. "I do not ask Keim to eat from one or the other, if he thinks one way would mar his fellowship or disrupt his digestion." She hesitated. I have come to know that look, the rare times when she cogitates. "It would not be this way in Indiana."

I gripped the arms of my rocker.

"Tell me. This Joseph Keim." She said his name, as if he were a wormy apple in her hand. "Does he not have a horse? Several nice horses?"

I closed my eyes and waited. When she outwaited me, I said, "Yes, Keim has a mare. A fine one with dark black coat. And others, well-groomed."

"He should be reduced to a nag! Should he not? A scraggly, dusty brown, slow one. Perhaps a donkey? The better to go about with the proper humility. Is that not so?"

Such response from a woman! I was forced to defend the man I am often at odds with. "He is a Minister of the Book and until such time as he has erred in holding forth the Word, he is to be held in honor. Look inward, Woman. I will speak with Keim and tell him to do the same."

A flurry of apple seeds spilled to the wooden floor. Mary sniffed but said no more.

I know she has pulled out her grandmother's six pottery plates on occasion, wrapped in paper and stored in a box under the bed. She runs her fingertips over the deep red and lighter pink of the painted rosebuds. But she insists she has shown no one. Still, she knows how words can spill, unintended. I must compel her to better discipline with the tongue. It may not be entirely fair, but obedience starts nearest the tree.

I have not had to counsel Mary regarding apparel. She has been entirely circumspect, even while other women in the church fall prey to pride over ruffles on their bonnets. And when I come near to despair, Mary is kind to console. One night she said, "We do *not* have differences on *all* matters."

"That is so; we are not like Ohio, overrun with cuffs showing up, buttons on overcoats."

"Nor do we have troublemakers over baptizing in a stream."

"True." The floor creaked beneath our rockers.

"And people follow common sense. It is too close for first cousins to marry," she said.

"So it is. And the documents from the Old Country back up what I have always said: There must be a probationary period before a deacon to the poor can become a full deacon."

"Yes, yes, you have held firm."

"But so many differences!" My voice rose in spite of my best efforts. "How many times must I remind: the utter falseness of members partaking of the bread and cup when they have not conformed to regulations? The last thing I want is to have to prohibit Communion altogether, but if dissension continues . . ." I could not say more of the dread that seizes me.

Mary jabbed her needle into her red pin cushion and placed an arm on mine.

I shook my head. "Some on The Bench even want to include unbaptized young people in our counsel meetings. That would not have worked with Emanuel."

"Your preaching has not been in vain. Do not let the Devil—" At that, Mary bent again over her sewing. She does not know—much, much she does not know.

Brother Goldschmidt had admitted another thing; he was the one who asked at the big meeting how stringently we should practice avoidance when a brother has been cut off from the body of believers. That very issue on which our founder, Jacob Amman, separated from other Anabaptists, came up again in Ohio! Joseph's exact words: "Should the ban be applied only for partaking of the Lord's Supper or used also in everyday affairs?" A bishop from Iowa manifesting uncertainty whether the ban should be observed in the case of married couples, a husband against a wife!

I had wasted no words with him that day. "*Not* shunning defiles the ones *not* observing the commandment."

He nodded, but his eyes blinked fast. "Some have asked for more freedom in the application."

"One sad case in Ohio, the ban wrongfully carried out against a brother, cannot mean we are to allow freedom from the rule. We cannot be of two minds."

He sighed and, at long last, seemed in agreement. But later I wondered again. It is a hard thing, not to know whether to trust a brother.

All these pressing issues troubling our church. And now, compounded by Caspar! I am not spared the basest of problems. My beloved horse, getting on in years. He never gave complaint until suddenly it dawned: he was unable to remove his waste. Such discomfort due to my negligence!

I ransacked my papers until I found Christian Engel's remedy for treating a constipated horse. What a blessing! I caught the problem before even colder weather set in, and I had kept solid notes on what North American plants to use in the treatment.

Mary wanted to hear nothing of the ordeal of colic treatment. So I proceeded alone and found cedum growing in the rock wall behind our house. I cooked it in watered wine and added oil. I could not have managed the next step without Jakob's help; he first shaved below the tail. While I rubbed the concoction on Caspar's hind end, Jakob hummed soothingly. After some bumbling, I applied the anal crease with a sweet cream and could feel inside. Just as I thought, I found the offending nodule, and Caspar allowed me to massage it.

Afterwards, Mary and I had ourselves a little chuckle. "You feel as much relief as Caspar." Yes, sometimes she still knows how to soothe. Two years now, living as man and wife. In a matter of hours, she can go from asking questions that confound—her tongue sharp as her knife—to letting her hair down. She says it is all part and parcel. "Loosen yourself." Her touch stirs the young man within, even if I cannot always complete the task. As she says, it is good I am not alone.

For now, we carry on as best we know how. I put her confusing words aside and have resigned myself to the bright red pin cushion. When I stand to wash, stooped in my nakedness, I give thanks for these legs and arms, even though my knees wobble and my wrists give out at the butter churn. Until the Lord calls me home, I must continue giving faithful oversight as bishop, even to the two Sunday gatherings, even for those who grow restless.

BETSEY — western Virginia, September 1862

Der Paep is widder do! After dark last night Poppa came again, but not to frighten. There was so much commotion, none of us could sleep half right. When Mother heard his voice outside the door, she fell in a heap, rushing from her chair. Tobias had barred the door—same as the other six nights. He scrambled to look to Mother's head, and Poppa had to rap again. Tobias yelled for me to undo the hook; I had been tossing but not asleep.

We children screeched and hugged Poppa, then each other. Mother stayed sitting on the floor, crying and rocking, gasping for breath, her hands tender to the bump on her forehead. No one paid Noah heed until he screamed with a shrillness, louder than ever from Gideon.

Finally, things settled right side up, and I fried potatoes for Poppa. He looked raggedy. He wanted extra butter on his spuds, just as we had been eating, with or without eggs. We have not gone out to bake bread once these days. Potatoes and eggs, every meal. Onions and turnips, too. Tobias ate again with Poppa, and no one put a stop. Lydia thought to bring Mother her shawl, and she quieted her wail at the table: "Lost to us; so long lost to us."

Poppa left his spuds and wrapped his arms around her again. He squeezed so much, I thought her chest might burst. Mary tried to wiggle inside to be a part, and Levi tugged on Poppa and said like an echo, "Lost?" Noah shrilled again.

"No, not lost," Poppa said. "Nor found. Set loose to walk. My own two feet." He pulled out his large handkerchief, crusty from a week, and blew hard like a goose honking. "We may never see the wagon again, nor the work horses."

"No!" Tobias and Mother said together.

"Stopped on the road that day," Poppa said.

"Exactly so." Tobias wiped butter juice off his chin with his night sleeve. "The last load of oak, the downed tree."

"Yes, the north woods," Poppa said.

"*Ferwas hoscht net—?*" Mother started to ask.

Poppa ignored her. "Made to haul for the gray coats. Another man from Brookside, obliged to do the same. But not allowed exchange; kept separate."

"What did you haul?" Tobias asked.

"Supplies," Poppa said. "Shoes and grain. The gray men want things in place before winter. A rough bunch— No stopping short. 'Wreck cars,' they said, gleeful."

"But our team?" Tobias asked.

Poppa's eyes got red.

Mother put her finger to her mouth. "No more, Crist. We have heard enough."

Poppa roused from wiping his nose again and looked around. "My children—safe. My good woman. You are the ones, cannot be replaced." We hugged and kissed again. Tobias picked up Noah and jiggled his legs, even placed a big smacker on him. And Levi—I kissed and forgave all his messes.

Mother said naught of Gideon's naughtiness. Earlier that day, he had pulled on Frank's tail. I had scolded, but a minute later he did it again, a quick jerk.

"Gideon, stop! You know not to tease. Never stand behind a horse!" I could not turn my back or he would have tried again. "I will put you in the pig pen," I said, but he giggled and ran away.

When I tattled to Mother, she sighed but said nothing. Now she does not seem to remember.

Poppa walked to the big clock and smiled that Tobias had kept it wound. He touched the butt end of his rifle above the hearth and tapped his hand to his heart. "*Gott is gut.*"

When I was finally on my pallet in the loft again and Tobias had lugged his bedding up the stairs, I watched jagged moonlight squeeze between tiny cracks of beams. Shadows moved on spider legs across heavy timbers. Sleep would not fall; this time I touched myself from gladness. Poppa will know how to fend, if Mother shows more *schpuckich* signs again.

Words like "hauling," and "Kingwood," and "Cumberland" drifted upstairs. Those must be places farther than Red House or Oakland. I strained to hear. "Slaughter" would mean a fat hog.

The voices quieted; I held my body tight. My ears snatched ". . . a gun . . . stationed . . . woods . . . whizzing."

"No!" Mother said.

Louder and of a piece: "Told to shoot the first man—'any blue comes along.'"

"You did not do!"

"Crouched . . . zing, like that . . . crackling brush . . . and whistling . . ."

"Crist! No!"

I heard no more words, but rustling below.

* * *

Today we have new ways. No one is to go anywhere without telling some-one. Not even Poppa. "Why or what for," Mother says. Her head has a goose egg. "Not to the outhouse, not the north woods. You must say some or such. I do not ever want— Promise: your whereabouts."

"Will they come again?" I ask.

"We are not to fret," Poppa says.

I try hard not to pout, but he does not know about Mother. She looks and looks on Poppa's face. I never before . . . how she touches his cheeks, as if she expects something besides a scruffy beard. She smooths and pats. I have to look away. We children take turns curling into his arms. Tobias is too big to curl, but he gives Poppa big smiles. When they disappear in the milk shed, Levi slaps his hand on the window, such that Gideon comes to keep watch, too, and blows slobber on the window. Then they both spit and rub with their fingers.

"Poppa will come back," I say. Sure enough, they bring full buckets; even Goldie is glad. I try to clean the window streaks with a rag, faster than fast.

After breakfast we go outside—Mother, too. She looks more herself. Green trees shimmer with orange and yellow in our meadow. I jump and turn myself about; Levi and Mary do, too. Mother props Noah in a bushel basket under a blanket, but when he fusses, Lydia picks him up. Tobias chases Gideon back and forth.

"Run, Gideon," I call. "Run fast!" I take my turn with Noah and bounce him the way he likes.

Poppa cuts stalks of corn for Tom and Frank; they will have to pull the plow now, too. And before winter Poppa and Tobias will build a new wagon.

But a bad thing: Poppa finds the potato fork. We did not clean it once. Poppa's face turns as dark gray as a storm cloud. He holds up the fork and says, "*Wer wees devun?*"

No one speaks, until I stumble to him. "Me, Poppa." He puts his hand atop my head like a lid, but not rough. "I hurried, for I was afraid."

"Hurry is not always for the best," he says. "Sometimes—"

"Me, too, Poppa," Tobias says. "Sorry. We were scared."

Poppa pulls Tobias to him, and we stand tight. I am taller than the start of Poppa's suspenders.

"I told them not to dawdle, Crist," Mother says. "They were to come back at once."

"Well, then, we are all in the thick," Poppa says. He leans down to me. "*Ich vergeb dich, mei Kind.* You, too, Tobias." He gives my shoulder another squeeze. All the little ones come running for hugs, too, jumping and clinging. Poppa is home all over again.

"Clean the fork," Poppa says to Tobias. I go with him and scrape dirt off extra good. But I stay clear of Mother, for fear her *schpuckich* ways will stay around.

J. Fretz — Chicago, October 1862

Revolting! I'm ready to pitch the war effort entirely. The bloodiest *day* ever, September 17. *Twenty-four thousand* casualties on both sides in twelve hours' time. How bad does it have to get? And to think, we despaired back in May over the destruction at Shiloh. That took *two days'* time with 16,000 casualties on our side, compared with 9–10,000 from the South. Those numbers left me numb. Each man, a son or husband—a father! Not just a body added to the count.

But this September battle—a cornfield, known as Antietam. I must be losing my mind. I see myself creating a story problem for my nephew, J. Michael. On average, how many soldiers at Antietam died in an hour's time? What a grisly thought for anyone, let alone a child!

Even Ross, an accountant at work, measures his words. "We mustn't lose faith in our boys."

"I'm glad my friends stayed near, not counting Shiloh," I say. "One disaster after another in the East: Bull Run again. The same place for the second try with the same result. Now Antietam."

"Pope was a mistake." Ross rubs his temple, a gesture he's adopted in the last several weeks. "No tactical skill, not able to command a large army. Better off, fighting Indians in Minnesota."

"But more men lost from our side, just like the first time at Bull Run. Even with standardized uniforms this time: red trim for artillery; blue, the infantry; yellow for cavalry. But our Army of the Potomac, routed again by this Lee fellow. And at the end, the same dire message: 'Lee, poised to invade Maryland and our capitol. Philadelphia's safety in doubt, too.' That's what my brother wrote from back East. Now Bull Run seems only a prelude to Antietam."

"Hold your righteous pants," Ross says with a sly grin. "This isn't over."

The same pattern, back and forth. I provoke him and his optimism; he jabs at my indignation. We've worked together almost six months, but everything about him irritates. He eats the same thing every day for lunch:

black bread, heavily buttered, and finishes with a red apple that he crunches, core and all.

"It's been a difficult year for Lincoln," he reminds me.

"I know, I know."

"His boy, Willie—they say typhoid might be traced to smelly, standing water. Might have been excrement from troops camped along the Potomac, corrupted the water supply." He puts a fist to his mouth, head down. "Our precious little ones. No one can bear to lose a child, or face the limitations that some are saddled with."

I pause, eating my own apples Mary Ann has cooked and sent in a small jar—easier for my teeth. I take a quick glance; sometimes Ross turns sentimental. One minute, his usual confident self, only to get teary-eyed. I forget the names of his youngsters, except for Gabriel, the oldest. I slow myself. "A difficult year—no question. Lincoln's wife, said to be at loose ends. And McClellan, no better the second time around."

Ross dabs his eyes with his carefully folded handkerchief. "That man still waffles, lacks fire. A wasted opportunity. This Lee follows his instincts."

My own emotions get the better of me when I read about it a second day at breakfast: Lincoln, furious with McClellan for not following Lee and crushing him. "Stupid men!" I say, spilling my coffee. Mary Ann hurries to wipe up my mess before it rolls off the table edge. "Could have been deci-sive," I mumble. "That general called it victory to force Lee south again. His second chance—lost."

Then I'm horrified. Am I cheering for a quick bath? What do I want—total obliteration of the South? *If it's a choice between sooner or later, maybe it's better to go ahead and do it sooner.* Shame fills me. I'm no better than a hard-nosed warmonger. I halfway support the war effort. My friends, out there somewhere; I can't let them down. Does that make me half right? Or only an inconsistent fool? Why don't I give Democrats in the North half credit? They accuse Lincoln of "tinkering" with slavery, saying he should care about making the war end more quickly.

But when I get to the office again, I follow the same pattern of disputa-tion with Ross. "Finally! A proclamation from the president that makes the war worthy: All slaves in Rebel states to be freed by the first day of next year."

Just as predictably, Ross repeats his favorite line: "Lincoln always wanted to abolish slavery as part of the rationale for going to war. Too divi-sive for him to say so directly."

I throw up my hands. "If Lincoln can say McClellan has 'the slows' when it comes to readiness for battle, why can't he see he's guilty of the same malady when it comes to openly supporting abolition? Every time he moves *toward* emancipation, he follows with sideways steps. I don't trust him."

All Ross has to do is point to his full ink bottle, dip his pen, and raise an eyebrow toward me. "You deliberate, too; you consider every possibility. No different: Lincoln takes one dip at a time."

"This is a *business*. I have to be a calculated risk-taker, too, even though the consequences don't affect nearly so many. But with the war Lee knows our side will be indecisive; he counts on it. He can divide his smaller army and get by with it."

"Lincoln will figure it out. You've said yourself that the man is wily. Right will prevail."

I hate it when Ross stays more even-keeled than I. I'm his boss! Sometimes I suspect he's gone to my partner Jim and mentioned my moodiness. I'm supposed to be the one keeping office folks clicking smoothly. But I hate this war. Everyone's out of sorts, and I'm tired of dangling. The fork in the road hasn't gone away. I still have to decide.

I visited Andy several times recently. I went to boost his spirits. Or salve my conscience. He ended up with an infected hand while still in camp. *Before* battle. I hate going there. Men eating at their peril. Sustenance for what? These camps with their close quarters carry so much disease, you're as likely to be killed before or after battle as during. When Andy finally left the city with his unit, I felt cheap saying goodbye. I wished him success, whatever that meant. Be an exception, I guess. Stay alive with limbs intact. I couldn't applaud his sentiments about enlisting: a chance to draw beads on Secesh.

Speaking of Rebs, I got taken by one recently. So far, Ross hasn't found out. I loathe the whole bunch of Confederates! They started it—eighteen months ago already. But last Monday a man came by, looking for work. He said he'd left the Rebel Army after nine months. I wanted to show him he'd made the right decision. So what did I do? I hired him on the spot. He had no money for lunch, and like a fool, I gave him small change from my pocket. He left and I was feeling good about myself. Of course, I haven't seen him since. And I accuse others of being tricked. I should have known better. I'm still too much like my mother.

When I've been grumpy all day, I take to walking again in the evenings. We still have warm fall days, and I know which streets to avoid. It only takes one hard rain for the ground to turn soupy. My city walking will never equal walking in the woods back home, but I can apply parts of Thoreau's essay, printed in *The Atlantic* a month after his death last spring. I can ruminate in the fading sun and store up toughness for the bitter cold coming. Ross likes to call me thin-skinned; I won't let it be true literally or figuratively.

When I get to the woods *in spirit* and breathe afresh to see new sides of the topics that vex, I often feel restored. Charles Dickens resolved issues in his head for years, walking around London, so why can't I do the same in Chicago? My questions haven't changed. How is it, after immense loss of men—Shiloh was supposed to be the end—the South can still put large armies on the field? And Grant's plan for complete conquest—no halfway! How is that humane? This is America—the grand experiment of opportunity!

Another thing: these men who go to battlegrounds and take pictures of the carnage! I feel sick to my stomach. I had no problem with Andy and Phil going to studios when they enlisted, having their pictures taken in their uniforms. That's understandable; their families need confident reminders. But photographs of war! It's one thing to *read* a newspaper's account of decomposed bodies and maggots swarming over corpses. But visual images utterly repulse. They cater to the worst: one animal devouring another. Yet two prominent photographers have set up exhibits in New York City and Washington. Long lines form with people *wanting to see* photographs of dead horses, huge piles of unburied Confederate soldiers. Why?

When I was a child, I'd gape at flies buzzing over a frog with its legs in the air. Curiosity, I guess. And today my niece, Estelle, pokes with a stick at such. But what is redemptive in viewing swollen faces and wide-open, blank eyes of humans? Does anyone need to make the war more real by seeing broken bloated bodies fallen on top of each other? Horses with front legs raised—their last moments of magnificence?

On my walks I try to sort through the endless confusion about the draft. I could be next! Three months ago, the president said he thought he could finish off the war if he had 50,000 more troops. I don't know how he calculates. The next thing I knew, he called for more volunteers: 300,000 for three years. And he added taxes: 3 percent on incomes between $600 and $10,000, 5 percent if you made more. My brother-in-law Jacob—Beidler as a business partner—was *not* happy. Everyone seemed to forget the 400,000 men Lincoln asked for little more than a year ago—so the war would be "short and decisive." I want to puke.

But now the War Department's plan has people turned inside out. When not enough men responded as volunteers, they asked for *an additional* 300,000 men between the ages of eighteen and forty-five. *A draft!* Sign up for nine months. My heart pounds.

I've felt relief at others' hostility toward the idea of conscription; some call it un-American or a loss of liberty. But as a result, the federal government passed the onus on to the states: let *them* decide how to implement the request. Don't people see the irony? Some of the same Northerners who've been caught up in curbing Southern states' right to secede, don't want the government telling *their state* how to run *their own militias!* Some states still haven't sorted it out, but Illinois continues to have enough volunteers. I remind myself: that could change quickly.

Some places have increased the bounties offered to volunteers for enlisting, as a way to fill quotas and avoid a draft. But if you're drafted, you have only two alternatives to enlisting: hire a substitute or pay a $300 exemption. But many a working man might not earn more than that *in a whole year.* Back home, Abe and Jakie applied for exemption certificates, in spite of the Doylestown newspaper making fun of that option. Abe says a substitute often costs *more.* You're at the mercy of the man; you pay whatever he'll settle for.

So even after my walks, I'm still indecisive. Much as I try to put matters aside, how can I be carefree? I hate not knowing. The war is all that most people want to talk about. I can't stay untouched. Rather, I'm desperate for someone to talk with—especially someone as conflicted as I. Martha's caught up in Chicago's hysteria, and I can't stomach prolonged conversation with her anymore. Jacob keeps his thoughts to himself at home, and Mary Ann stays too busy with Augustus to pay attention to the news.

One Sunday afternoon, though, I was out walking with an assigned purpose. As part of our Reuben Street Mission school outreach, some of us teachers distribute tracts after the morning classes. We each cover certain districts to spread the word about our program and efforts to acquaint children with the Gospel. I had completed my work in the vicinity of Oak Street on the north side when I happened upon another teacher, Dwight Moody, who had also finished his distribution. We'd first met a year earlier, and his energy and self-confidence made an impression. But he's a clerk in a shoe store on East Lake Street and I'm still committed to the lumber business, so we rarely do more than greet each other on Sunday mornings.

That afternoon, though, we both planned to attend the evening Young People's Meeting at the Methodist Church. As we walked toward Clark and Washington, we soon realized we face some of the same dilemmas: both abolitionists, both supportive of the Union cause, both urged by friends to serve our country. *Loyalty!*

When Dwight said, "I can't conscientiously enlist," I stopped walking. "You, too?"

He spoke directly. "I've never felt I could take a gun and shoot down a fellow being. More of a Quaker, I guess."

I nearly tripped but caught myself before I completely misstepped and sank into oozing mud. "You're so calm. You've never wavered?"

He looked at me directly. "What if I killed someone who didn't know the Lord as Savior? How would I go on living?"

We fell into step again, scuffling through leaves atop boards. My long-stifled words tumbled out. "I don't know what I'd do if I had to defend myself or a dear friend." I looked at him shyly; he's stocky, has a healthy beard. "I keep a pistol in my bedroom and shoot it skyward every July 4th." His face didn't change. "Sometimes I go to the range to practice on the first day of a new year. I grew up in a family with two rifles above the hearth. My father hunted, but I never enjoyed going with him. He was thrilled to get a buck, but I hated the gutting. Even a fat rabbit for stew could please him. Of course, I grew up with predators: coons in the corn, foxes in the hen house." I stopped from sheepishness. "I don't know why I'm saying all this."

"Some of my former business associates have formed a company," Dwight said. "That puts pressure on me."

"All I've done—loan a man fifteen dollars to help *him* raise a company. My close friends have joined. Me? I write letters to them."

Since then I've learned Dwight does much more; he goes to Camp Douglas, preaches and holds prayer meetings with the boys, gives them hymnbooks to replace their playing cards. Very tenderhearted, that man—maybe because his father died when Dwight was four. One of nine children, close in age, his mother had to send some of them away to work for porridge and milk.

We'd reached our destination early for the evening service, and he suggested we sit on the side steps. "Tell me more of your background."

I pulled my coat closer; late afternoon temperatures drop off quickly. "I grew up in a family with scruples about killing—other than hunting for sustenance."

"Scruples? Not that I don't know the word."

"The belief goes beyond. It's a refusal to act—refusal to kill another human, based on principles of conscience that go back to the Ten Commandments: 'Thou Shalt Not Kill.'" I reached for a stray maple leaf, its veins a dark brown. I twirled it, stripped off one side from the center stem. "My church, Mennonite, takes this literally; our history includes persecution back in the late sixteenth century. Perhaps you know the German word *Wehrlosigkeit*."

He shook his head, and I said, "Defenselessness. With time, though, the church's pattern has turned to some form of equivalency—usually an extra tax—if the government demands military enrollment."

"You won't do that, but you'll pay this instead?"

"Exactly. And another basic belief: God ordained government. That means we're to obey the government, unless—here's the difference—unless it asks us to do something that's against God's law."

"So the question becomes whether to obey government or your conscience against killing?" He nodded to an acquaintance going up the steps to the church building; everyone seemed to know him.

"Right." I pulled out my pocket watch and hurried to finish. "My conscience won't let me volunteer, not with what I've been taught about peaceful living. But if there's a draft, do I obey the government if it calls?"

"The way I see it, you don't *have* to do anything," Dwight said. "Free will, as the Quakers say: Do what you believe is right and then take the consequences."

"Simple." I ripped off the other side of the leaf, spun the stripped stem in my fingers.

"I know, it's not simple. But the decision's yours. Mine. The responsibility. Conscience, its own law. Pay the price in order to be faithful."

I nodded; I've heard the same from Oberholtzer. "But my friend Phil thinks the North must *force* the South to get rid of slavery."

"Lots of Northerners believe violence is God's will." The church bell rang.

I lowered my voice, so as not to be overheard by strangers passing by. "At first I refused to enlist because the government was slow to state the goal of righting servile conditions for the Negro. Maybe I was hiding." I hesitated. "But now, if I'm drafted—"

"What if you are?" he prodded.

There was no getting around him. "You're right—personal responsibility. Lincoln said last month: 'God's purpose is something different from the purpose of either party.' That much I agree with. But then he said, 'God wills this contest and wills that it shall not end yet.' That part makes my stomach churn. That's not the way I know God. Jesus commanded us to show love, overcome hatred. Force can't *make* the South want to change; it only fosters more hatred."

"Can any leader, either side, claim to know the Almighty's design? I only know for myself. Not others."

I leaned closer. "Lincoln seems to think that since neither side has been decisive in victory to this point, *therefore*, God *wants* the war to go on longer. That would mean God *wants* more men killed. I can't accept that. I used to think Lincoln used logic and facts—those debates with Douglas. But now I hear vengeance."

"Yes, I've thought, too, Lincoln's Quaker blood is losing out to what he likely heard from his father. But Lincoln has himself to answer for. I have myself."

I heard singing from inside the building. "I've kept you—selfish for your time. I can't thank you enough."

We stood and he brushed off the back of his coat. "You've reminded me: every day I choose for myself. I need convictions more than opinions."

I nodded but held back, checking my pocket watch again. "I think I'll skip— Sorry again, delaying you."

"No need to apologize."

We shook hands warmly and agreed to talk again. "*I* may need more bracing," I said.

With some of the cobwebs cleared away, I walked with more energy. What I'd heard was as good as—better than!—some earnest soul inside the meeting, telling of his release from sin. If Andy or Phil, out in the field, believe their commanders are appointed by God, and that makes it easier for them to do their job, I shouldn't try to dissuade them. But *I* don't have to believe Grant—or any general—is acting on God's behalf. I can't stomach it for myself. My conscience—my law. What's required of me: willingness to suffer for my faith.

Of course, my uncertainties soon came roaring back. My thoughts turned homeward, and I gave in to *Fernweh*. Why don't I have more friends who think like Dwight? Sadness swept over me. Why did I let things turn out as they did with Salome? Was I wrong not to move back East? But then, reality hit. I still don't want to be a farmer. Salome's likely found other interests—a *good* man, someone reliable. For all I know, she's nursing a babe. That's the nature of past acquaintances. They seem important at the time— and truly, they are—but people drift apart.

Still, I pictured the porch where Mother made soap and filled tin molds to make tallow candles, the wooden benches on two sides, the work table Father had made. That huge kettle where Mother put lye from slaked ashes and added fats she'd saved all winter. I used to help her stir apple butter in that same kettle through long hours of the night. How did we pass the time? Talking of everything and nothing, I suppose: the neighbors, Fretz relatives, my latest notions of grandeur.

Mother would approve, though; I plan to travel to Indiana this weekend. Deacon Good wrote to me again last month and invited me to the yearly conference of Mennonite ministers. Other visitors will be there, too—folks from Ohio and Illinois. Ordinary people. I won't know anyone; it's likely a waste of time. But if I'm ever going to make connections—see for myself—this will have to do. David said they'll have Communion, and quite a number of young people have asked to be baptized. He invited me to stay at his house those nights, so that solves that problem. But the closer the time comes, the more I don't want to go.

* * *

What a weekend it's been! I can't yet take it in. A slight whiff of the white flower I dreamed my sister Margaret pointed to? So much happened and I met so many people. Far too many names to keep straight. Strange feelings. The ease with which I talked about the war with Peter Nissley—almost my father's age. He'd come all the way from Lancaster County, Pennsylvania. A bond with a stranger!

Part of the jolt, simply getting out of the city, away from the oppressiveness of the war's call. I told Peter I go to war meetings at night. But now I've spent four days of putting that aside, surrounded by people in rural Indiana, intent on staying *out* of the war. They appeared prosperous—productive land and plentiful timber—but more conservative and plainer dress than most Mennonites I know back home. I felt out of place with my good broadcloth suit, my tie knotted under the collar of my white shirt. I'm not accustomed—my best clothes as an obstacle? Still, I enjoyed the way some of the young ladies took a second look.

What a time I had getting there, though! The train ride to Elkhart was fine and I stayed Thursday night at the Elkhart House. But muddy roads the next day! Everywhere I go, I'm hounded by mud. I hired a carriage and two horses to take me to the home of a Moyer, where I was expecting a further ride. But till I got there—those poor overworked horses! The Moyer man had already left for the conference. I couldn't keep the carriage longer, so I dismissed the driver and started walking. Seven miles to David Good's house on roads that became progressively worse. No recourse but to make guesses as to which oozing spot might prove to have solid footing underneath. When not avoiding mud, brambles on the side snagged at my coat.

I finally reached the Goods' house—two in the afternoon!—but *he* had left already. I had to content myself and wait for David to get back that evening. His kind but portly woman offered a beef stew. I fretted: *why had I bothered?* Finally, David arrived, bringing another house guest, John M. Brenneman, a Mennonite bishop from Elida, Ohio. Four sermons from him over the weekend—such impassioned preaching! Small in stature, he's not polished like ministers with smooth tongues in Chicago; he kept saying *irregardless*. But his earnestness far exceeded anything I've ever heard.

That Friday evening we had opportunity to converse in the parlor of the Goods' large farm house, sparse in its accessories but comfortable enough chairs. "I joined the Mennonite church over three years ago—my home church in eastern Pennsylvania."

John M.'s eyes blinked rapidly under raised eyebrows. "Three years, you say?" His white hair, flattened from the hat he'd been wearing.

"There's no Mennonite church in Chicago. I'm sorry, Sir." I hurried to add, "I worship with many Christian denominations. Prayer meetings, too."

"Call me John, please. Do you find food for your soul—those other churches?"

"Yes and no. Much praying and exhortation but also encouragement to warfare."

"And that is a problem?"

"Most definitely. I cannot in good conscience enlist."

He nodded but fixed on my tie. "Tell me, do you believe Jesus Christ is the Son of God?"

I leaned forward, my arms resting on the wooden chair arms, and managed a soft "yes."

"And do you walk humbly before our God in newness of life?" His eyes flitted to my closely trimmed beard, then closed.

"As much—" I hesitated. "As much as lieth in me." His dark eyes opened abruptly. "Chicago isn't known for green pastures. I'm human."

His shoulders sagged and he stroked the center point of his beard.

I rushed ahead. "I've never taken part in Communion, but I'd like to— very much. If you could see fit."

"Never, you say? Highly unusual. Three years." In the end I must have answered his questions satisfactorily enough, for he gave permission.

On Sunday when he read the words of Jesus to those gathered—"Take and eat, this is my body given for you—"a hush fell. I can't imagine having stayed seated, not after he said Jesus's words: "This do in remembrance of me." I went to Indiana out of curiosity, but I soon wanted to be more than an onlooker. All was solemn as we walked to the front, row by row, to receive the bread and cup.

But the footwashing made the morning service unforgettable. I don't understand why churches in my home community have neglected this part. The instruction is clear in the thirteenth chapter of John: follow Jesus's example of washing his disciples' feet. I didn't know the first thing of what to do, but Brother Good had instructed his son, Gideon, to stay with me.

There in that Yellow Creek meetinghouse, some forty by eighty feet, overflowing with 300–400 people packed in the plain frame building—nothing ostentatious—older men washed each other's feet, as did the older women on the other side. The overflow waited their turn outside. We younger men took off our shoes and socks—the bare wooden floor, exceedingly cold—and went to the back of the meetinghouse where more buckets were lined up. As we stood in line waiting our turn, I tried not to gawk but watched how others did.

At last I followed Gideon. He pointed for me to sit down on the bench, and he knelt before me on the other side of the bucket, motioning for me to lift my bare foot. He cupped water over it into the bucket, then dried my foot with a towel. In the same manner he followed with my other foot. He seemed as awkward as I. How humbling, someone performing such a menial task! I silently thanked Mrs. Good again for having brought warm water in a basin after my muddy walk on Friday. Then Gideon and I exchanged places and I washed his feet as he had done mine, taking care not to spill water outside the bucket or drag the end of the towel. His toes looked like claws; mine are short and stubby.

I will never be the same. The singing, the solemnity. Brother Brenneman's warnings of possible suffering ahead. Was it—could it be another step in my conversion?

Once home again, I could hardly wait till evening to tell Mary Ann. She was still working in the kitchen that Monday evening and listened silently until I got to the part about washing feet. "I did as I'd observed others." I paused. "When we rose again from washing, so that others could take our places at the bucket, I gave Gideon a kiss on the cheek."

Mary Ann turned from the raisin filling she was preparing for pies, her brown eyes wide with surprise. "You kissed him?"

"On the cheek. The Kiss of Peace, like ministers back home give each other when first greeting. Brothers in the Lord."

"And you didn't know anything about this Gideon?" She turned away to pour a thick mixture into the cooked raisins.

"Not to any extent. Only that he was a believer, the deacon's son." I suppose she tried to picture such a ritual among Presbyterians. "Very solemn, done in an orderly manner. Kneeling to wash, showing you don't think you're better than the other."

She shuddered as she added another dab of butter, stirred the boiling mixture with a long-handled spoon.

"It's in the Gospel of John; you can look. How Jesus loved his followers; how we're to do the same—those of like faith."

"Mennonites back home don't do that," she said, banging the wooden spoon on the edge of the pot.

"And that's a pity. The Amish still practice it. Completely opposite from our thoughts of power over another. Jesus wanted to make a point—knowing he was going to die: his followers were to think of him as their servant, not Lord or Master." Mary Ann wouldn't look at me. "Some people came in buggies; some rode horses. They traveled for miles, some by oxcart—two miles an hour!" I paused. "I looked like a city dandy."

At that she turned slightly and said, "The young ladies are probably still talking." But her smile faded. "It's time you found someone, J. Fretz."

She's said that for weeks, badgering me to bring Martha for a meal. A few months ago I nearly did, but lately I've not been tempted. "Listen to this;

we rode on a farm wagon to the Saturday meeting—a few miles south of Elkhart—each given a biscuit to put in our pocket for dinner."

At that she thumped the stirring spoon loudly and set the pot aside to cool. She sighed as she sat at the table. "That was your noon meal?"

"It sounds strange. The biscuit was to tide us over through the long morning service; it lasted until two in the afternoon. We'd gotten up at five and eaten a huge breakfast. But Mary Ann—none of that matters." I reached for her arm. "Do you remember when you were baptized? The excitement within."

She sat up straight and adjusted her hair, piled fashionably but marred by the day's loose strands. "Of course, Fretz. What do you think? I have no appreciation?"

"I meant nothing negative. Only, do you still feel that newness of life? That fervor?"

She rubbed her fingers as if they were sticky, covered a yawn, and looked toward the kitchen clock. The strain of tending Augustus at all hours, placing the needs of Jacob ahead of her own.

"I'm sure you're tired, but I need to say: forty-six new converts baptized on Saturday."

"Forty-six?" She started to get up but paused. "How was there room for that many? Their families?"

"The applicants came to the front in five groups, nine in each, except one group had ten. Two groups of girls in white dresses. The rest, boys or young men. All freshly scrubbed, untouched by the world. I felt old and worldly by comparison. Stained." My insides tugged.

"What is it, Fretz?" she asked. It was her turn to put a hand on mine.

I shook my head. "I can't say. But I saw something—been missing."

Her eyes drooped with weariness; she waited. Mary Ann's been a mother to me, feeding me, looking after my clothes. She tells me I should use my first name, John; it would carry more respect.

"Something changed within. The solemnity." I shook my head. "Seriousness of purpose. I don't know. It seemed everyone had gathered with the same desire to do God's bidding. Maybe only a facade." My hands gestured aimlessly, tightened into fists. "Willing to go against the government's wishes."

"That's it, isn't it? This war. Your friends enlisting." She lowered her voice, "I'm thankful J. Michael is still young."

"Indiana has a draft," I said.

"Oh?" Her eyebrows arched; she stood slowly.

"A $200 commutation fee in their state for exemption—conscientious objectors. Over 200 young men signed up. Others still buy substitutes, like some Mennonites back in Pennsylvania. But those rows of earnest young people in church. It still startles. They're naïve—maybe a false humility—unprepared." I suddenly felt overcome by fatigue; Chicago's heaviness pressed in. Had I been duped again?

I stood to watch Mary Ann spoon pie filling into the crusts; she asked no more questions. I excused myself and soon crawled into bed. I went over everything again. My talks with Peter and John—they don't think *either* side is right. They don't believe God *wills* this contest to go on longer. Two elderly men—my heroes? Peter said he's had his sixtieth birthday; his black hair covered his ears, but no sign of gray.

Yes, I connected with them, but I didn't tell them I'm an abolitionist. Peter may have guessed. I told him I'd been a teacher. I mentioned Phil and Andy, now Joe, gone to war. Peter spoke with heaviness of Lancaster County—his way of pursing his lips without sounding judgmental—the pressure on conscientious men with scruples. He mentioned their Republican congressman, Thaddeus Stevens, and his belief that God might be punishing advocates of slavery.

The whole weekend—inspiring, disturbing. *Unsettling.* Back to Illinois's unpredictability about a draft. Where am I? Carrying a new question: What does God *ask* of me? Not, what do I want God to *do* for me?

I made myself recall the singing, in hopes of falling asleep. My bad ear had kept me from joining in fully, but I had turned my head to hear the women on the left, the men on the right. The warm mellow tones of "*Oh, for a closer walk with Thee*" sung slowly. The plainness of fresh faces. No expensive cravats. A peacefulness—no arguing it away—not a frenzy such as Chicago knows. "*A sure and heavenly rest.*" Gentleness like my mother's.

I shook away sadness, though, as I drifted off. I'd never be satisfied with such simplicity. I wouldn't fit in; I've changed too much.

ESTHER SHANK — Shenandoah Valley, November 1862

My bones have let go their shaking. First Simon, then our first-born Andrew returned—the second flight for each of them. But we still keep watch; soldiers linger, looking desperate in torn pants, shoes flopping open at the toes. Cruel, not to give from our apples, crisp and juicy.

My man Simon had the least distance and heard first. Last month the Confederate Congress passed an exemption from military service for us Mennonites and Dunkers. Nazarenes, too. Like unto the earlier exemption from our state—the one, soon nullified—each man must pay $500 or buy a substitute. But this time the government agreed to accept the commutation fee paid earlier—that first time, when Simon and Andrew were released from prison in Richmond. Such a relief! Now when either of them must do business in town, they carry papers. Simon is much to extend the hand and help others in church who are weighed down with extra hardship.

He wants us to go see his brother Gabriel, since the roads aren't clogged like in the spring. But I protest. We don't know who we might happen upon, asking questions. Why stir things up? Simon could go by himself, but I don't want him out of sight. It's enough when he checks his traps every day. Zigler started him on that habit when they lived in the cave.

I told Simon of our new one—it could be another month—but the youngsters don't know. At first, the furrow deepened on Simon's brow, but then he smiled, almost as broadly as long ago. If we were to go to Gabriel's family before winter sets in, Harriet might put questions. Another mouth during uncertainty? In our forties and starting another family? But my milk has always been at the ready, and I've borrowed garments from women at church; our baby clothes went to the rags years ago. Now the kicks have taken on persistence. I'll soon place Mary Grace's hand on my belly and watch her surprise. I may put her to knitting a cradle cap.

Frances has made promise for the birthing, but it won't be the same without Genevieve. So long ago, when we three were back and forth and I trusted her more than Frances. But now, even midst freezing rain and snow this month, Frances hitches up her skirts and swings her leg on her horse like a man. What would I do without her? She knows uncertainty, too: her man, Samuel's, whereabouts. She thinks he's still in Maryland but says he could have gone to check on relatives in Greenbrier County.

What a story Frances told of Genevieve! Algernon Gray, a lawyer in Harrisonburg, had kindly come to inquire about Samuel and told Frances of the tumult. A letter had come to George and Genevieve, telling of their second son Henry's death in battle. Even worse, no remains were to be had. The parents bore the burden, knowing passage to heaven could not be assured without proper burial services.

But after the first shock wore off, they recovered to hold a funeral service at the Methodist Church. What do you know—their son walked in! The very hour. Glory be! But to behold his family in black . . . Word from the Confederacy had been botched. Algernon insisted the letter had come in a black-rimmed envelope and carried the official seal from Richmond. This newly returned man walks with a bad limp and goes without an arm, but he lives! He'd been in a hospital in Maryland, not knowing the wrong name had been sent out. If ever an official envelope comes regarding our Peter . . . Mercy!

Much as we long for word from him, the other son who has returned gives little satisfaction. One boy of ours or another—a mystery. Andrew's been tight-lipped, except to say he hitched rides coming back when he could. Last summer he'd sent a short letter about his trip north, so we knew he'd made it. He and Bishop Samuel had stayed clear of Confederates, and Andrew had walked the last part alone, welcomed by my brother. Matthias had never written aught of needing to make do with only one hand. His right one caught in one of those new-fangled threshing machines several years ago. Being one-handed disqualifies him from military service, so that's a blessing. But Andrew said there's no equivalency fee for those who claim conscientious scruples in that western part of Pennsylvania.

I thought he'd be full of stories, but I've had to pry to learn that Matthias and Lena have the seven, and Shem is their oldest, the same age as our William. Simon got Andrew to say Matthias plants more wheat but less corn than we. And they'd been delayed putting in their crops when ten inches of snow fell early last April. But as for Lena, Andrew only shrugs. Simon thinks Andrew might have lost out on a girl. I've wondered if he's dissatisfied to be home again, but that can't be true; he gave me a bear hug and helps with bread like always.

Sometimes, though, he gets up from the table and paces for no reason at all. But if I ask directly, "Were there troubles? Soldiers and such?" he becomes stony.

Only once he said, "Always in the wrong place at the wrong time."

When Simon pressed about Andrew's route north, he said, "I could find it again." We waited, but all he told was a time he and Samuel found lodging with a Quaker family. We had not known: Quakers fleeing North Carolina have an Underground Railroad that relies on handshakes and oaths; even red has meaning. With us it's word-of-mouth.

Andrew said, "The man's house had been marked by red strings, but he took a long look at us. 'Appears to me, you're no Quakers,' he said. The man relented, though, and took us in. A pleasant enough night of conversation and the woman outdid herself with breakfast."

"A stubborn bunch, those Quakers," Simon said.

"I'd stay there again—that Hoskins fellow," Andrew said.

"Not what I've heard," Simon said. "They could take part—the exemption."

"Their church doesn't believe in paying an extra tax."

"That's what I mean," Simon said. "Stubborn."

"Made sense, the way Hoskins told it. They live their beliefs, harm no one, expect neither penalty nor accommodation. Their principle is sufficient."

"Hogwash," Simon said. "No need to be martyrs."

Andrew clammed up, so I didn't ask what their Quaker women think of the risk.

By the time we did our butchering a week ago, Andrew was a big help. We had four good-sized hogs that hadn't been snatched, so our smokehouse now has hams and sausages again. It used to be, when I walked past, the emptiness put a hitch in my breathing. But now I'm thankful for what we've stowed.

Long ago, when back and forth with Genevieve and her George, we'd start at three in the morning—our boys and theirs working together. This year, only half the help, but we had water boiling in the iron kettle when the sky barely showed light. And by mid-morning, we'd not only killed and scalded but finished scraping and hanging upon the scaffold. The taste won't be the same, for we have to make do with as little salt as possible. Simon says not to add sugar when I bake either, but with sour cherries I slip in a smidgen.

William turned out to be our butchering surprise this year. He got it in his head we shouldn't kill any of the four surviving hogs. To be sure, he'd been the one who'd kept watch over the pen. But there was no reasoning with him, not even my "saved for the purpose of sustenance."

When butchering day came, William disappeared. I found him scowling in the woodshed. "Come now," I said. "Your duty: build the fire."

"I'll go hungry," he said and bolted for the house.

He doesn't know whereof he speaks, but I knew no swaying would be accomplished.

Simon turned red. "The boy is to help!" I had to stand between my man and the door. "You coddle him," he charged.

"Not everyone takes to everything," I said. "We have enough hands with Andrew."

Simon knows how Mama taught me well. Never one to shy from blood, she passed on her skill with the knife. I don't mean to contradict my man. I'm a good woman. I put up with Simon's tobacco spit; I don't want him ever hiding again. But in his absence I learned my own ways of doing; I didn't always follow the usual. Yes, we teach the fear of the Lord, but it wasn't in me to pick up the rod. I could exact cooperation without making a scene.

But Simon said, "You stand up for the lad—a bad example."

Two days after butchering, Andrew was the one to get crosswise, when he rode to see Joseph Funk at what's now called Singers Glen. Not asking Simon for the horse, Andrew went of his own accord in the afternoon drizzle. "Going to see the man's print setup."

Simon groused. "Why the boy can't knock that hare-brained idea from his head—"

But Andrew burst out, "Old man Funk translated our Mennonite Confession from German to English and printed it up; otherwise, we'd be ignorant oafs."

I was as taken aback as Simon. "Must have been new ideas in the north," I ventured.

But when Andrew returned, he still looked sour. All I could pry: "The man has sons." Later, I learned Joseph Funk had walked with Andrew to his print shop, a short distance behind the man's house. But all too soon the man wanted to return inside and lie down.

"A feeble one?" I asked, but Andrew gave his usual shrug.

* * *

Yesterday on our way home from church, Andrew opened more of his dam. Our cold rain from early morning had turned to a sprinkle, and we didn't get drenched as before. But fog still sat in the low areas with clouds to disorient. Joseph took the reins so Simon could motion when we came too near the edge of the road.

Soon enough, Andrew shouted from the back wagon bench, "We're behind, always behind here in Virginia. Why is there no instruction about peace?"

I turned sideways from the middle bench where Mary Grace and I huddled. Andrew spoke as in an argument, and William sidled away from him. "Mennonites in Franklin County use a book called *Gemüths-Gespräch.* Young ones are instructed before baptism—three sections on peace. Here, nothing. People must think the war's over."

Our team had slowed, pulling uphill. "When he's here, Bishop Coffman preaches about turning the cheek," I said. "You read Christian Burkholder's *Address to Youth.*"

"That's all." Andrew tucked his chin against his coat.

"The *Martyrs Mirror,*" Mary Grace said, her light voice falling flat in the heavy air. She tapped her feet on the wagon floor to keep warm.

"That's in German," Andrew said. "Nothing bold this morning."

I turned frontward again; he only wanted to criticize.

"Only *one* way we're *not* behind," Andrew said, near to a shout again. "One Sunday, Bishop Coffman came north and preached in English. First time for them. Matthias said so."

I had to turn and look again. "Samuel? With you?" Frances had not said a word.

"Several times at Chambersburg," Andrew said. "Came from Maryland where he stayed. But even before that, Lena said they instructed their young with diligence when armies surrounded the year before."

"Soldiers? Thereabouts? A whole year before?" I asked.

Andrew lowered his voice. "Union Army used Chambersburg as a supply depot."

"The summer before this last?" I asked again. Matthias had not written of living amidst.

Even Simon turned back fully to look, while Joseph guided through a low stretch. "Must have made farmers and merchants happy—extra demand for grain and meat, those soldiers."

I wanted to dispute. Simon doesn't know what it's like—soldiers milling. He's never stayed the duration. But we had reached our lane and the talk stopped. I busied about with Mary Grace, frying cooked potatoes with a chunk of beef, some beans and onion. All stayed quiet as we ate, but I determined to ask more later.

That night I stopped Andrew from refilling his mug. "Does my brother drink that much every night?"

"What of it?" he asked sharply.

"What went on?" Simon asked. "Soldiers."

Andrew pushed his chair back and folded his arms. "I told you: I'm never at the right place. I went to Uncle Matthias, thinking I'd get safe harbor from Rebs. What did Lee's men do? Raided farms, came after horses."

"Right there? Why didn't you tell us?" I asked. "All these days."

"What difference?" he replied. "People around here think the war's moved on."

"We remember Peter every day," I said.

"What do you want?" Simon asked Andrew. "Us to stay in the cellar? Ignore harvest? You can't live, looking backward."

"You mean soldiers came to Matthias's farm?" I asked. "Snooping? Asking about your birth home? Lee's men."

"Only had eyes for horses," Andrew said. "We'd heard cannons and bugles for days. Most of a month, coming from Hagerstown. Already in September, people were agitated."

"You lived that way?" I placed my hand on my belly, but all stayed quiet. "My nerves a jangle here—the rattle of artillery last spring. One army or another."

"Chambersburg was under martial law; local folks, wild-eyed." Andrew pushed unruly hair behind one ear, then the other. "Lots more people there, even in normal times. Folks from Maryland fled there, too. Thought sure that their farms were next. Lee had come to Frederick, then crossed the South Mountain." Andrew crunched into an apple, wiped juice with the back of his hand. "I learned that from Mennonites fleeing north."

"People on the run?" Simon asked.

"Whole families in wagons," Andrew said. "People believe anything. Abandoned their farms so fast—no thought for provision. Most evenings Matthias sent me out to dig potatoes."

Simon snorted. "I'd never uproot my family. Better to stay put, hide at home, not be on the run."

"People scared," Andrew said. "You know how it is. Not always thinking straight. Children crying, whatnot. We did the best we could. Built a huge fire in a pit, roasted corn for anyone. Folks stayed four or five days; finally went back."

"You leave your farm, you give soldiers permission. Take whatever they find." Simon spat beside his chair. "Could be worse, what you run into away from home."

Andrew stared at his father, opened his mouth, closed it again, sucked juice from the apple core. He looks so much like my brothers when they were young—the brown hair, wide nose. "Did your Lesher resemblance help?" I asked.

Andrew began pacing. He followed a track: the cookstove, the fireplace, the table. He never answered my question; his talk came in spurts. I expected footsteps coming down the loft anytime.

"Turns out, Rebel troops had been in western Maryland last December, almost a year ago. Skirmishes along the Maryland-Virginia border. Stonewall and his men tried to blow up Dams Four and Five. The B & O Canal. Come spring, people still jumpy. Loud noises, most any hour. Matthias said people held their breath. Not normal."

"Signs aplenty last year. Remember?" Simon asked. He poured another drink; he says this crop of currant wine is weak. "That whole year, full of portent. You know what I mean."

Andrew stopped pacing; his hand fidgeted in his pocket. "They saw the ball of fire."

Simon swiveled toward Andrew. "The ball of fire falling toward the south? The same?"

Andrew braced a hand on a chair back. "The very same; Matthias saw it. July 4th. Same for us." He cracked his knuckles.

No one needed reminder. Even Simon had been shaken, that day of the omen. A bird in the house may be only a slight disturbance, but falling fire—far from usual. Especially so, happening a few months after our state seceded. Simon and the big boys had been out thinning corn. The sky overcast, so much so, the sun barely shone that day. A strangeness. My men came in breathless.

"What?" Mary Grace and I had asked together.

Finally, Simon spoke. "A line in the sky from east to west." He'd pointed. "To the north, the sky showed clear."

The boys stood stiff, nodding solemnly. They all insisted: the tail of the comet had exploded like a ball of fire, moving toward the south. No one said more, but they stayed inside, restless.

Now Simon tossed back another quick swallow.

I looked to Andrew. "When did you say those Rebels came looking for horses?"

"September, this year. Didn't hit hard, though, for another month." Andrew sat again, chair tilted back on its hind legs, his fingers gripping the table edge. "Matthias had a plan. In case. I was to take the two best horses into the woods north of the house. Keep 'em quiet. Shem was to help his father with the work horses. Only if . . . I never heard exactly how that was to be."

"That never works," Simon said. "A horse has to be on the move."

Andrew half-nodded. "I did what was asked, trained the two in my charge. Did the best I could. Took them out of the barn at nighttime, clapped two pieces of board together." He slapped his hands together, so sharp, I jumped. "The bay got better at it, like she came to expect. I'd offer grain and apples from my pockets if she stayed quiet. Her sides would shake, but she'd only let out a faint whinny. Never put much stock in it, though. Streak, the black one, little more than a colt, would jerk his head and rear his legs every time. Matthias wouldn't let me fire a shotgun into the woods. I never told him, but I had half a notion to keep Streak in the barn and only take the bay to the woods. If it came to that. Or turn the colt loose; they'd never catch him and he'd come back eventually. The main thing: save one, not lose 'em both."

"What happened?" Simon and I asked as one.

"Came in broad daylight. Two Rebels on foot. All quiet. Through the south woods in back. Must have cut across Horst's land. We were cradling wheat, late afternoon. Never expected a thing. All the horse gear in plain sight."

"Took everything," Simon said.

"Almost. Several weeks after that awful fight at Antietam. Nothing we could do but watch those two soldiers, on the scrawny side, unhitch the horses, take harnesses, most everything. Matter-of-fact, like it was theirs. No asking. Shem cried."

"All the horses?" Simon asked.

"The two for work and the bay mare." Andrew shrugged. "What could we do? Men with revolvers. One talked so fast and had such a thick accent, I couldn't make out half what he said. Matthias begged to keep the oldest horse. Nothing doing. The other guy kept repeating, 'Need remounts, need remounts.' As if we'd be sympathetic. A work horse as a remount! That was sad. That guy—nasty, red scar on his neck—he said, 'We're the Army of the Confederacy. We do what we want.' No interest in Streak, jumpy as all get out. The soldier with the southern talk handed Matthias some paper money—we knew it was worthless—said it'd be up to face value when the South won. Matthias kept looking toward the house, as if he feared Lena might come out. He showed me later; he had a very nice watch hidden away."

Andrew got up to pour a dipper of water, guzzled it. Simon glared at me. "You know to stay inside with the children, if ever . . . War is for men, Esther." Then he said to Andrew, "What was that—Antietam?"

"Maryland. You don't know? One day of fighting. Part, on farm land some Dunkers owned. Took their corn crop." Andrew looked toward the loft, lowered his voice, and sat down again. "Thousands killed. A holy hell of bodies." I looked away, but Andrew continued. "All accounts: Lee went back to Virginia with survivors. Left his badly wounded on the field. Folks in Chambersburg made a makeshift hospital. Took care of some 400 or so."

"Must have been like here in Harrisonburg," I said. "They used the high school building back in the spring."

"Ma! Thousand times worse!" Andrew said. "Thousands and thousands—did you hear? The badly wounded left untended. Thousands died at Antietam. I haven't said nearly all." He spoke the way Simon chides Mary Grace. "Matthias sent me into town with two days' worth of eggs. I saw it, Ma. Butchered men. Mangled. I still—" His face drained of color.

"Oh, Andrew," I said. What nightmares he must have. The clock ticked loudly. Kicks came again; my breathing quick.

"When I told Matthias, hundreds sick—some said *800*—he sent me back the next day. A dozen dressed chickens. Lena baked extra bread for days. The nicest I've ever seen her; she can be brisk. Soldiers coming through our parts all the time. Sad boys—stumbling."

"Why didn't you tell us?" I asked again. "Most of the soldiers here, polite. But the longer things went on, the louder the ones in blue. Butter—the main thing to keep 'em quiet. Night and day we fed strays, nibbled at what was left. Nothing like Lena's ordeal, though."

Andrew stayed sallow in the lamplight. "Only one thing frightened. Still does."

Neither Simon nor I spoke.

"Fear of seeing him." Andrew barely spoke above a whisper.

I knew—my fear as well. My boys coming upon each other. Blue and gray ghosts.

"People there call this the brothers' war," Andrew said softly.

"Brothers do not war." Simon stomped to the fireplace and added another log. We watched the burst of flame, turned from the loud pops, hissing. Finally, Simon spoke again. "Rebs wrecked the train system, didn't they? The North's? What I heard."

"I can't say what happened elsewhere," Andrew said. "Some said that wrecking was part of Lee's plan. But nearby, they lacked the right explosives to destroy the iron bridge at Scotland. Had to settle for burning railroad buildings in Chambersburg. Several locomotives set fire."

"How could men . . ." I shushed under Simon's dark look.

"This is war," he said, harsh. "If the railroad furthers the North's cause, the South will destroy. Seek to waylay it, cut off supply lines. The whole Cumberland Valley, crucial."

Andrew nodded. "No Northerner wants to hear of Confederates crossing the Potomac. The *worst*. Yet Lee had over a thousand cavalrymen where I was, led by a man named Stuart. Two thousand horses taken in two days' time. Twenty-some Mennonite farmers hit."

My brother Matthias, one-handed, losing three horses, hiding a fancy watch. Long ago, how eager he was, going West. Always the daring one, skinny-dipping, poking a long stick at a wasp's nest. Now a wife and young ones to shield. "We've stayed peaceful here," I said quietly.

Andrew's loud laugh broke in. "Soldiers don't make distinctions, Ma. They don't ask: 'Are you kind-hearted folks?' Nobody says, 'So sorry to bother your peaceful little life. Give us a minute here.' Union men? Not one inch better. Take whatever they want. Either side."

"I didn't mean—"

Andrew's laugh like a bark, interrupted again. Bitter like Peter's on his one-day visit. Andrew didn't say the two had met; he stopped short. *My boys, oh, my boys.* Had they set eyes? How do you live, when you fear your brother? When will this ever be over?

Andrew wasn't finished. "I mean what I say about Union. Soon after the Confeds raided our horses, the blue coats came. Matthias and I worked several days cutting up dead trees in the woods, sawing lengths for Union fires. I spent all of a Sunday hauling wood." He was up, pacing again. "Lena made bread all day, that same Sabbath. No one went to church. I doubt any church gathering was to be had." He paused. "What would church people sing? Huh? Some of those Union men—never seen a madder bunch. The man in charge—where to put the wood—cursed something awful. 'Now we're fighting for the—' Words I can't repeat."

"That's so, isn't it?" Simon said. "Lincoln wants to free all the dark ones in January."

"Who knows? I'll tell you this: not everyone thinks the same. Not in Chambersburg. Farmers who've used slaves, and others, *opposed.* Not for the Negro man's sake, opposed. No! Opposed because freedom would be a threat to that farmer's, *that white man's,* easy labor. Men gone from there, either side—soldiering. The ones left, scrounge to get field work done." Andrew sat slumped. "Think about this: one part of Chambersburg called Wolfstown. Uh-huh. For deserters, former slaves. From the very start, Matthias warned me: 'Best keep your mouth shut; you never know.' Spies, one side or the other." Andrew buried his head off to the side.

We'd had no idea. No safe place to be had for my boy; not even my brother could provide. I had to ask, "How does Matthias make do—harvest with a crippled hand?"

"That's why I stayed as long as I did," Andrew said. "He couldn't complain. Finished the crops before I left. Not good wheat, not with their late start in the spring and trampling later on. Bound as many sheaves as we could; Shem's a pretty fair worker." Andrew took on a faraway look, cracked his knuckles again. "It worked out, I guess. He gave me lodging, fed me. I gave free help. He said I'd be welcome next summer." He shook his head. "I couldn't wait to get back here. But now . . . Backward."

"Our Shenandoah, all part of the same," Simon said. "One long valley, one country—north and south. No border but what manmade. You must have been a brother for Matthias."

Andrew flinched. I got up slowly. Would Andrew have looked the other way? Or pressed a drink to his brother's lips? Peter could have been with Lee and his men. Could have been one of those left behind. The paper with his name tucked inside.

David Bowman — Shenandoah Valley, December 1862

The worst storm has passed from our immediate surroundings—near to six months already—but my mind finds no rest. Am I to take off my shoes, pretend to be in awe for having been kept safe from last spring's adversity? Or must I build a stone circle, stand inside, and listen for a voice? In spite of the church's call, I still lack fervent desire to seek the mind of God.

Brother Kline drew me into a quandary back in the fall. He wanted to visit Joseph Funk and wondered if I would accompany him. He had heard the man's health was failing, but all I could think of was their tiff over baptism—five years ago or more. This Joseph's grandfather Heinrich had been blinded in his writings on baptism to say the Old and New Testaments suggested no *one* method. Out of love for the truth, Brother Kline had defended our German Baptist practice of triune immersion—three times forward—taking place at a riverside or stream. It is clear: the New Testament example to follow.

But these two men had gone back and forth—hundreds of pages in rival publications—excess wording, to my way of thinking. Exaggerated aspersions had been assigned to John's character: arrogance and a haughty spirit, even the false charge of prevarication. Why would I want to meet this Joseph?

Making things worse, John's request came in the middle of harvest work; I only had Delilah and Abigail's help—my boys still gone from home. No word of their safety, since the letter last June. I felt put upon; visiting a sick Mennonite seemed an unnecessary intrusion. But I did not want to sound sniveling toward John, our church elder, so I agreed to go. I packed my small saddlebag as usual, for we never know what unexpected injury we may encounter along the way.

My ride on Ruby to John's place was enjoyable in the brisk morning air, although the forest's colors had lost their vibrancy already from rains. When John and Nell joined us, we proceeded across the gentle inclines and slopes of Turleytown Road to Singers Glen—well-named with its steep hills and deep coves, as well as a fitting residence for Mr. Funk, given his years of educating young people in singing schools.

His wife, a small woman with heavy shoes, met us at the door but pulled back when she recognized Johnny from his days under Funk's tutelage. Of course, John is portlier now and his hair has turned gray, but the woman—a Rachel by name—recovered to say Joseph was resting. We waited outside as she asked her man about receiving us. Theirs is a small log house, very plain; I stepped down from the porch to better assess the gable roof.

After the wife instructed us where to secure our horses and ushered us inside, we found Joseph covered with pillows and a large velvet cloth and propped in a large chair that had a semi-reclining wooden back. I had never met him, but it came to me on the ride, he had declared as an individual that he did not need to practice footwashing. When Johnny introduced me as a minister from Flat Rock, I found the man's grip entirely lacking in firmness. My "Pleased to meet you" also lacked sincerity, for I felt far removed from pleasure. Joseph might have been tall at one time but now carried a look of wasting away—his blue eyes glassy, his sparse white hair askew in the manner of one who sleeps for considerable lengths of time.

The two men reminisced warmly enough about their years when Joseph had instructed Johnny regarding the rudiments of vocal music. I did little more than shift in my chair and offer an occasional comment about the value of music in the church; I know little about shaped notes and faw, sol, law, mi, let alone the various editions of *Harmonia Sacra*. The old man had trouble picking up my voice, so I contented myself with assessing the exposed joists and wondering at the unevenness of the floor boards. The one window offered little natural light.

When Brother Kline asked regarding Joseph's health, the man said he had trouble with both breathing and swallowing. As if the thought spurred the problem, the man's breathing quickened and he took to coughing—short little barks that soon became loud spasms of hacking. The wife was upon him immediately in her loud shoes and offering a mug, as if she had lingered at the doorway, knowing such an episode would commence. Johnny and I both declined the woman's offer. He only partakes of fermented wine at our Communion, and I have been careful to exercise moderation since becoming a minister.

Finally, Joseph's discomfort eased and Brother Kline reached for the man's arm. "We will not be long." He paused. "I thought it needful to make repair. You remember, I am sure, our disagreements over the manner by which Christians are to be baptized into newness of life."

The man's eyebrows barely flickered. He pulled on the heavy cloth—black with squares of dark green, red, and blue—to better cover a shoulder.

Johnny spoke slowly. "This year our churches have been tested as never before on the matter of nonresistance. It has been no small satisfaction that when pushed to the brink, our two groups have cooperated, making known our defenseless posture to the government. I had the privilege of hearing earnest expressions by Mennonite men while in prison. We share the same desire to live no more by '*an eye for an eye*.'"

I wanted Johnny to manifest more hurry. Sometimes he weighs each word, as if it must pass clearance with the Almighty. Joseph's eyes had closed again, and I feared he meant to shut his hearing as well. I fidgeted and cleared my throat, even though I had no intention of speaking.

Johnny continued at his deliberate pace. "Some young people from our two church groups have intermarried in the past." But then he surprised me. "I need to confess—" Mr. Funk's eyes popped open, bluer than before. "I have held onto enmity toward you, my beloved teacher, of all people. All because of differences over practice."

Funk's eyelids fluttered and closed. He gripped the mug on his sunken chest.

"Will you forgive me?" Johnny asked. "I humbly beg you to accept my contrite spirit. I brought David as my witness."

The man fumbled to extend a hand from under the cover. Johnny steadied the elderly one's shaking. My eyes brimmed.

Funk's voice wobbled. "I have been in the wrong, too. Pride in my insistence. Now reduced, this poor state . . . Nothing of worth to show before my Maker."

"You have given much," Johnny said quickly. "Your translation of the Mennonite Confession of Faith is one thing our friend Algernon Gray took with him on our behalf to present to the Confederate Congress in Richmond."

The man let out a sigh that seemed more of a groan. I relaxed at the return of Johnny's usual voice—doctor and spiritual minister, not sinner. "Your love of music has infected many a soul, eased countless burdens," he said.

The man's hand shook; he half-sobbed to regain himself. "Music is my soul. All my emotions, major or minor keys, even folk tunes."

The floor boards creaked outside the room; I knew the woman listened.

"I have noticed the minor keys on the increase," Johnny said.

"Everything that matters is in those pages," Joseph said. "My belief in God. The poetry of my soul." He fumbled to spit into his handkerchief and took short swallows. "I do not always know about doctrine. I allowed my children to have musical instruments but tried to divest myself of party spirit regarding religious matters." He closed his eyes.

"Joseph, will you forgive me?" Johnny repeated. "I need assurance."

The man did not hesitate. "I forgive," he said, adding quietly, "the method is but an outward expression." His eyes drooped, then opened wide for Brother Kline's response.

"We will continue to disagree on the method," Johnny said.

I could not avoid my sharp intake of air. Who was this speaking? Repentance, I could understand—we are all human—but forsaking years of insisting on our triune baptism? That is whence our nickname comes, Dunkers or Tunkers. How often I have heard Brother Kline explain with fervor the three dips: repentance, forgiveness of sin, washing clean with regeneration.

Joseph coughed weakly. "Sometimes I am too hard." He paused as a great rattle of pans erupted in the kitchen. "Given to stubbornness," he continued. "Words in the past—" he shook his head. "I wanted with all my heart to preserve the understandings of my grandfather. Is that so wrong?"

Johnny leaned forward, hands clasped tightly; his chair squeaked under his weight.

But Joseph was not finished. "A heritage is a precious thing. Sometimes hard to know—what to keep, what to let go."

I peeked from one to the other.

Suddenly, Johnny began to sing, "*How firm a foundation, ye saints of the Lord.*"

In a raspy wavering voice the old man responded, "*Is laid for your faith in His excellent Word.*"

They studied each other, then sang together, the weak and the clear voice, more of our shared hymn, "Protection." "*What more can He say than to you He hath said—*" Johnny motioned for me to join the repeat line: "*Who unto the Saviour for refuge have fled.*" Joseph lost breath, but Johnny and I finished. We touched the inner recesses.

"I fear we have tired you greatly," Johnny said. "Thank you for receiving us, even though you did not know—"

"I expected one last tirade," Joseph said. "The proper administration—"

My heart sank; the old man was about to undo everything. The smell of onions frying hung in the air along with the man's unanswered question: *Is that so wrong?*

But Brother Kline refrained from the usual teaching. "I have been told for years already, I never preach a sermon without saying something about baptism. It is very dear to me."

Joseph's eyebrows flickered.

"Our strengths can be our weaknesses," Johnny said, as he stood to retrieve his coat. I followed his lead and looked about for my hat as well.

But Joseph took to coughing, and the wife appeared as suddenly as before, helping him sit upright. Finally he whispered, "Pleased to—would you see fit to break bread?" He looked to his woman. "We have potatoes enough?"

"I only warmed broth," she said, "with onions. Given more time, I could add potatoes, a bit of beef."

Johnny waved his hand to the woman. "Your offer, generous. We will gladly share broth."

With that, she added bowls to the table, and we helped Joseph arise and walk to the kitchen, a separate room at the back of the house with more light.

We did as the wife did, breaking bread into our soup. I will tell Abigail, for sometimes her black bread gets exceedingly dry by the end of the week. Little was said as we ate. The man had difficulties and asked that the onions be fished from his bowl. When finished eating, Johnny could not help himself, folding his hands and offering thanks. "Bless this nourishment to its use intended, and this dear friend to your honor and glory."

I could not have added a heartier "Amen."

Johnny and I rode home in silence. The briskness of the morning had brought vigor, but the early afternoon shade across our mountains cast a chill, such that I pulled my coat and hat tighter. But an upsurge from melancholy stayed with me; I was grateful to have been lightened from our country's vale of warfare. Brother Kline might have betrayed a precious precept, but he had showered the blessing of not holding on to ill will.

A month after our visit, Joseph's son Benjamin became a minister among us German Baptists. Now two months later, the day before Christmas, news comes that Joseph Funk has passed from this earth at the age of eighty-four, some thirty years my senior. Who can explain?

But my upsurge—how quickly it has disappeared. After only two months' time, my renewal has dissipated. Partly, I have learned more regarding our German Baptists in Maryland, caught in the mix back in September. Sickening reports of our church's meetinghouse along Hagerstown Pike, full of bullet holes and wracked by artillery fire. Now, abandoned. They call the place Antietam, where Union men were ambushed in West Woods, just north of our folks' meetinghouse. Farmers' fields torn up—bodies left for dead. Sickening is not the right word. I am terrified. Stricken. I have not found escape—the questions raised by this deep wound of strife. What if something similar happened to us at Flat Rock?

And another nightmare has come to my attention. What if we had in our midst, wealthy members who think like the Hildebrand men in Augusta County? They are cousins, I believe. On the one hand, they have donated land for a church building among their Mennonites. But on the other, this forty-year-old Jacob purportedly supports his son, a Benjamin, giving service to the Confederate Army. Brother Kline shakes his head at such misplaced loyalty, subordinating themselves to a worldly government. How can they believe God's will could be accomplished by exacting vengeance?

What must these Hildebrands think when they hear of death by the thousands this very month of December? The terrible winnowing at Fredericksburg—not far from here—halfway between Richmond and Washington. Citizens had to flee when Feds ransacked the town, making off with flour and pork. Thirteen thousand dead from the North, plus 5,000 Rebs. The mind cannot comprehend these numbers. Mine cannot. Is there no reason left on the face of this earth? Slaughter justified? Word is, they dug shallow trenches—the ground, frozen already. A man would have to be liquored up to throw masses of bodies in a ditch. As mindless as my neighbor Winfield, tossing animal carcasses onto my land? Why is there no uproar? Why cannot *someone* put a stop? Countrymen looking to butcher each other—so far from the ideals our nation was founded on.

I sit staring—questions I have never entertained before. How can anyone be fully at peace, partaking of food, when such brutality continues? No matter the scale of death—one or 1,000—lives are changed. Families altered forever. I am changed. I *must* do more. *I must oppose and resist, not leave to an angry God.* And yet, I seem unable to rouse as I did back in October. Instead, I meet someone on the road and calculate: what harm can this man do to me or my family?

Abigail says, "Your walk has slowed."

"Why would anyone hurry in this vale of tears?"

"Are you going to stay in the dark all winter?" she asks. "You need to be about."

"I need rest."

"There are walnuts to pick," she says.

"And a long winter to do so."

"It is not your nature to sit idle."

I point to the new wooden board for checkers. "No one has need of another barrel."

My daughter Delilah shows more acceptance of my spirit: my swings from sadness, to anger, to relief. Then I am back to wretchedness and resignation. "Might Brother Kline be of assistance?" she asks.

I shake my head sharply. I cannot say what I think to Brother Kline; he would lose faith in me. "*Perfect love casteth out fear,*" he would spout. "*Wherefore, love the more.*"

He is sincere; there is no doubt. But I cannot achieve his elevated state of mind. I sometimes despise the tranquility oozing from him. He cautions not to describe the past year as dreadful. He makes pious statement: "All is within the hands of our loving Father."

I want to say how useless we are—little more than ants. How infected by the blister beetle, sinking its poison. Helpless when an enemy steps in our direction.

I know to humble myself before God, but I am selective with regard to my fellow man. I try to open to the stranger at the door, especially when there is rain and freezing snow, as we had already last month. But I fear for Ruby's safety, when I allow stragglers to use a bed of straw in my horse shed from time to time. Joel's horse must be here when he returns. But these fleeing Rebels with torn shirts and shoes pass through. I do the best I can. I tell my women, we must think of it as mending a shirt for Joel or Amos; we cannot let these men leave the next day as poorly clad as they came.

Other times, slaves show up—on the loose for their lives, what with the high demand and prices offered. None has refused a half loaf of bread when morning comes. They sing their songs softly; I catch snatches. A man and his boy's "*like a motherless child.*" Again and again. Not certain, if the boy was the man's; they could have been old and young brothers.

A woman with no front teeth hummed and muffled words. Delilah claimed she could make out "*. . . other side . . . Jordan . . . bound for the promised land.*" She thought the meaning might be, heading for Northern states or Canada. Another time, after an old woman left, Delilah kept singing, "*Children, go where I send thee . . .*" Most of the next week yet, she whispered, "*Where I send thee . . . one by one*" or "*two by two.*" Other times "*send thee . . . seven by seven, never got to heaven.*"

But other folks find our place also, and I can muster no good will. Last spring's mass of soldiers, replaced by ruffians. Some, locals. Call them bush-whackers, what have you. They are up to no good, some months already. Could be deserters among them. Not uncommon again, come home from church . . . hams taken from our smokehouse. Locals know our patterns— when a house will be empty of people. No respect for property, not even this distance from the turnpike. Not even our stacked wood is spared.

Once, these were but random happenings, but now Stonewall Jackson employs thieves to be his eyes and ears—nuisance-makers!—in our Valley. (His former spy, Ashby, gone.) Other folks say these scruffy molesters are led by John Imboden with headquarters at Staunton. He started raising companies west of the Blue Ridge back in the spring; nearly the status of army men, they are ordered to wreak havoc on citizens. Imboden's latest broadside at Cootes Store appeals to men "whose conscience would not be disturbed" by the sight of a "vandal carcass." Some insist, though, that he and his men have moved elsewhere. Whatever the case, dishonest men continue as regular citizens most days but cause mischief and terror by night. Abigail says I am too quick to blame Winfield for everything. I say I cannot stomach evildoers.

Traveling merchants, another unwholesome lot. That Ricketts boy and Acker fellow—the latter a relative of Winfield—come from near Broadway. I do not like the looks of either one—a shiftiness whether peddling furs or guns. Their slick hands spread bolts of cloth for display, always with a sly smile and outrageous prices. I cannot say too often to my women: "Do not open the door. If you hear pots and pans jangle, that is no time to do business."

And the ravages of diphtheria have worn down my spirit also. Still no cure! When I add up my end-of-the-year numbers, I will doubtless find I have participated in as many funerals as last year. The price of laudanum, gone so high, Johnny makes no effort to purchase it anymore. Our dear church children, the weakest, offer little resistance. Why some can survive while others perish . . . I scratch at unanswerable questions. How can anyone remain serene? *Why?* A thousand *whys*.

Despite all, I must attain a readiness for January first of next week at Linville Creek church. Brother Kline calls it a public offering of thanks to God for deliverance. Yes, of course, I am grateful for the new exemption, more generous than the previous one; it does not include the 2 percent on all taxable property. Nor does it insist men must serve as noncombatants in place of a fine. Nor be required to declare an oath—our practice has always been to affirm—to show loyalty to the Confederate States. All these changes are an enormous relief for members of our church, as well as Mennonites, Nazarenes, and those from the Society of Friends who wish to avail themselves.

As usual, we give credit to Brother Kline's persistent letter writing and petitions to the Confederate Congress, especially Colonel John B. Baldwin. Brother Moomaw and others in Botetourt County have done the same with their Congressman. John's petition pointed out the coincidence between civilized society and its respect for conscientious convictions. The Confederate Congress knows well our reputation: good farmers and peaceful citizens. But John's letter to Baldwin also included ominous words: "If we cannot be faithful to God here as noncombatants, we may be compelled to seek shelter outside of the South." What was he thinking? Where would we go? I do not want to move. My walnut trees—

Brother Kline's recent upset called to mind his dismay last spring when the quartermaster had persisted in dirty tricks—harassment!—demanding a *second* payment of $500 or forcing into the army those who had already paid once. Without belittling, Johnny had pointed out that we were helping pay the fines of church brothers not able to come up with the heavy sum on their own. His members at Linville Creek alone had raised almost $9,000 to provide exemption fee money. Arrangements like that cannot be forked over in a matter of hours, sometimes not even in weeks.

But to think of leaving our Valley with its wide-open beauty! *My home!* How unlikely that we would ever find our sons. *Oh, my boys.* They are the ones, young enough and spirited for travel. Why do they not come back? Why do they not write again? Surely they know how we pine. Only one poor letter. All this time, knowing not. Have they prevailed? Was their path on West ever made clear?

Abigail has stopped saying, "Maybe we will hear today."

That is the hardest. I wearied of her saying it every day, or asking if I thought they might have turned homeward. But now I wish she would dare to whisper anything hopeful. I am overtaken by distrust and fear, but she is the one, consumed by sorrow, having given them up.

She turns her mind to flour. Several times a month she asks, "How many barrels yet?"

We both know, flour costs over twelve dollars a barrel some places. I try to practice forbearance and offer solid reason. "We can always raise more wheat."

But I am not the man for the hard task. I hear the traveling woman's song: "*Roll on, Jordan.*" How can good overcome bad, when running from *bound* is the way to the promised land? I say uplift will come—next week, next year. I *must* say such. But I do not always believe. "*Three by three . . . for the Hebrew children.*"

Yet, barring a terrible snowstorm, my women and I will attend the day of thanksgiving. We will offer our feeble praise, while perplexed and seeking reassurance within. If only, soldiers would return to their senses and bushwhackers go back to fruitful occupations. If only we knew the worst was past, for certain.

J. Fretz — Chicago, January 1863

My homesickness finally broke through untethered. Whenever it tugged before, I shoved it under. Most of last year I stayed preoccupied with war developments, wondering what would be required of me, questioning my worth as a man. Even after my weekend in Indiana, whenever I thought of Pennsylvania—my brothers, my aging parents—I followed nostalgia with: I don't want to live there. As if a visit might suck me in against my will.

But the persistent tug became a loud knock. I wanted to see the hills of my youth, even if the trees were bare and the meadows covered with drifts of snow. Most of all, my thoughts ran to Salome. Her blue eyes. Could there still be attraction? I had to find out, rather than wonder. I'd grown despondent in my single bed, grumpy from cold, restless nights. My cheerless, one-horse bed. I feared I was losing all the finer feelings of human nature. I'd spent time in barns, on wagons—horseback!—that were more pleasant than in that bed. I didn't want to be a bachelor for life.

Professor Fowler influenced me also. He made clear: "Marriage would be the best of all means to improve yourself. You've become nervous from overwork." One time I misplaced my office key; lost it another time. "Not a serious problem," he said, "but signs pointing." I first heard him lecture on phrenology a year ago at Metropolitan Hall. His ideas fascinated me, along with his collection of skulls from men and animals, his busts of distinguished men and women. This past November I went to hear him again and soon set up a time for him to examine my head and give a delineation. By using physiognomy and assessing outward appearance, he's able to indicate one's character. It came as no surprise: I'm my mother's son.

My disconsolate bed and Mister Fowler's advice conspired. I made plans to be gone from work for a month. I secured the necessary papers to leave the city. I must have looked honest enough—it helps to be a business owner—for I was able to retrace my first journey to Chicago. December 15th I started out on a sleeping car through Detroit to visit relatives again in Vineland, Ontario. Like that first time, I stayed with my father's sister, Betsy Rittenhouse, and her family—twelve children. But this time I couldn't stay two weeks or take in the splendor of Niagara Falls again. Their boy Moses, now sixteen, shows great interest in Chicago, but he's such a talker! From Canada I went to Elmira and other points before arriving in Philadelphia. In spite of the usual irritants, smoke and dirt, the long train ride gave me ample time to contemplate my twenty-seven years. How could I possibly appeal to a woman when our country is torn apart?

I arrived in Bucks County on Christmas Eve and felt reassured by smiles from my home folks. Jakie punched me in the belly, kneed me in the thigh, our old forms of jabbing and tussling as brothers. Only now he stands fully grown above me. He brags about his horse, Arrow's, speed down the straight stretch of Hilltown Pike, but he hasn't attached our country's flag as others have. Mother remains as before, warm and affectionate; her rye bread, as good as ever. But I'm stunned how slowly Father gets around. Both my parents, past sixty, but Father only carries short lengths of wood inside. Not many years ago, he wouldn't let anyone touch his fires. Now he makes no protest when I get up before him, or restack firewood so he won't need to lift logs down from as much height.

He looked startled, though, when we shook hands. "What's this?" he said, my smooth palm in his rough one. "Soft as a woman!"

"Time to toughen me up," I managed to say.

Since Christmas Day, I've seen old friends and helped relatives with their butchering. One day my brothers and I threshed rye with a machine, but then the snows came. Ever since, we've been cooped up. Father tells his favorite stories, although I squirm when he tells again of the Doane brothers and their revenge against guerillas back in Grandfather Funk's time of the Revolutionary War. We all laugh like usual, but given what I hear of irregulars in the South today, I'm not sure merriment is called for, especially when variations about the Doanes leave me uncertain whether they were the outlaws or victims. Sometimes they seem both in the same version. But we all laugh when Father recalls how the neighbor jumped out of bed, frightened because he thought the Doanes were after *him*, and forgot to put clothes on before he ran for help across the fields to Grandfather's place, the next farm over.

But the best part of being home: I've stepped up my courtship, taking Father's carriage several times to see Salome. In fact, I surprised her on Christmas afternoon. I hesitated at the Kratz back door—*slow and easy*—but then knocked and walked in like old times. When I saw Salome's sweet face, I wanted to crush her to my chest. But good sense prevailed, and I took off my hat and kissed her hand instead. She's slightly smaller than I remembered but still has a spark in her eyes. Three days later I went back—she had nodded eagerly at the suggestion—and we've taken up nicely for these two weeks.

Every day I remind myself: *keep your hopes in check.* She has no commitments; my fears of Harry were unfounded. I must have looked relieved, for she touched the back of her hand to my cheek. With that warmth my old feelings returned in a rush. Some nights I'm tempted to think she realizes the same for herself. Could it be? She's twenty-three now. Could we possibly have arrived at readiness? The professor told me to follow my instincts, but I don't want to seem desperate. Mary Ann reminded me, "Calm yourself before any visit; don't overwhelm her."

After more times with Salome, my assessments seem reasonable: she's tall for a woman, but not too tall for me. And *not at all* thickset, nor showing any sign of curliness in her hair. For certain she meets Professor Fowler's ideal of "well-developed in the upper portion of the forehead." Something else sticks with me. He said to marry a woman who's like her father. His point was to avoid too much of the feminine or emotional between us. She's definitely fair, compared with my dark hair. And she's quieter. But then, I talk too much.

Her father, Jacob, likely thinks me a city slicker. I paid attention to his work with leather, although he uses it for harnesses and work shoes, not book bindings. When I commented on how he doesn't waste a scrap of lumber, he smiled. And it was my turn to be pleased when he showed the Kratz family coat of arms his ancestors brought with them to this country.

I can't say yet what his politics are, but my brothers have made their ideas known. Neither has had trouble with his exemption, although the Pennsylvania legislature still hasn't settled on a commutation fee. We all agreed, it's been helpful that Europe has stayed out of the war, not recognized the Confederacy. But when Abe mentioned this new recruiting song, "*We Are Coming, Father Abra'am,*" he scratched his arms like a cat with fleas.

Other times, our talk has veered toward strain. One day I asked, "How can it be fair play for a sniper with his Sharps rifle to look through a scope and target an officer at a far distance?"

Abe nodded. "Like killing for sport."

"And that Union general by the name of Sherman," I said. "You heard of him? He retaliated against guerillas last fall in Mississippi, just over the border and south of Memphis. Destroyed houses and barns, even crops for a fifteen-mile stretch."

"No good way to fight guerillas," Jakie interrupted.

"But destroying farms?" My question didn't soften his scowl.

"Vicious, those guerrillas," Abe added.

I let it drop, but another late-night conversation made me wonder even more. "You might remember, I met some Mennonites in Indiana last October. One man came from Pennsylvania."

"You wrote that," Abe said. "Did he mention our state's Thaddeus Stevens?"

"Yes, this new acquaintance, Peter Nissley, told me about him—their Pennsylvania representative in Lancaster County. He's said to look out for peace people. Right?"

Abe nodded, but Jakie swung a leg over the arm of his chair and said nothing. I went on to describe the Mennonite meetinghouse in Indiana, people's plain dress.

Jakie scratched under his beard. "Not even ties?"

"Much like our mother, retaining the old ways—dress and bonnet— here at Line Lexington. A genuine meekness," I said. "She wouldn't have to stay so plain."

"Suppose not," Jakie mumbled, chin in his hand.

I had also looked forward to seeing John Geil again; as expected, he goes about with none of that puffery I see in the Chicago churches. At eighty-four he wears the same, long white coat and still stands with only a slight slump in his shoulders. His sermon the first Sunday of the new year took me back to when he instructed me in the faith before my baptism at Line Lexington. The same forcefulness of delivery, although he didn't go on as long. But his words touched me when he spoke of arranging our affairs so that our work and labor serve and glorify God. My mind flitted to the lumber business and my slightly impaired constitution that Professor Fowler has noted. Over five years of time in Chicago my patterns have become set: politics, Sunday school teaching, war meetings, lumber, church socials, money-making, more politics. But still, there's plenty to unsettle me at times.

It was when I spoke with Geil after the service—he stood at the stove lighting his pipe—that I felt a jolt. I reminded him, "I'm Jacob's oldest son, the Funk who lives in Chicago."

He nodded but asked, "Have you joined the enthusiasm for making war?"

I must have stiffened. Had he expected me to enlist? "For a while," I said, but my voice trailed off. "Not much of late," I added. I told him about marching with Lincoln's supporters, the Wide-Awakes, and about my friends signing up. "I'd make a poor soldier. I couldn't fight to kill—my scruples."

His reply puzzled me more. "Yes, that has always been our privilege to decline such; we shall probably always retain it." A casualness, like talking about variables in the weather. So different from John M. Brenneman's passion about the need to maintain what has set us apart. Did Geil not know about slippage in the church? Only later, when Father mentioned that Geil has a grandson who's enlisted, did I begin to guess at what might have split his loyalties.

Of course, no one stays exactly the same: not John Geil, not my brothers or parents. Father's aging is probably natural enough; it's not that he's going to expire soon. Still, he mentioned with soberness, a relative, Joseph Funk—same age as Geil—who died a few weeks ago. Father hadn't kept in touch with him—this Joseph had moved to Virginia long ago—but Father knew of the man's influence. Far beyond Mennonite circles, the man had taught music and published song books.

I calm myself: there are far more ways in which Father *hasn't* changed. When we sit around at night smoking cigars I brought from Chicago, he wants numbers on our clients and lumber accounts.

He pounds the arm of his rocking chair and fairly shouts, "Capital, my son!"

"Prices keep falling, but we always sell our lumber for more than we paid to buy it. Your son-in-law, Jacob, is sharp as ever. Never tires, even with all his business affairs."

"And you're happy to be a rich man!" Father declares.

My head drops for a second. "Well, yes—some discomfort, though. Many folks suffer."

He looks puzzled but then switches to talking about *Uncle Tom's Cabin*. "Might be one of the last books I read in its entirety. Too much eye strain. Very sad story, though. That Tom—the very definition of loyal. Wouldn't you say? Not one hint of vengeance. And Topsy—such a happy slave."

I snuff out my cigar and straighten. "Considering what a brutal sort Tom's owner was—" I take a deep breath. "I guess you could say Topsy *seemed* happy."

Father takes a second look at me but asks, "Did anyone write you about those two deacons who made a house call when they heard I was reading a novel? Called it frivolity." Father laughs like he's twenty years younger and leans forward in his rocker. "One of 'em thought I should spend time reading the Bible instead. I put on my poker face and asked what he thought the end time would be like." Father laughs so hard, we all laugh along. "Those two ended up arguing: what the Bible says, or what it means. What they *thought* it means. Finally picked up their tails and left. Completely confused."

"I was outside," Abe says, "and missed hearing it. But seriously, Father, you should get spectacles. I've been telling you."

"What would I want with a fool bridge on my nose? Old Susie's tail would knock specs off in no time."

"You know what I've said," Abe counters. "Wear them when you're inside. If they help, it's worth a try. No sense having trouble."

"Hard to think of you not reading, Father," I say. "Is it your eyes? You only wanted me to send copies of *The Tribune* now and then? I thought maybe you only had time for Republicans in Chicago, not uncivil Democrats."

"As long as I can read your letters and scribble a note back," Father says, "good enough. Old age teaches. Soon enough—learn what you can do without."

I shake my head. "But fuzzy letters—why put up with that, if there's a remedy? I'm fortunate; can't complain. Only my right ear. Well, my teeth sometimes."

"An abscess that time, wasn't it?" Father asks. "Bad rupture—your ear."

That's how our conversations go. I'm pleased with Father's praise, but we all tiptoe when differences show up around the edges. Maybe I've changed even more than I thought.

Abe adds another uncertainty; I don't know whether to encourage him or not. He hears grandiose claims about opportunities in Chicago, just like our cousin Moses, and compares that with the low pay he's getting as a teacher. There's truth in what he hears, but plenty of exaggeration, too. Sometimes I wonder if he's always going to follow whatever I do. I need to get through to him how lonely it becomes—my best friends gone—even though there's endless activity. Long nights might not bother Abe so much, though. Just so he doesn't blame me if he moves and it's not a good fit.

But right now, I must push family questions aside. My short time left with Salome presses. Less than a week until I return to Chicago. I dread taking the train back through Ohio—that hotbed of rabble-rousing Democrats. It will save time, though—the most direct route back.

* * *

With more than the usual trepidation I went to Nace's Corner again—how can someone both quiet and excite me *beyond words*? My greatest fear: botching things. This time I took Father's sleigh and best horse, Sir. Ever since it turned cold on New Year's Eve and the snow has stayed, our hills and woods have glistened. I wore my Chicago hat and coat along with a green neck scarf Mother recently knitted. Countless times I've reminded myself: whatever happens, *do not beg*. It hasn't worked before; it won't work now.

The crisp brightness and stillness of the morning seemed to support my scheme. I'd scarcely entered the Kratz home before I suggested a ride with Salome. Her mother Mary's eyes blinked fast at the idea, my own heart aflutter. I mentioned that the bricks would still be warm for our feet, but Mary hurried to find an extra blanket. I'm often freezing in Chicago, but if all went well, I planned for beauty to circumvent coldness.

I steadied Salome as she let go my arm and stepped up into the sleigh. In the slight jostle, she lingered before withdrawing her hand. She looked smaller as she sat bundled in a warm coat and blankets, her hair pulled back tightly under her hat. Sir pranced, with all the grace befitting his strong legs, the little more than twelve miles to the Delaware River, a place that draws couples in summertime. I knew of a lookout, elevated and between two wooded areas, offering a splendid view of the river any time of year. I'd reviewed in my mind where the winding path down to the river starts, should we choose that. One time we bounced, the sleigh's left runner caught in a rut, but Salome took it in good spirit, even pressed willingly into my side. Her blue eyes twinkled as I'd hoped.

At another point we had to backtrack—I missed the proper turnoff—but otherwise, we found our way easily. Once at the lookout, we sat in silence, taking in the sparkle of sun on a snow-covered, frozen river. I pointed to the drift of smoke from cabins nestled on the other side.

"It's so quiet," she said, barely above a whisper.

"Like the breath of a new year," I said. My tongue felt thick, and when I tried to recall lines I'd memorized from John Greenleaf Whittier, my mind went blank. I had to fall back on what I'd written in my diary at the end of last year. "The wheels of time roll on . . . they heed not our presence but onward . . ." My words sounded overly formal, but Salome's eyes, soft and gentle, stayed fixed on me. "May we so live, that though the circle prescribed for us be past, we need not fear to enter upon the untried realities of an unknown future." I took off a dress glove and reached for her hands inside her muff.

She squeezed in return. "Heaven whispers to a scarred earth and blesses it with freshness."

I looked at her, astonished. "You are lovely to me, *beyond words.*" I hadn't intended that last part. "I hold you, dear as my own life." I loosened blankets and reached to put my arms about her. She did not resist; her lips welcomed me. In spite of layers, I felt her body breathing against mine. The time for rehearsing had passed.

"Will you marry me and be my wife?" My cold breath billowed above her face.

"I will," she said simply. "Will you be my husband?"

I gulped cold air. "Most honored. With all my heart, I love you."

"And I, you," she said, not a blemish on her face. No false vein would ever be at home with her.

That was the easy part. We've been close to such declarations before.

"I loved you already when you were my student. You stood above all the rest."

"I always respected you as my teacher. Admired you even. But now we're changed."

"Yes," I said quickly. "That early attraction, nothing, compared with asking you to live your life with me." I couldn't put off the rest. "Will you come to Chicago with me?"

"Yes, but on one condition. Two," she added quickly.

The conditions had to wait, however, as we kissed and fumbled more, my hunger swift.

Finally, she straightened and pulled herself together. I couldn't look away. My desire pounded. Such soft skin, tender to my touch. I wanted all.

I thought she might scold, but instead she continued as if there'd been no interruption. "The first condition is that I remain in Pennsylvania another year. By then my sister, Annie, will be thirteen; I can finish training her to take over for Mother and Father."

I inhaled so much cold air, I had to turn my face away to muffle my cough. How could she speak so calmly of separation? Another miserable year alone in Chicago—that wretched single bed. How did she dare—so businesslike? I shuffled my feet to keep blood flowing.

She ignored my distress. "The second condition: I must be allowed to visit my parental home once a year. If I want." Her deep-set eyes looked steadily but still carried warmth. She's exactly what I need: hearty but judicious, far more refined than I.

"The second is an easy one," I said. "I get lonesome for my folks, too. And we have a responsibility." I took her hands and kissed each knuckle. "The first condition—a difficulty." Sir stamped his foot and the sleigh rocked slightly. I felt no amusement but smiled wanly. "Not one I can't manage, though, for the promise of a lifetime. I'll wait. Not gladly, though. Put off life with you?" I pressed my forehead into her coat. It's true. I'd made no arrangements for taking a bride back to Chicago. One ticket is all. I couldn't have presumed a month ago that such good fortune awaited. The best I had imagined—maybe next summer. But a whole year's delay—? "I want to marry you now, today even. But I'll pray the year passes quickly."

"And safely," she said, a shadow crossing.

But it was her turn to act; she unbuttoned my coat and reached her arms around me. Her fingers pressed through the back of my vest, my shirt.

Oh, no, not another year. I closed my eyes and took in her kiss.

I won't let myself dwell on the wait. She's the one I've wanted. I knew it over five years ago. All the fine ladies of Chicago, their beautiful dresses, can't compare. Sir fairly flew over snow-packed roads and fields, back to Salome's parental home, as if he knew to make each minute of delay pass quickly.

The uncertainties abound. The lumber business—I've laid bare my doubts. The draft—we've talked of every possibility. Yet I've more of a plan for my life than a few weeks ago. Salome has agreed! I'll see her again in two days to make certain of our promises. I must speak with her father alone, but then Salome and I will go together, make known our plans to both sets of parents before next Monday. Before I catch that dreaded train in Philadelphia.

I almost forgot. When we neared Nace's Corner, I tugged for Sir to stop and pulled a small delicacy from my outer coat pocket—yes, smushed chocolate. "Take and eat," I said. I couldn't wipe the silly grin from my face.

"Where did you—?" But then, she quickly unwrapped the flattened morsel and placed it in her mouth, one end extended, her blue eyes beckoning.

I understood at once and bit off a tiny piece of sweetness.

"Uhm," she said. We sat, hands locked again, savoring what I'd purchased weeks before on a whim in Philadelphia. Suddenly she held up my hand. "Your middle finger is shorter than the one beside it—the one, some call the ring finger."

"I know. But it's only one hand. I've made it this far in life."

She laughed with delight. "I still love you."

I sat there, grinning like a young lad—all that had befallen me. Sir grew impatient and started his trot. Neither Salome nor I know aught of the obstacles. We've much more to talk about. I need to hear again her thoughts of Sunday schools and evangelistic meetings; she knows I've been superintendent at the Milwaukee Depot Mission school. She's said nothing of her father's views.

But her gentle ways and words stay with me. Chicago! I'll have her to come home to! No more coldness in bed. But one year yet!

Jacob — Iowa, February 1863

The cold of winter has made its home in my bones; we stay braced for deep snows that may measure up to last year's worst. Almost a year ago it was, early in March, a severe storm lasted most of a week. I thought the snow had stopped, only to see a blizzard resume the next day.

Now in the throes of my third winter with Mary, I sometimes walk to Frederick's house. He looks surprised, but I cannot say all that bothers. More than the red pin cushion, more than dishes from the Old Country. I watch Frederick tinker with one machine or another. We say little. On the way home, I pause at the fresh tracks of fox—oval-shaped prints, longer than wide.

Once inside my house again, burned meat may show up. The worst: a fat rabbit several of the young grandsons brought after their hunting outing on the first day of the new year. Extra special to my way of thinking, but Mary ruined it with too much heat, as if my latest request for quiet had been unreasonable.

I miss my oldest grandson Samuel; he left us right before Christmas, heading East, as he had desired. One time I dreamed he grew a mustache like Emanuel's. The postal system is unreliable, but he might not write, not even if he happened to come upon soldiers. We pray earnestly that he will not be pressed into any unwanted duty.

It cost $11.45 for him to take the cars, first from Iowa City to Chicago, then on to Indiana. That is what it would take to send Mary to visit her relatives; double that to bring her back. Already two months ago, she said she was homesick for her daughters. I was sorry to hear, of course, but I could not see fit to put her on a train by herself. Even more dangerous, if soldiers were on board.

But Samuel's lack of concern regarding money remains a great puzzle. Not that long ago he spoke with such admiration for Diogenes's simple style. But before Samuel left home, he seemed nonchalant, whether about his purchases or his income from construction work. He copied records for me and showed no embarrassment. I could see he gave four dollars for new boots

63

and the same amount for a travel valise. I can picture his gold pen glittering alongside his new Bible. And last fall when Samuel and a friend had gone to Homestead and bought woolen clothes, he had not blinked an eye when he told of parting with twenty dollars.

It is true: his records showed unheard-of-generosity also. He paid out sixty cents a day or eleven dollars a month when he had to hire help for the work he did at Abe Kauffman's. The same wages went to men who helped with the new barn for Big Chris, as well as the brick house for my son Joseph. All of that in greenbacks, this paper money that showed up last year. I could not say half my fears: too much cash at the ready for one so young. And during warfare!

Now my only daughter's oldest, Noah, has reached twenty and has the itch. He wants to go to Indiana and find work! He will have to wait another year until he is of age, but even so . . . When I reported this news to Mary on the way home from meeting with the Deer Creek group, she said with a glint, "You should know: Indiana is a good place to find a companion."

I only said, "I do not see the humor."

But she leaned forward in the buggy and looked me square in the face. "You were prone to change locations when you were young."

That sizzle in her replies is not uncommon. When I commented on the number of women absent from church when we met at Anna and Daniel's house—Susanna Hochstetler was not the only one missing—Mary passed it off with a wave of her hand. "Oh, they had sick ones." In truth, she speculates, even when she speaks as if she knows all. I learn later, only a part came from a reliable source.

During that same time of aggravation in the buggy, I said, "If the members continue to be of many minds, we will not be able to hold our spring Communion."

"Warmer weather will bring better attendance," she said, as if that is all it takes.

"Our church dare not hide its face from disobedience."

"You will wear yourself out being the gatekeeper. Loosen yourself; you forget again."

"I cannot be a part-time shepherd."

"You do not need to take everything so seriously," she said.

"Authority comes from God. Can anything be more serious?"

"Do you never err?" she asked, her eyes blinking fast.

"Of course, I am human."

"But I am not to question?"

"Not if you seek to undermine," I said.

"My first was an able listener."

"I am called as bishop. I cannot choose to obey God four days of the week, and please members the other three. Your Daniel never—"

"My first never achieved your importance?" She smacked her lips. "My first knew to distinguish willful misdeeds from harmless failings."

I looked away to snow-covered fields. This woman does not know what a frightful member the tongue can be.

But greater alarm had stirred earlier that Sunday when we gathered at Anna's. I took opportunity to converse with Peter Swartzendruber and Henry Hochstetler after our noon meal. They were inspecting the brick frame Anna's Daniel had fashioned at each end of the fireplace mantel. He took clay from the hillside behind his hog stable and ended up with a house solidly built from bricks. A far cry from my stepson Daniel's first chimney, made from a clay mortar mixed with split sticks of wood.

I had been wanting to ask Henry about Emanuel, and I remembered how warmly the lad had spoken of his Uncle Peter. "How does your young man fare?" I began.

"Minor complaints," Henry said. "A Selby fellow from Iowa City is afflicted with the eye problem—enough so, to be in the hospital."

Peter stood with his Sunday coat open carelessly in front. "Emanuel mentioned sore eyes already last fall in his post mailed from Missouri. One of the Fry boys, almost blind back then."

I motioned for us to move farther from the heat. Someone had added an unneeded log. "I missed hearing of such. Most of the talk has been how Copperheads have quieted around here."

"Hard to get word," Henry said. "Some aggravation about stamps, though. Emanuel asked us to send some."

"How do they pass the time—winter and all?" I asked.

"Mostly guarding trains, commissary stores," Henry said, his arms crossed in front. "One time, a big snowball fight amongst them. Much idleness." He added more quietly, "You surely heard—the Iowa boy who died? A Coons by name. Clothes sent back to the parents."

"Very sorry to hear," I said. "But these eye problems—?" I waited. Neither man showed interest in saying more, so I mentioned my granddaughter Barbara instead—next in line after Samuel and Jakob—her first babe last year, found to be completely blind.

Peter grunted but turned to Henry. "What of your boy Christian, the married son who enlisted with that unit back in Pennsylvania?"

"Still in a hospital," Henry said. "So far as we know. Not certain, whether Maryland or Pennsylvania. Tried to get him sent back to his woman for recovery."

"Is that so?" I began, but Henry stepped away to spit at the hearth.

When he returned, Peter stretched his suspenders over his belly and said, "You know what Emanuel would say about that." With barely a pause he added, "One time he wrote: 'A man may try as well to roll the Alleghenies into the ocean as to get a discharge.'"

"Sounds like Emanuel, all right," his father said. "A brick wall, when they tried to get a discharge for the Iowa fellow who ended up dying."

"You mean—Emanuel would need to desert to escape? Face being chased?" I asked.

The men barely glanced at me but continued their back-and-forth.

"Had to pay forty to fifty cents on the dollar, to get a dollar bill changed to silver," Henry said.

"Nothing good to say about Missouri pens either," Peter added. "Wouldn't trade an Iowa pen for all the pens in Missouri!"

"*Ja*, homesick. Disgusted to shell out twenty-five cents for the same kind of tobacco he'd given fifteen cents for in Iowa City."

Peter briefly glanced my way. "Told me he'd given up smoking and chewing."

"*Ja, ja.* Heard that one before, too," Henry said.

I looked for a chair to clutch but did not want to miss out.

"Not cheap, that army life." Peter pulled on his suspenders again and hooked his thumbs inside the top edge of his pants. "Twenty-nine cents for a pint of molasses!"

"And twenty cents for a dozen eggs! That one riled Susanna."

"Are they not fed?" I asked. Neither man answered, so I stumbled on. "Sometimes I feel a chill, the back of my neck, thinking of the lad. I can be out brushing and feeding Caspar, and my mind wanders. Do they run into Rebs?" I asked hastily.

"Only one time I heard about." Peter turned fully my way. "Rebs bothered railroad cars passing by, and Emanuel's company responded. Nighttime."

Henry nodded. "No officers with the boys that time they heard shots. No lieutenant or sergeant to give commands, but the boys went out to look anyway."

"Not afraid to stand up, that boy of yours." Peter turned a moment to a commotion in the kitchen. A child had come running in, breathless, to tell of the lad Joseph's fall on the pond. Peter continued, unhurried. "Proud to stand up to the Rebs. 'Stand up to the mark,' is what Emanuel wrote. Said they hunted for Rebs in cornfields. Disappointed—nothing more than coons."

The kitchen racket increased—a crying child, carried by older boys. Women bustled to give attention. Henry pulled out his pocket watch and signaled to his boys to get their horse and carriage. Before he left, though, I said I would appreciate further word. He made no definite response one way or another, only a slight lift in his shoulders.

Anna's little Joseph had broken his arm on the ice. Now he will need to fend with his left for a while. We have the best hills for youngsters' sledding in Sharon Township, but Anna's man and their big boys developed their own pond where the children scoop off snow and play their games of tag or what have you.

But this unnerving news of Emanuel and the other Iowa boys! So much I did not know. I have since repeated to all the ministers, especially now that we have added Jacob Marner and Peter Brenneman to The Bench at Deer Creek, "We do well to share word of each other's concerns, not yield to any manifestation of the individual spirit. That goes for withholding information." I looked each man in the eye, but I could not be sure.

Benjamin Schrock is newly come from Pennsylvania and helps out here in Sharon Township. Sometimes he gives newsy reports from his brother Peter, part of that young church I was blessed to visit at Red House, Maryland. Benjamin works exceedingly hard; in two years he has enclosed all his prairie with board fence. His cows do not need to wear a bell about the neck to be found for milking. But when it comes to Scripture, Benjamin claims apt words fly away. I do not mean to chide, but he hangs his head like one of my boys as a lad. If only he would not repeat the same words so much.

Marner is little better. One Sunday he sat down after only twenty minutes, and I had to give additional thoughts, for he had omitted much Scripture. Afterwards, his hands still shook when I gripped them; he claimed he could not think what else was needful. "Do not lose heart," I said, "but more diligence is needed. Study, so you can make application. Then you will be able to fill the proper amount of time."

But these men are learning; neither is as much a thorn as John P., a seasoned minister. The effects of age may be taking their toll, for he is past seventy. I would never want to bring grief to an elderly one—I am less than a decade behind—but his gears may have slipped a notch. Something recently provoked his loose lips, for he said to my face, "*Du hast Stolz!*"

The Lord gave strength and I replied, "*Ja,* I keep watch to avoid pride." No one else heard his outburst and I decided to ignore; I could not be sure if his lips curled in amusement. But if he oversteps again, I may have no choice but to take it up. What would my Barbara say of her own stepson! I cannot let myself think what John P. may divulge to others in a reckless moment. I fear he bends Mishler's ear with falsehoods.

It is far better for me to dwell on the new calendar year, for we follow the pattern set forth long ago—which Scriptures to use when, for what sermons. In January we turned once more to the Sermon on the Mount. I marvel at how Jesus showed no fear of being misunderstood by those in his hearing. Some of his parables still baffle, almost as if he wanted his message shrouded from those who wished to tear him to shreds. I seek to adopt the same courage, even when some want to cast scurrilous doubt about me or ignore the Lord's teaching.

And courage with family, too. My woman's sizzle and Samuel's stubbornness. If he ends up penniless and comes scuffling home like the prodigal son, I will gladly go to him. Even if the worst happens—embroiled and needing to desert—I will welcome him back. Daniel would surely rustle up a fatted calf for his part; we would consider it a sad lesson for everyone's edification.

ESTHER — Shenandoah Valley, March 1863

We've had our baby most of three months now, but I'm slow to gain back. I couldn't manage without Mary Grace—thirteen next month and standing taller than me. She fixes most of our food—her pie crust, as good as mine—and scrubs our clothes with the washboard and large tub when we have need. William fills the lamps, but we're running frightfully low on oil. All winter that boy has stayed stubborn, turning up his nose at pork.

I should be gearing up for outdoors, but I can't seem to make headway. Mary Grace still needs a bigger dress, but I might take in one of my own instead. Simon says the sheep will soon be ready to shear. I can't expect Mary Grace to do all the washing and picking of dirt from wool. Even when two people work together, the carding is tedious.

I don't know what ails. I do little more than care for Jephthah. Spots of blood show, but Frances says she took care with the afterbirth. Simon watches every day for a mess of greens. He calls it the best tonic, from those days when he lived in a cave a year ago. Mama always counted on chamomile tea for female troubles, but I'm still lagging. It might take dandelion mixed with egg and vinegar to bring cure.

My time of labor started on the up and up, but went to the bad. Frances came right away when William rode to her. But after the good start—all was laid out—the pains stopped. I drank hot concoctions and Frances insisted I get up and walk. But when darkness came, everything quieted. The next morning I made effort to milk cows. Pulling on teats did the trick, and the pains started again. I had to call Joseph, though, for help getting up from the three-legged stool; he carried my bucket, too.

Four hours later we had our boy with the weak cry, Jephthah. All our others cried with a fierceness but not this one. The children tiptoed up to look, but none lingered. No defects, not even a red birthmark. But his color—no good from the start, more yellow by the day. Frances stayed an extra night and said to rock the babe directly under lamplight. Now when the sun gives warmth, I bundle him and go outside to sit. Simon sees improvement, and my milk comes better. But we have a lazy sucker, Mama would say. I chose his name, not that I want Jephthah to grow to be a warrior. But his name reminds me to teach the ways of love.

I had wanted to send the big ones to school for the winter months; Andrew stayed restless. But back in December, Simon surprised me with the ten-plate stove. "More ease," Simon said, his jagged teeth jutting out in a grin. The boys helped him replace the old and affix the new—three wide sections, plus a deep hearth in front. It stands a few feet above the floor and has a broad flat surface that holds heat from the hot air in the uppermost section.

I was overjoyed; we don't make a habit of spending on elaborate gifts. (Mama might be alarmed.) But later, when I mentioned schooling again, Simon shook his head. He pointed to the stove, as if I would understand his bargain. "All of ours can write their names; the boys have learned to read and cipher. Good enough."

"We don't have work to keep them busy all winter."

His eyes gleamed and he smacked his lips. "Our own fertilizer in another year," he said. I had no inkling, but he'd put the boys to building a lime kiln—that clearing in the back woods.

Around the same time as Simon bought the stove, our bishop returned from the north. He and Andrew embraced at church, like father and son. But Samuel's worry lines had deepened, his eyebrows gone white, save for stray black hairs. He told of new friends along the route of our Underground Railroad and remained steadfast: "War is repugnant in the sight of God."

But the times have not been smooth. Two months ago, Brother Samuel had to rebuke the Hildebrand bishop in the southern district. Only twenty-some miles separate us, but they've turned more to supporting this stand-in government. This Hildebrand, a cousin of the one who'd offered a blessing for Peter, caused a ruckus when he invited our Weavers church, plus Mennonite churches in the northern district, to join them in Augusta County for a service of thanksgiving near the end of January. Straight from the pulpit, Bishop Coffman objected.

Hildebrand had called the exemption for men of conscience a privilege or kindness. But Samuel said, "*God* is the one who bestows blessings, *not* the actions of a Rebel government. *God* is to be the recipient of our prayers and thanks."

They must have far more wealth in Augusta County, for this Hildebrand is said to have referred to the exemption fee as a small fine. Few of us at Weavers would look on $500 as anywhere near to small. Frances has said since, the southern bishop apologized, but feelings have stayed bruised.

How can people get turned so opposite? These differences in leaders, as wide as between my two oldest boys. All winter I worried over Peter. Did he stay warm? Did his shoes hold up? Did he need to scavenge? It's been most of a year since we've seen our boy—only that one visit. But when I pine, Simon tells me to shush. He says spring is when armies make ready again.

"The 52nd was in Maryland back in December," he says.

"Where 'bouts?" I ask. "Why didn't you say?"

He shrugs. "You were busy with Jephthah. One man said Fredericksburg; another said Frederick. Better to know nothing than to think we know something."

"Across the Blue Ridge?"

"If Fredericksburg. Or Frederick to the west."

"Nowhere is it written to stay ignorant."

His reply comes quick. "If we were to know for certain, we would have been told."

He puts unknowns aside; all his energy goes to getting a head start. "This year we'll overcome deficits," he says. "Weather is promising, not like last fall's freezing rain and early cold."

He and Andrew have taken the plow shear to be sharpened; the boys have hauled manure to the fields. They follow Simon's directions: prune apple trees, stop worms in peach trees, spade part of the garden. Every day he checks if moisture has gone from the soil. How can he tell a mud ball has changed from one day to the next?

But when I want to dispute again, last spring comes back—abandoned here with three youngsters. I dare not let him think I doubt; he'll heap scorn.

"Hurry it up," he says to William, harping at the lad.

To me he says, "Be ready with the sheep."

I get up slowly, but I mumble, "You said before." We never properly cleaned the sheep shed last year. Now with warmer weather, I must force Jephthah to speed his sucking. I must be about.

* * *

He came as in a dream, the way Mama's presence sneaks in. He left like a gray ghost. I couldn't rid myself of the thought: *he can't stomach us.* Peter walked in right before our noon meal and walked out halfway through the afternoon. He took to Jephthah right away, talked sweetness and said he misses little ones.

All but Andrew crowded round. Simon looked his son over, raised both eyebrows. He'd not seen Peter in a year, hadn't known him slimmed down and shaggy-haired.

Joseph noticed Peter's canteen, watched him slip out of boots with tarnished buckles.

"Fredericksburg," Peter said to him with a grin. His shabby jacket hung on his shoulders.

"You were there?" I asked.

William interrupted, fetching an extra chair. I motioned for Mary Grace to put the pork and kraut on the table. My heart beat hard through Simon's prayer.

We'd barely helped ourselves to food when Peter took up my question. "Fredericksburg, way back in December, Ma. Yankees made fools of themselves, sacked the town but lost men by the thousands. No business whatsoever. Not one of 'em reached that stone wall. Kept sending waves of soldiers across the open field. We were right there, sending them back. If ever anyone asked for it! We showed 'em; only lost a third as many. Their corpses abandoned two days before they finally asked for a truce."

My mind went to shambles. Simon studied his plate; Andrew picked.

"What happened to your tooth?" William asked.

"My teeth!" Peter opened his mouth wide. "Lost two and chipped another; I chew on the other side now. Jumped up too fast. A sudden noise behind. Before Fredericksburg. Walked right into a low-hanging branch. Must have had my mouth half-open. Caught it such, ripped the corner and knocked out teeth. All healed now; my buddy knew to use dried yarrow."

"What was the noise?" Joseph asked.

Color spread on Peter's thin face. "On picket duty, stationed on the side of a steep hill. I'd been walking up and down but took a short break. You have to. Tiresome, keeping an eye out for Blue Coats all the time. Must have dozed. My own man came to relieve me but got his feet tangled in underbrush. His curses sounded close. Lucky I didn't fire." Peter busied himself, slabbing butter on bread.

I couldn't think how to get us elsewhere. The story of Genevieve's boy, Henry, came to mind, but that didn't seem right.

Peter broke the silence. "You saving that for last?" He nodded toward a small pile of meat William had scooped aside from his kraut.

"I don't eat pork," William said.

"What's wrong, man?" Peter asked. "Too young to have bad digestion."

William shoved his plate toward Peter; Joseph usually gets the extra.

Simon kept his gaze on Peter but finally said, "When you going to put this aside?"

"Never, Pa," Peter said. "Not till we finish. We don't quit. Oh, some do. Some skip out—cowards—say they're homesick, some other excuse. But the 52nd—our commander says we're the best unit ever. Fearless. Wouldn't trade us. We know we're good; that makes us even better. Over twice as many Feds killed at Fredericksburg proves it." His brown eyes dared anyone to disagree. "They were fearless, too, I guess, but their officers—stupid. A general named Burnside—goofy sideburns, they say."

When Peter reached for more bread, I said, "Mary Grace made that."

"You should be our cook," he said to her. "Nothing half this good in camp. Days of eating slosh."

"Severe shortages here," Simon said. "The sea blockade."

"Not my fault," Peter said. He reached to add apple butter.

"Shoes, flour," Simon continued. "Fortunate to have our own wheat. Not a lick of salt."

"Don't blame us," Peter said. "You ever eat hard tack? Flour and water? I guess not. Baked into thin cakes; might have a little salt but no flavor, unless from worms. Best to dunk it in coffee, if you can stand the swill that passes. Helps to be hungry."

"Whose fault then?" Andrew asked quietly. "You started it."

"I didn't start anything," Peter said. He glared at his brother. "Lincoln started it."

"Boys!" Simon said.

Everyone knows that voice: raw and rasping, cutting through disputes. Simon doesn't settle things; he cuts them off.

Mary Grace stumbled to get up—eyes red. She brought two pieces of leftover peach pie and a fresh custard to the table. Peter helped himself, a piece of each, but little more was said. From the woods a mourning dove called; not the kind of bird, though, that the devil can't change into.

The others soon went out to work—Mary Grace, too. Simon wouldn't veer from sowing flax seed.

Peter stayed at the table with me. He held Jephthah and sang to him. "*Yo! ho! Yo! ho! Yo! ho!*" swinging the babe's arms with every note. He said they've been building earthworks; sometimes he called it breastworks. They mound up earth like a fort, behind which they can crouch for protection from enemy bullets. Other times they've cut down trees and piled branches high, making a shield around their camp. He wouldn't say where.

Jephthah grew fussy and couldn't be quieted, save by feeding. Peter inspected the new stove and offered to heat water for clean-up.

"I can do it later," I said.

"No, Ma, I'll wash up. You look tired; you work too hard." Peter bent to me and kissed me on top. He rolled up his torn jacket sleeves.

Tears blurred my eyes. Simon hasn't kissed me in months. "Slow to recover from birthing is all." I couldn't say *low in spirit*. "Pa bought the stove last December." My voice came stronger. "That open oven section, middle part, circulates heat better. Check, though, if the firebox needs more long sticks."

"I'm glad for you," he said. "The stove."

Tears sprang again. I had thought life would go better with Simon home. But that only lasted a few weeks. The stove—his impulsiveness. It never made up for the dearth of tenderness. Now kindness—my absent son.

When he sat again, he took Jephthah, put a thick finger inside the baby's fist and rested his head on the back of Mama's rocker. "I miss you, Ma. Everyone. Even Pa."

"Yes, Peter. You, too."

"One side, going to win; the other—" He shook his head. "We can't lose. We won't stop fighting. We know we're in the right."

"But, Peter." I closed my eyes, wiped fingertips across my cheek. "It's ungodly—"

His rocker stopped creaking. "One time, Ma—" He stopped short. I opened to see him press a fist to his mouth. Jephthah wiggled, and Peter grabbed him close. "You don't understand," he said softly. "Couldn't." But a hardness crept in. "Feels good, doing as we're told. Animals on the other side." His eyes stayed fixed far away.

My boy—sad and angry by turns. A grown man, a full year's beard. His own ways.

"I'm only a small part, Ma. Replaceable. The 52nd—another small part. But when I stand at attention and the colonel walks by, looks me in the eye—it's something, Ma. I'm where I'm to be." He closed his eyes and rubbed a sock-covered foot on the rocker rung. "Time may be coming—" He jerked his head and his voice hushed more. "Something, all right, to be a part."

I couldn't take my eyes off him.

"The Army of Northern Virginia. I go where asked. An enemy decides, or an officer. I won't let my brothers down." He leaned forward, made big eyes at Jephthah. "No, you couldn't see—can't—how it is." He slowly rocked again. "Not so low as to run."

"Your brothers are here."

"No, Ma. I know my brothers."

He made a noise that sounded like a sob, but collected himself. "I lost one—a brother. All the thousands that die—I lost my closest. Burton. Loved him like a brother."

I pressed fingertips to my forehead. "I'm sorry. I don't know what you've been through, Peter. What you've chosen." I couldn't cross over. Not even if my words had been better. Somebody else's boy.

Jephthah whimpered and Peter started to croon, "*Sure he'll come again / And cheer my weeping eye.*" He turned to humming, then sang more words: "*Mourns the loss / Of a southern Soldier Boy.*"

I held out my arms for Jephthah, but Peter shook his head. "Words meant from a sweetheart back home."

I nodded, as if I understood. They could have been mine.

"Burton had his banjo in camp. All winter he taught us songs. Kept us going, when spirits sank." I reached again for Jephthah, but Peter paid no notice. "We have revivals, Ma. Ministers come to camp, one church or another. Tell us to live righteous lives. Not drink so much. They leave tracts or Bibles."

When Jephthah had finished messing himself, I took him to the back room. I heard Peter rustling in the pantry. What more could I have said? While I was occupied, he must have grabbed his hat and haversack. His shiny canteen. He'd never removed his jacket.

I don't know if he really called out, "Tell the others—" I held still to catch more, then hurried with Jephthah.

He didn't say what to tell—not that I heard—didn't say goodbye. When I finished cleaning Jephthah, Peter was gone. I didn't give him a kiss back. He left. I would have sent more cheese than what he took. More of Mary Grace's bread. But no shirts to spare, no extra jacket. Peter slipped out the door, must have put his boots on while on the porch. I thought he'd wander to the fields. But none of the others saw him again. When I went looking, he was nowhere to be found. My tears came full, mixed with Jephthah's cries over his red bottom. I let him nurse the other side. I dreamed a stranger sought consolation.

Peter didn't know where they'd be going next. "Maybe out West." But another time he had said, "North, most likely. Maybe Stonewall; could be Lee. Marching anywhere, better than stuck in camp all winter."

Simon will never go looking for Peter; he showed no dismay at Peter's sudden departure. He's given him up. Nothing like that Hildebrand father keeping track of his Benjamin.

Mary Grace couldn't stop her trembling lip. "I wish he'd stayed the night."

I nodded but turned from her, my sorrow welling. I could have done better. I could have grabbed the oil cloth from the table and given it to Peter. He gets soaked on wet ground at night.

BETSEY — western Virginia, April 1863

They came for Poppa again, but this time we knew. Not where exactly, but pressed into service. Our new wagon, and Tom and Frank, all gone, hauling for gray coats. Mother said Poppa was farther away than my home-home, but added, "More than likely."

When I asked, "What if it happens again?" she said short-like, "Hush, child." I am not a child, for I am in between like our state.

But this time we big ones were older; we knew more how to do. And church folks knew of disturbances, so they kept alert. Peter Schrock brought his team and plowed our garden in no time at all. Tobias did not know how Peter had slipped past troops. The other Peter came, too, like a miracle. He and Tobias sawed firewood from downed trees. They stacked so the ends did not point to our house. An older one at Red House got *verhuddelt* with booms last year. When he looked out his window at his stacks, he thought cannons pointed inside.

Sometimes Mother skittered away, but she did not get so worked up. Not one sign of bewitched, only distracted. I told her Levi was picking his butt again, but she barely shrugged. Noah grows better now; he had his first birthday while Poppa was gone, but he did not get hoisted.

"No tossing, no romping," Mother said. When Mary would not stop sniffling, Mother said, "Maybe next year." She did not look like she would remember.

Tobias slept close to the door again, and Levi got to sleep with Mother in the rope bed. He is almost four and promised not to puddle, but after two nights, Auntie Mommie came, so that was the end for him. I had to make sure he did not bother in the loft.

The first night Mary scooched against my straw tick and put her wet face on mine. Lydia slid close on the other side, and we three slept tight. I took extra care with their hair, too, for I did not want scolding. Auntie planted a patch of onions and radishes, but Mary took on the rooster—she does not like radishes. She whispered that Auntie was bossy, but I said it had to be.

Auntie Mommie surprised me, though; she brought her girl Magdalena's slate. But only for us to borrow. When I did not have jobs, I taught Mary and Lydia how to spell their names. And I taught bad, worse, and worst. "Do we say: each day Poppa is gone, it is badder?" I asked. "Or worser?"

"Yes!" Mary said. "Badder."

"No," I said and rubbed the slate clean. "We do not know why, but it is not ever gooder, badder, or worser. Somebody made a big change; it is only *worse*."

"Was it Satan?" Mary asked.

Auntie Mommie overheard and laughed. "*Ach, du Kind!*"

One afternoon Sarah came to visit with her mother, Elizabeth. They walked all the way—Elizabeth's cheeks, bright red—and brought a big rhubarb pie and cinnamon treats. They did not meet any unwanteds trudging on the turnpike. Sarah said their new baby, Lena, grows like a weed; her real name is Magdalena, like my cousin. When I whispered to ask if children can be witches, she looked startled and shook her head fast. "My sister says not to talk such."

Poppa finally came back after two whole weeks gone. Each night I made a mark with my fingernail on the bottom of the loft railing. The fourteenth day was the *best* because he came in daylight without scary noises. We have our team and wagon again, too! Mother cried for joy, but we did not make as much to-do. Auntie Mommie said to Poppa, "About time they set you loose."

But nothing is for sure. None of the adults give much cheer at church either. One time when men were huddled tight, I sidled up and heard talk of a bridge at Oakland that got burned. Peter Schrock's voice stood clear: "McNeill's Rangers." I turned away fast.

Poppa has said Rangers are the ones who carry guns and talk mean. They do not belong to the army, but they do bad things to give soldiers aid.

Mother said a new word, ravenous, for soldier men, when we had to part with bread and butter. After they left, Gideon and Levi pretended to march around the table, lifting their knees extra high. Mother sat them down immediately. "Do not ever!"

And another time since Poppa is home, Mother scolded *him*. He lets strays have shelter from rain but calls them "good-for-nothings."

She said, "It should be one way or another: no shelter, or good for something."

"We do not need a kettle from a peddler," Poppa said. "But anyone needs protection from the elements—lightning or what. We must be kind to strangers." Then he mumbled, "They would sell a cat in a sack, if they could."

One thing has stayed the same: we are always to be on the lookout. Poppa says strangers could be spies, and we do not know what their business is. Even a nice-looking man could smile and hold out a mint horehound. We are to run inside. Poppa would not say if we children will get to seek after blue flox and trillium this spring—only "Time will tell." I know right where the best patches of pink and dark red grow. Only twice have I seen a yellow.

Even though Poppa is home, Mary still has bad dreams and sometimes calls out at night. Tobias can turn to the wall and sleep on, but I do not want Mary to waken the big folks. I pinch her or give a bump. Even if she whispers, it could be the start of louder. She does not like it when I put a hand over her mouth. Mostly, her words are mush, but one time I heard "Run, run, fast!" I wanted it to be Momma. It has been over six years already since she hugged and clapped for me. Then we had happy times.

Some Sunday nights Tobias and I are allowed to stay up thirty minutes longer than the little ones. I asked Poppa, "Will we be safe when we have our own state?"

"You have not forgotten," he said but pinched off his smile. Mother sat with a big frown. "It depends," he said. "We may be *less* safe. Some neighbors still favor the South."

"Oh, Crist, must you?" Mother said.

"Better for the big ones to know whereof we must take caution."

Mother's eyes flashed dark. "None of the children will sleep."

"These are not little anymore; we may need their help." Poppa turned from her. "When we separate from Virginia, we will be part of the North, stuck between the enemy and the Red Sea."

Tobias drew himself up and sat tall, but Mother clicked her teeth.

"The railroad at Oakland attracts soldiers," Poppa said. "Some want to hurt train cars; they do not care what happens. What I mean—" He barely glanced at Mother. "They do not care if regular people are in the way. Our friends at Gortner, five miles from Oakland, have had it handy to be near the rail. They have ridden cars to Wheeling a good ten years already. That will be our new capitol." He rubbed his beard. "But now—handy for danger, too."

"Crist!" Mother hissed.

I held my breath, for fear Poppa would stop.

"A train is not the problem, by itself. But the B & O—that is the railroad name—becomes a target. You see? Southern soldiers, or sometimes these Rangers, tear up tracks. Or they burn locomotives to scuttle plans: wreck lines or engine houses." Poppa looked right at me. "*Verschtehscht?* To protect, the North places pickets for important bridges and such. Men walk up and down, guarding equipment."

I nodded, but I did not know about lines or pickets.

"When men have designs, they stoop," Poppa said. "One thing leads to another."

Mother jerked her head to Poppa and whipped a finger to her lips.

Poppa stopped, but only a minute. "Here is what to remember: God is on the throne. The sun comes up every day; the geese find their way home each night."

Like always, Tobias dropped right off to sleep. But every noise made me think soldiers and tramps were coming to our door. Even skittering on the roof made me hold my arms tight to my body. Mother says not to make up stories about bad things, but I do not want the Gortners to have to take a train to that Iowa.

* * *

"Things have taken a turn." That is how Poppa began a week later. This time it was a Monday evening, and we four oldest were told to sit quietly at the table. We three girls, tight in our sleepgowns, a blanket wrapped about us. Poppa calls us stairsteps: Mary is six, Lydia is eight, and I am a big ten. Tobias will be twelve by the end of the summer; he and Poppa had the whole bench on their side. Mother let Levi fall asleep on the rope bed, so he would not be alone in the loft.

Poppa looked serious, like when he sits in church and closes his eyes. "Yesterday was a sore trial, but the Lord kept us safe." I reached for a hand from Lydia and Mary under the blanket. Mary kept her other thumb in her mouth.

Mother came from checking on the littlest boys in their trundle bed and cradle. "Do not be long, Crist."

I did not know what had happened yesterday, except Poppa came home very late. He was the only one from us who went to church. Without being asked, Tobias had dragged his pallet down by the door when it was dark. We girls trooped silently to the loft, for Mother was having a time with Noah. She had tiptoed to the window, even when it was too dark to see anything. My throat felt scratchy, like a big straw ball had rolled inside. I did not want another two weeks without Poppa. Tobias sometimes makes our house smoky with fires.

"You know how soldiers go by on our highway, any time of day," Poppa said.

Of course, we know. The Saturday before, we had watched more than the usual strays—soldiers, too—passing by, even though rain pounded.

"Too close, that turnpike," Mother said. "Anyone can see our cabin."

I wanted Poppa to hurry, but he talked as slow as ever. "Daniel and I started for church in Maryland yesterday. He rode his mare, Baldy; I had Frank. We planned to stop at Joseph Slabach's place, but before that, we met gray men." Poppa closed his eyes, as if to blot out.

Lydia squirmed. "What, Poppa?"

"Not unusual, of course—gray men. But the road was muddy from rains and extra traffic. This was before we reached the Maryland state line, when we met the large group of Confederate soldiers led by a General Jones. We stopped our horses at the edge of the bank where it goes down to the ravine. Our custom, of course—let the men pass."

"Do not dally over the unnecessary," Mother said, her cheeks a dull crimson. She had brought her knitting—new stockings for Poppa—but her needles stayed quiet.

"Most of the soldiers marched straight by, paying no heed, but one man on horseback stopped directly beside us and dismounted." Poppa's eyes twitched. "This tall one stood on tiptoe and quick as a flash, jerked off Daniel's church hat. Just as fast, he reached up and slapped his officer's cap on Daniel's head. Then he placed our dear brother's black hat on himself. Others gathered round, slapping their legs, thinking it a time of merriment."

"What did Brother Daniel—?" Mary blurted.

"Do not interrupt your poor poppa," Mother said. "That only makes for longer."

"Nothing, Mary. Neither Daniel nor I said aught. Baldy snorted and breathed hard. I could barely look at Daniel with the wrong sign of loyalty on his head. But the soldier, the grumpy sort, turned meaner and said he wanted Daniel's horse. He smashed Daniel's good hat for not fitting tight enough." Poppa rubbed and rubbed his forehead with the heel of his hand.

I squeezed Lydia's hand and pulled Mary tighter.

"Daniel stayed polite; not once did he shout. 'Sir,' he said, 'I cannot give up my horse. I need it for farming.'"

Tobias cracked his knuckles and Mother gave him a dark look.

"At that the officer became angrier." Poppa's eyes looked ready to pop. "The man said he would knock Daniel off his horse. 'Dismount at once,' he commanded."

"Crist," Mother said. She motioned faster for Poppa.

"Those gathered spoke ugliness. Filthy talk, defiling the Lord's name."

Mother clicked her teeth, like when Gideon pesters.

"I must tell all," Poppa said sharply. "Another soldier came by and started to unbuckle Daniel's saddle girths. 'Hold still!' he yelled at Baldy and made as if to kick her." Poppa slumped. "I should have spoken sooner."

"What?" Mary asked.

"I said—I was very respectful—but I said, 'Sir, we are on our way to church; this man is our preacher. How shall he get there, if you take his horse?'" Poppa's voice wobbled, but then he straightened. "Well, then. You could see—the man who started the ruckus looked about, as if afraid." Of a sudden Poppa's voice roared, "'Why didn't you tell me sooner?'"

Lydia jerked and Mary squealed. The little boys stirred about, restless.

"I do not mean to frighten you, precious ones. But the man's words—" Poppa hid his face in his hands. Mother ran her hand again and again over the unfinished sock. Finally Poppa uncovered his eyes and said softly, "The two men rebuckled the saddle bags and told us, 'Git on.' Daniel exchanged hats with the officer; I could breathe better. We started again slowly, keeping to the edge of the road, not looking back."

"Now you children know what can happen," Mother said. "You must always obey."

"Even if we tell you to do something that is not usual," Poppa said. "*Gfaehrlich* times."

I sat up straighter but held my grip on Mary. Brother Daniel uses that same word, perilous, in church. There is dangerous and ravenous, and now *perilous, perilous.*

Poppa's upper lip twitched. "We do not want you unaware."

"Do not ever question," Mother said. "Do you hear, Lydia? And Tobias, if we say, 'Put the saddles in the bake oven,' do so at once."

No one giggled. Lydia leaned against me.

"If we say, 'Betsey, look to the little boys,'" Poppa added, "do not delay. Your mother may need to help me outside. One thing or another."

I wanted to give Poppa a big hug, but Tobias asked, "How did you get home in the dark last night?"

"Crist," Mother said, staring at the clock and shaking her head.

Everything had been off kilter that Sunday; Mother did not want any extra noise. Tobias and I took care of the animals like usual, and we girls played quietly with our straw doll. But Mother did not want us to sing church songs. Only Tobias was allowed to show us pictures from the Bible story book. When he showed people walking through the Red Sea, Mother called it *Befreiung.*

"Deliverance," I said to Mary.

"Like if the Cheat River divided by itself—a path in the middle," Tobias said.

Mother nodded. "A miracle."

All that Sunday afternoon we had stayed cooped up. Mother let us use dry beans for counting, but Noah hid one in his mouth and Gideon frightened me when he pretended to stick one in his ear. I do not know what happened when Tobias and I went out to chore, but the three little boys were all lined up with their faces down in bed when we came back inside. I made *Brockelsupp* for supper—the last of our cherries with milk—but only Gideon devoured.

At last I had drifted off to sleep, only to startle awake when Tobias tiptoed up the ladder. I sat up straight but lay back quickly. For once, he stayed restless—side to side and back again. All the time I could hear Poppa and Mother whispering—Poppa had come home on the sly—but I could not make out words. Only sniffles and nose-blowing. Next thing, Noah called out and it was daylight.

All Poppa would say to finish his story, "Daniel and I stopped for Joseph Slabach—but late. We tried to restore Daniel's mashed hat before we went on to add Peter Schrock to our sad group, riding to Red House. We said little to spill our tale until we met the few others who had gathered in Maryland. Daniel preached only a short time; those living closest to Oakland had not come."

Mother kept her head down; her boney hands clutched the ball of gray yarn.

"We waited till dusk before starting homeward," Poppa said. "Daniel and I took the cut-off, away from the Oakland Road—said to be much clogged." He stopped, as if lost. "Our horses made it," he whispered, "streams rushing out of banks."

I covered my mouth. All the times Mother has told Poppa to stay off back roads! And Poppa's warnings to Tobias: never attempt an overflowing stream. *Nimmand dutt was gwhenlich is!*

Of a sudden Mother's needles clicked fast. "Say yet about the animals."

"Yes, in the event—the unexpected—" Poppa looked at each of us. "If we need to take horses and cows behind the barn, you, Tobias, head for the back woods. You, too, Betsey, be ready; you could handle Frank."

I nodded solemnly, my hand clammy in Mary's. This would be worse than any hex on the animals. Frank is slow, and I do not like to rub my arm against his sweaty flank.

"Lydia, are you awake? You might need to look to the little boys," Poppa said. "If Tobias and Betsey must help outside with Mother and me. Only a short while—*verschtehscht?* We cannot have Gideon and Levi slipping out and getting tangled in briars again."

"Who will watch the hens?" Mary asked.

But Mother interrupted. "Your frown, Betsey—you could burst a vessel. We do not expect— Every one of you, say naught to the little boys. Did you hear, Mary?" Mother stood slowly, her free hand gripping the table's edge.

I gave Poppa a hug, but he did not wrap me tight. I did not want to hear of him being reckless ever again. If Momma were here, she would know to tell me the safe places to hide with Frank.

When we big ones trooped to the loft—Levi got to stay downstairs—I started the Lord's Prayer very quietly. *"Unser Vater, der du bist in Himmel."* Tobias joined, and Mary and Lydia added words. No one stopped us. But I still could not sleep. I promised never again to hit Goldie on the side to get her moving. And I made vow to talk extra nice to Frank, so he will listen and not stall.

J. FRETZ — Chicago, May 1863

Our seasons, upside down because of human plots and misdeeds. Springtime brings its usual green growth, upstaging gloomy winter. But warmer weather means battles are picking up—more bloodshed, death, and suffering for innocent civilians. Nothing good will come from this. Already last month, Robert E. Lee and his men surprised our men at Chancellorsville—another disaster in Virginia. Butchery, as happened in Fredericksburg last December. The boldest die senselessly.

No word from my friends who signed up a year ago. But desertion is a big problem—said to be up to 300 of our men some days.

I needle Ross. "No hiding the dire truth from deserters."

"Just wait. We're having success at Vicksburg, Mississippi."

I shake my head. He knows as well as I, we're far from controlling the big river. And worse, I heard Joe was on his way there back in March.

Lincoln keeps juggling. He says he detests slavery but adds, that's his personal view. Compromise and manipulation—necessary evils, supposedly, for the greater good. Whose greater good? Even the Emancipation Proclamation comes flawed. Is it for the purpose of winning the war and restoring the Union? Is it an excuse for all-out war? When will *all* Northerners care about righting injustice for the black man? Sometimes I question my fellow abolitionists, too. How much of our desire for emancipation is a case of easing our Northern white conscience? Where's the evidence, we want to treat all people fairly?

When I get overly agitated, I force myself to look to my own motives. I want racial justice, but what have I given up personally? It makes me squirm. Did I really come close to joining the Northern army, or was I simply torn when Andy and Phil left? Would warfare be a better way to fight for what I believe?

My rebuttal comes swiftly: it's not *my* war. And yet, it's *our* war. My mood improves when there's a Union victory—even a near-victory will do. These opposite pulls tear me apart. I desperately want this war to be over, so I can get on with my life. I want something in the news besides death.

I'm sick of chaos. But am *I* all I really care about? Maybe I *should* move to Canada. Or not read so many newspapers. In that case, I'd have to convince myself I don't need to know what's going on.

Salome's promise is my best escape. Only eight months until January! I want her beside me now! I want to unpin her hair, feel her next to me. I want the sun to speed us on our way to next winter. Even I can laugh at that: me, eager for another cold winter when it's only May! I rarely worry about Salome staying true. But those few times I do—trying to imagine what betrayal would feel like—my rage rises. I'd be lost. I hardly ever see Martha and don't miss her. I'd never go back.

When I told Mary Ann and Jacob about my plans to marry Salome and bring her to the city, Mary Ann bubbled with advice. "For sure now, you must let go of Fretz. John carries more authority, befitting the stature of a married man."

I put her off, as usual. She comes from Father's first wife, a Haldeman, so she doesn't have the same attachment to Fretz, my mother's maiden name. But I made clear, "If I have a son, he won't be named Jacob. Not with our father and brother, your husband, your firstborn, my father-in-law to-be. And those are only the living ones."

But I can't dismiss other questions. My mind makes its rounds. Where will we live? Salome says to make whatever arrangement is convenient for my work and budget. Back in February, I was so eager; I rushed to buy a residential lot. Now I've retreated; it's only an investment. I don't want to build a house without Salome's help. Once she's here, she can better assess a room arrangement to her liking.

Both Mary Ann and Jacob offered my second floor room as long as needed. It's large enough for Salome and me with the addition of a double bed, but the situation wouldn't be ideal. The two women would likely be compatible in the kitchen, knowing it'd be temporary. But the ongoing noise and hubbub of children . . . Then I get sidetracked: waking with Salome—sheer delight!—rising from the same bed. Has ever man entertained greater sweetness? How will I force myself to get out of a warm bed and go to work?

Of course, I still care about my business. But there's no confidence in money these days—banks might bust again. Back in February when I bought that housing lot, I followed Beidler's lead and took out $3,000 in treasury notes. He withdrew almost three times as much as I; we keep the notes in a safe here at the house. I couldn't afford to start over.

When Jim's out of the office collecting bills, I drift back to questions about our national disarray. Ross is as pre-occupied as I. "Is war the only way to free slaves?" I ask. "Have we ever tried to understand what Confederates want?"

"Now you want to support evil?" he asks in turn.

"Of course not," I reply. "But sometimes answers come by looking from different angles. If Southerners want to preserve their way of life and mistakenly think they're elevating the Negro by their ownership, wouldn't it be more effective to *educate* them to see Negroes as equal? Harder, true, but more effective. Killing only makes all sides angrier."

"That's naïve to think education's the answer. You've said yourself, the South's tired of being told what to do by us Northerners. Here's the problem: we keep underestimating them. Only *more* force will be effective, awful as the result will be."

That's when I pull out the latest issue of *Harper's* and turn to the oil painting by Winslow Homer of the Seven Days' Battle back in November. "Look at that Union sharpshooter targeting Confederate officers," I say. "A murder scene. That's who we are—murderers."

Ross's snort echoes in my head. "What an exaggeration! You think there can be fair play! For all your business savvy, you still think like a child."

"Wait behind cover and then shoot? Because it's *only* a Rebel's head?"

"You can't be conservative in war, Fretz. Even you criticized McClellan."

"The war changes everyone," I say.

"Right. You've become more cautious." When I refuse his bait, he says, "Look at it this way: the North's been given power *for a good reason*. When a soldier keeps a stick in camp and adds a notch when he shoots a man, that's natural."

I shake my head. "*Un*natural. No different than those Southern whites who think they have power over black people for a *good* reason. War twists people. It's perverse."

"Your perfect world doesn't exist!"

"Never said the world could be perfect," I mutter. "But is it too much to expect *civilized* behavior? We're losing our humanity. Thinking war is the way to make progress? We can do better—*be better*—than create chaos to get us to *restoration*."

"You're forgetting. Call it brutality if you must. It's for a reason—our survival. Sometimes we have to use the animal in us to get to the good for everyone."

"The *good!*" I say. My voice shakes. "From killing!" I turn away. Another pointless argument. Why did I let myself start it? I need to focus on my summary of our April numbers. Forget how soon Illinois might have a draft.

Ross doesn't know the extent of how I'm changing. Or *trying* to change. Of course, I told him about Salome, but there are other things, too. Sometimes I'm frightened—where I may be heading. He thinks I'm cautious; I *have* to be.

I still keep up with my Sunday school work as superintendent—a steamboat excursion coming up for our students—but other entertainments have little appeal. Why would I want to go by myself? And war meetings? I've only been to a scattered few this spring. Marching and shouting slogans?—almost entirely put aside. The fervor of some people there is unbearably excessive. If someone asks regarding my absence, I pass it off—"an old man" or some such.

The truth is, though, I haven't been going to bed early. Many a winter night I stayed up—one blanket over my legs, another around my shoulders—translating a book from German into English. John Geil had mentioned a Doylestown man, Abraham Godshalk, who'd written about regeneration. I've enjoyed the challenge, searching for appropriate English words to convey the original meanings. Treasure in every sentence. An old man's work, indeed. *Regeneration.* When finished, I might write up my notes in a more formal way.

I've scoured all the noun forms with the *re* prefix that means *again*— *re*birth, *re*newal—to translate Godshalk's ideas about spiritual growth. That's what I do with my free time! I've added countless verbs: *re*place, *re*store, *re*fresh, *re*vise, *re*create. When I crawl into bed and close my eyes, I see my handwritten scrawl. Some nights I'm so gripped, I can't fall asleep. Wakeful because of stark words, not cold feet or a lonesome bed. A prefix! I've been so bold as to send an early part of my translation to Deacon Good in Indiana.

Some days it feels like foolishness. Sometimes this solitary experience reminds me of what must have happened with hundreds at Yellow Creek Church in Indiana—some form of escape? Other times my prefix obsession takes me back—my distressed walk on a January winter street in this city. Maybe everything since has been connected, even that prone leopard lily. *White,* not orange or brown. Why not ongoing *re*awakening to earlier awakenings? *Re*born!

When I make myself think back to my first months in Chicago—my intention to adapt, put myself first—all that seems far away. Yes, I came here wanting success. Now I see how far that road falls short. I'm teaching myself to *re*adapt. It's self-knowledge of my early self-ignorance. My flaws, more obvious. Even now, I fight a form of evil by using methods that put Ross down. I probably sound self-righteous. I must stop belittling him when he says white people are superior. I don't agree, but I can't excuse my bad behavior as righteously battling ignorance. In truth, I could be taking in— *becoming*—the evil I'm fighting. Then I tell myself: stop overthinking! Step back; take more time.

I still read newspapers to stay abreast. I need to know. Bread riots in the South last month, even in Richmond. Several hundred demanding food grew to a thousand looters. Jefferson Davis threatened to call in soldiers with orders to fire. And the awful news that Confederate General Stonewall Jackson was shot accidentally by one of his own. Imagine! Jackson's own sentry pulled the trigger, not knowing it was the general returning from a night reconnaissance. Even after they amputated Stonewall's arm, doctors couldn't save him from pneumonia. What folly, his death! I took no pleasure in it, even though it perfectly illustrated Melville's line in his poem "Shiloh": "*(What like a bullet can undeceive!).*"

I turned to my greatest consolation: if we're still at war next year, I'll have Salome with me—a helpmate for warding off troubling thoughts. Right now I can only dream of —total joy!—her sitting on my lap. No cross words. Well, she might tire of me talking so much.

And there's Abe to think about. It sounds like my brother might move here before Salome! He's convinced Chicago is his answer and signs his name A. K. on letters, as if to make himself look bolder. But as is true for everyone, his decisions aren't entirely his own; events outside his control might push him to move our way sooner than he wants. He might end up coming here to avoid paying a heavy commutation fee in Pennsylvania. He'd rather wait another year or two—for sure, finish teaching this school term. But like the rest of us, he's holding his breath.

* * *

I woke up this past Sunday—another bright, sunny day—my mind on the special anniversary program we'd planned at the Milwaukee Depot Mission. But what actually transpired took me in directions I couldn't have imagined. While I sat eating breakfast, Jacob went to the front door and found a stranger knocking. The man, dressed in a plain suit of clothes, asked for me. It was John M. Brenneman. I was dumbfounded. *What was he doing here?*

I recovered to greet him warmly, and he apologized for the intrusion. "Peter and I—you remember Peter Nissley?" He took in my nod and continued. "We arrived in the city last night, but all trains heading east had already left. We found a room and thought perhaps you would be available today. The next train leaves tomorrow morning."

"Of course," I said. "And Peter?"

"He wanted to look up friends—a Moyer family from Pennsylvania. We've been in Sterling, Illinois," John added, "bringing encouragement—a small church there." He took in his surroundings: the entryway with the high ceiling, the sparkling glass chandelier. He apologized again, this time to Jacob, for coming unannounced. I hastily introduced them.

"We were lingering over coffee and the newspaper," Jacob said. "Please join us. May I take your hat?" He glanced ever so briefly at the worn lining under the broad brim.

We headed for the swinging door to the kitchen, but John lingered to run his hand over the oak pedestal of the open stairway. I'd forgotten how small of a man he is—nearly as tall as I but with finer features. Except for his nose. Unfortunate in that regard—pointed and overly large for the rest of his face.

I introduced Mary Ann as well—she and Jacob are both interested in news from Sterling. "Remember, I told you about some of the folks I met in Indiana; John comes from Elida, Ohio."

As it turned out, he went to Third Presbyterian with us and returned for Mary Ann's dinner of Cornish hen, which he found quite to his liking. John made no comment on the church service, but during our meal conversation it came to light that his wife was a distant relative of Jacob's. John had also looked at family records since we met last fall and concluded that he and I are third cousins. "My roots are in Rockingham County, Virginia," he said. "Grandfather Abraham owned 800 acres there."

In spite of these pleasantries, I picked at my bread pudding, anxious about my afternoon commitment. I should have told him from the start: I can't miss the anniversary program. He accepted a second cup of coffee about the same time there came a knock at the door. It was Peter Nissley, wearing the same dark coat and gray vest—a tie at the neck—I'd seen last October.

Flummoxed again, I had to be straightforward. "I very much want time to visit, but I've promised to attend a Sunday school event this afternoon." I knew neither man had such a program in his church, and I assumed they'd be skeptical, if not offended. To my surprise, both wanted to come along.

My Sunday school boys recited their Bible verses well—I made sure my guests had good seats—and I relaxed that my friends could witness the boys' childish innocence and enthusiasm. But near the conclusion, I received another jolt: I was called to the front and presented with a photographic album as a token of regard for my work as superintendent. My boys jumped to their feet and cheered lustily. I was flabbergasted. The album contained photographs of each teacher, some of the pupils, a few dignitaries. I hardly knew what to say; indeed, I don't remember what remarks I made. I couldn't look at John M. or Peter. Of course, I'm grateful for the kind gesture—the book makes a fine memento—but I couldn't help but think the school would be better off, and a better impression made, if the money had been spent elsewhere.

My unease built as my guests said little about what they had observed. I reminded myself, though, that restraint is likely their nature. Still, I feared I'd jeopardized our friendship. Then I wondered why I cared. All day I couldn't shake the sensation of being scrutinized, not that the men were unkind or nosy. But I was thrown off. I'm the one who plans others' work at the lumber yard; I decide what my Sunday school boys will study. On that day I had little control.

I was disappointed to learn that Peter had accepted an offer from his friends to return for the evening meal. John M. went along back to the Beidler's house. We ate cheese and bread and then retired to the parlor with a plate of dried figs. He prefers tea to coffee in the evening, so we settled with a steaming pot on the small table between us. Mary Ann had put out saucers, too, likely having noticed John's fumbles with his fork at the table.

He can sometimes be reticent to speak, but he made no pretense of delay or effort to obscure. "I've given some thought to sending a petition to our president."

I was struck dumb. "Oh?" Unnerved again, I managed a more drawn out "Ohhh" of acknowledgment. I blew softly on my tea. I didn't know any Mennonites back home who would be so bold as to write directly to President Lincoln, unless maybe John Oberholtzer.

"With regard to seeking exemption from military service," my guest added.

This time I nodded, although far from understanding. I shifted on Jacob's wingback and reached for another fig. John likely referred to the federal government taking conscription out of the hands of states. Formally called an Act for Enrolling and Calling out the National Forces, the order made no mention of conscientious objectors. I'd avoided talking about it with Jim and hadn't mentioned a word to Ross about the details. But some of our work force could be tapped; men between twenty and forty-five are eligible.

"Some of the brethren in the western part of Ohio—I believe you met Brother Rohrer— entreated me to be the scribe or spokesman. Some of our number struggle. Their neighbors say, 'You've drunk and voted with us; now fight with us.'"

My mind flashed to Joe and Andy. Randolph Smith, too. "Yes, exemption can create a rift in friendship. Even bitterness."

"Very true. But sending a petition is a path fraught with peril. I've not seen my way clear. Some of our Mennonite farmers are becoming wealthy with rising prices. Naysayers wonder how our people can seek exemption in good conscience."

I pulled back from hot tea on my tongue. "You've written it, though? The petition?" Shadows spread across the parlor; I could only guess at his nod.

"Already last year some ordained ministers in Wayne County sent a petition to our Ohio Governor Tod, asking exemption for our people on the grounds of religious belief in non-resistance. Others of us did the same." John held his tea cup with both hands. "I wrote a draft last summer when rumors first swirled. Now I've been advised to hand deliver it to the president." His eyes looked watery. "I don't want to ignore my brothers' wishes, but neither do I desire to go to Washington."

Nine months of holding onto this letter while matters worsened! "You would be a citizen exercising your rights. You might need a military pass, though, to enter the city." I couldn't picture him, ushered into Lincoln's executive mansion, doubtless gawking.

His cup clanked on the saucer. "I don't know about *rights*. That has to do with the earthly kingdom." He pulled his small frame upright, his back as straight as the wooden chair he'd chosen. "The letter could be sent by mail. But whatever the method of delivery, it will require a better scribe with a better style than I. Someone to copy and make presentable." He leaned forward. "A delicate balance, submitting to the powers that be. Not expecting privileges while maintaining ultimate allegiance to God. Would we make matters worse, bringing our plight to the attention of the president?" He stared at his shoes, worn from many miles. "If it's to be sent, I'm not at all certain I want my name made public." He dropped his chin to his chest.

I stared at his bald spot, fringed by darker hairs. What could I say? This bishop in the Mennonite church. "I'm sure you heard this morning, many who name the name of God see no conflict with also serving in the military."

"Yes." He put much effort into clearing his throat, finally returning his handkerchief to his pocket. "We don't condemn Christians who disagree with us; that judgment is God's." His voice became stronger. "Nor would I want to convey to the commander-in-chief a revolutionary spirit. Or support for secession. I've even said—" He stared straight ahead. "If there are Mennonites in our state who support rebellion, they're guilty of treason and should be treated thusly." His voice broke; his fumbling hands cradled his head.

I drank sips, my tea now lukewarm. What did this torn man want from me?

John saved me from quandary, reverting to basics. "We trust our government—its good policies and rules. But when government laws militate against the Word of God, we must follow our conscience."

I nodded and held up the teapot, but he covered his cup with his hand.

"We understand, Mennonites in the South have received an exemption. Some of our brethren in Virginia had been pressed into Confederate service earlier, even taken by force and tied up, loaded onto wagons." He fiddled with a discarded fig stem between his thumb and finger. "Surely we in the North will be treated with mercy."

"Citizens, yes, as is our due." But my opinions are worth little to John. Why was he here? I have no authority in the Mennonite church. Maybe he only needed an outside sounding board.

"I digress," he said. "In my letter I tried to convey that we would be willing to assist for the *good* of the nation. My *proposal:* give aid by providing relief to the homeless or needy. Our men would be at the ready for such service."

"An alternative for good. I've practically given up; I don't visit the camps anymore. It's too discouraging with my friends gone."

"This would be an organized option. Church folks could visit wounded soldiers, reach out to women and children left behind in dire need."

John may have heard of Clara Barton and her nursing work, but some strongly oppose a woman going to battlefields. "Do you know of this Walt Whitman fellow?" I asked. "He went to Fredericksburg after the battle there, searching for his brother. Ever since, he goes to hospital wards, reads to soldiers, changes their dressings, writes poems."

John seemed not to hear. "My delay is not knowing whether appropriate. A request like this. Some call it a plea. We don't want to be a burden; many weighty matters fall to the president. Nor dare we murmur. Yet our people, sorely distressed. Someone needs to speak."

"Do you think it's morally wrong to petition?"

"I wouldn't say entirely wrong. But is it *right*?" he asked.

"The prospect of being forced to take up arms—repugnant. Thus far, I haven't had to be faithful or unfaithful. To government. To God."

"That could change."

"I know. Ever since the meetings in Indiana—Communion, footwashing—I've been weighing questions, scribbling some notes on paper. Nothing polished." It suddenly dawned on me. "Did you bring a draft of your petition?"

"Oh, no, I don't carry it with me." His eyes looked tired, as if I were one more person who didn't understand. "I wouldn't want to have it on my person."

That was the last thing I expected. Last fall he preached with such passion, offering calm assurance. Maybe the Copperheads have ratcheted up their dissension in Ohio. Something has reached inside this man. Afraid for his life?

"Is it true?" I scanned John's lined face. "Are there Mennonites in Ohio who've joined? They want the Union restored, but they don't want slaves freed? I've heard that," I added lamely. In truth, I knew from Peter it was worse. Some Mennonites follow the line: if slaves are useful to Southerners, owners should keep them. Worse still, some church members have applauded vicious racial slurs, made open reference to "the Nig."

"Yes, some." He spoke slowly, as if delivering a funeral sermon. "We are not all of one mind, Mennonites or Amish. Not at all. Rabid ones don't adhere to peace principles. Some want Union forces to crush the rebellion. Others think the federal government has been *too* meddlesome. There's a group of Mennonites in Holmes County; they come from Bucks County, your home." He looked long at me. "More of them going off to war than Amish in that same county."

"I can believe most anything. Some say, do as the government bids, consider it patriotic duty. Others see the commutation fee as a tax due Caesar." I hesitated. I didn't need to describe my brother Jakie or mention some of Oberholtzer's followers. "My studies as a youth took place where that thinking prevails." I couldn't admit to some of my own ideas when studying at Freeland Seminary, my desire for revenge against those tearing apart our country. The *good* I thought we could be.

"Some Swiss families—recent Mennonite immigrants—came to escape forced soldiering in Europe. They're staunch, want nothing to do with warfare. But even they"—John's voice dropped—"have given money to the military committee in Wayne County. Bounties or what have you. A very sad day. Sad for those who fight and lose life or limb. Sad for our church, so far adrift."

"Is there sufficient teaching?" I asked. "I don't mean you. But those earnest Mennonites in Indiana. Are they typical? Their professed willingness to suffer."

John's shoulders jerked, as if chilled by a sudden draft in the room. "Many members crouch." He returned to twirling spent fig stems. "If the president could remember: People need to be respected regarding religious liberty." Then he whispered, "Yes, some given to hypocrisy."

I wondered if I should slip out, let him deal with his torment alone.

He inched to the front of his chair. "If the president could do that—a great favor. Never to be forgotten. Given respect, we would pray to God, the righteous judge: Look favorably on Lincoln and richly reward him." He slumped back.

"I've wondered, too—it doesn't seem consistent to hire someone to do what I can't conscientiously do. That bothers me."

"Yes. I mean, no, it doesn't." His face gaunt, bags under his eyes. "Not consistent."

We sat in near darkness. "You've talked with Peter?" I asked.

"At great length. This past week again. His advice: 'Do something, or say you're not going to do it.' He reminds me that Paul appealed to Caesar when in danger from the Jews. But —" John put a fist to his mouth; his words muffled. "If this war represents God's chastisement—not having adequately taught our young the ways of peace— We should not plead for escape if the punishment is deserved. If men break in to plunder, we should not defend our property. Nor our physical bodies. If we lack the proper humility . . . Slowly waking up; it may be too late."

I wanted to get up to light a candle but knew not to interrupt.

"Who is the president?" John asked wistfully. He turned to me directly. "Only a poor dying mortal like the rest of us. If we lean on him"—John's voice a whisper—"I fear we lean on a broken reed." Minutes passed before he added, "God is our guide and shelter, a very present help in time of trouble." It seemed a plea more than a promise.

Since then, I go back over everything that was said. We talked about what *John* should do. But what am *I* to do? I wait, fearing a drawbridge will suck me in with official word. I want to direct my own passage. I don't want to merely stand with Beidler, uncertain whether to withdraw assets from a shaky bank.

I should be used to this feeling of being split apart. Riven long ago, over whether to come to Chicago, become a Presbyterian, move back and take over Father's farm. Whether to pursue Salome. But now, having encountered another's trembling . . . A draft of a letter hidden in John's desk. Is he waiting to be struck blind?

I wish I'd said: It's not going to go away, John. A broken reed for a president or not. We're *all* thus. Tormented and at a loss. *Send it.* None of us is equal to this Damascus Road. No one can fully prepare.

Not my Sunday school boys, so many with fathers gone from home. Not the families of men I met in camp. Not any of us. Not the soldier, Ben, boasting about how a nine-month term of duty wasn't very long. Has he *re*-enlisted, like Phil and Andy? Is Joe at Vicksburg?

If John doesn't speak or write, who will? The Mennonites have no overall organization, no official spokesman. Any void fills with rabid voices; confusion seeps in.

I wish I could read John's draft, but he didn't offer to send it. It's probably not safe to do so. Before he left, though, he showed me hymns he'd written. Those are safe to carry in his bag, bringing solace. After reading them, I knew not to show him my latest poem, not the way it begins: "*Dark is the world, Dark its scenes / Dark is all that Beautiful seems.*" That's where Fretz Funk is. Naming the darkness, not lighting a candle.

What a strange turn of events. John missed a train. Delay brought him to my door. He hardly knows me, a young whippersnapper in the city. Perhaps a rising rich man in John's eyes, tainted by worldliness—the trappings of this house. I can't argue; I've paid seventy-five dollars for my new brown mare, Phoebe. I gave up on Horace when I couldn't tame him as I'd thought.

Serendipity—the word comes unsolicited. The faculty or phenomenon of finding valuable or agreeable things not sought for. Discovering by accident or sagacity—one thing, while looking for another. An unexpected coloration. *Why me? Why here?*

I can't criticize John M. I'm afraid, too. My own limbs, *my* turbulence. *Exercise caution, Fretz.* There's Salome to think of—our commitment. This isn't the time to let elevated thoughts of *regeneration* lead down a too narrow road. Nor does it seem *enough* to stay informed, use my education as protection.

David — Shenandoah Valley, June 1863

I feared I would never say this—we have *letters*. Two from Joel and Amos this spring; each time, Delilah wrote reply. Now Abigail admits: it is good we did not know of privations. She can be as fickle as the wind. The boys say they wrote of tribulations after Indiana, but we received nothing until early this spring, the same time we learned that Timberville had a different postmaster. Word of the boys' survival has given me courage to press on with my own efforts.

Our boys are in the state of Iowa at a place called Cedar Rapids—some sixty miles north of the Brethren folks in South English where they spent the winter, living off the minimum. "Table scraps," Abigail said. Now our boys shell last year's corn for a large outfit. They board at a hotel, but Amos calls it an improvement. He said nothing more of needing to keep Joel from recklessness.

It turns out the South English Brethren do not hire out much. That, in itself, is not surprising, when families have sufficient children to fend for themselves. But when they do hire, the pay is less than skimpy. I thought for certain one of the boys could have hired on with a cooper, but that was not the case. Instead, Amos found work with a shoemaker, and Joel was hired for building furniture and other odd jobs. But no steady pay. For a while, a farmer and his wife took them in, but arrangements sounded spartan: a mat to sleep on and one meal a day in exchange for helping saw and haul chunks of ice from the river. The pay went to the man with the ice cutter.

When Delilah read that aloud, Abigail burst into tears. "Skin and bones," she wailed. "We should never have let them go."

"Better than the army coming to our door and demanding a son. Or more money," I said. "Why must you repeat endlessly?"

She knows as well as I: a substitute can cost over $1,000 these days. And men like that may get a sudden notion to desert. Some make a business of it, always on the move, paid again as a substitute in a new location, only to jump again.

"No mention of German Baptists in this Cedar place," Abigail said.

"But, Mother, the boys are somewhere; we have been granted word," Delilah said.

"Yes, they have survived," I said. "Perhaps a goodly measure of craftiness, knocking on strange doors, sleeping in the forest. 'Better,' they say."

During the winter I increased my own form of deception. My horse shed has always been available for stragglers. But this past winter more runaways came, sleeping by day and traveling through woods at night, using the North Star to locate their Drinking Gourd. "Summer has too many chiggers, biting flies," one man said. These desperate ones and their songs finally brought understanding.

One night late in January, after Delilah and I had played our nightly game of checkers, she read aloud from the Matthew account of Jesus sending forth disciples. Abigail says I do tolerably well now at reading Scriptures on Sunday morning, but Delilah's voice reassures us both. None of us has appetite for fiery battles from the Old Testament.

Jesus's new dispensation showed me I can do more than tuck a blanket under my chin. His advice was akin to what any father might give. I could have said to Joel and Amos: "*Into whatsoever city or town ye shall enter, inquire who in it is worthy: and there abide until ye go thence.*" Or another verse: "*Behold, I send you forth as sheep in the midst of wolves; be ye therefore wise as serpents, and harmless as doves.*" That night I could scarce sleep. A fire burned inside me.

I was so taken with that advice, I read the same for devotions at Flat Rock. The disciples had been told they would be brought before governors and kings, "*for the Lord's sake.*" As if a natural part of their calling! I said to the gathered, "We survived the spring of 1862; that is well and good. But more"—my voice trembled—"we are not to fret over what to say if more trials come and we are called to give account." I admitted I have not overcome my reticence to speak publicly, even as a minister. But I said, "I must trust: Words will be given." What captured me most: the need to be ready, not caught in surprise. As surely as Abigail had crouched in silence last spring, I could do more. And yes, *wise about the extent of my wiliness,* even when not setting out for travel. Winfield might come snooping again. More soldiers would likely pilfer.

To be sure, there are reports of craftiness I cannot condone. Some farmers, especially to the North, have been accused of profiteering from wartime shortages. And *some* of our German Baptists, not the majority, have stooped to overcharge for grain by scandalous amounts. For us in the South, worthless Confederate money is often at the heart of duplicity. But if we want to use it for purchase, we must also accept it as payment.

For my own wiliness I first considered a trap door to the cellar with a piece of carpet to cover the opening. But knowing that the barn and cellar are the first places authorities look, I gave more thought, turning an eye inside my house. The serpent and dove came together over my seasoned lengths of wood. I set to, using the remaining winter months to prepare for an influx of visitors—more deserters—come spring. I do not think my project oversteps the bounds.

I studied our bedroom space carefully before explaining my plan to the women. Delilah was at once enthused; Abigail took her time. I was ready for her objection. "What is done for a brother, is done unto the Lord. Our boys have benefited from the kindness of strangers. Not to the extent we wished, but nevertheless, benefited. This is but payment."

Abigail's forehead stayed wrinkled. "An extra closet brings trouble inside."

"We cannot lock out trouble. We are to give a cup of water in Jesus's name."

"Men will take advantage," she said.

"We are to test all things—*wise as serpents*," I replied. My fire breathed anew.

"You know how Pa and I stagger," Delilah said, "carrying loads of produce to the loft."

I nodded. "You have cautioned us against such lugging of kegs up the stairs."

Abigail wilted. I took from my boards, measured carefully for the same width, and rubbed stain from my walnuts to darken. My greatest fear: Winfield might surprise me while working in my wood shed. How would I explain? But I pressed on: No one does a difficult thing without the will to make difficult effort.

Now we have a new closet off our bedroom and have harbored three men at separate times, all from increased foot traffic this spring, as armies have picked up again. The new wood is near to a match with the original. Only when light streams in from the west late in the afternoon, a difference becomes noticeable. If we need a heavier curtain, Abigail has agreed to make one.

To enter the closet, there are two modes. One is to pull the large wardrobe to the side—yes, it takes Delilah and me—and enter by stooping through a hidden half door. The other, a small opening with a latch two feet above the floor that a desperate one could wiggle through under the rope bed. Abigail has made no protest about the headboard of our bed now sitting smack against the long side of the new closet. Nor has she complained at the room's shrinking size. Come fall, we can store flour and sweet potatoes along the inner wall of the closet, still allowing room for a person to stretch on the floor.

Those of the darker race—Delilah's favorite is still Lila—prefer the horse shed for eating and sleeping. They say they must listen and keep watch. A few times Delilah has spent parts of the day or night with a woman and infant, keeping Ruby settled. But deserters have increased, just as I expected. When a barefoot man knocks, I look him over and tell him to milk a cow with me. From that I can take his measure, know whether to invite him inside to sup with my wife and daughter. Sometimes I send a man away with only bread or a small portion of last year's walnut meats.

One time Delilah asked, "Is it not like playing God?"

I could not tell if she meant to criticize. "Better to do nothing?" I asked.

"No, of course not," she said, her eyes lowered.

I do not like judging worthiness, but I exercise caution. Anyone must look me fully in the eye before I will offer extended time to recuperate inside. I do not know if I have spared my family heartache or disobeyed the command to always welcome the stranger.

Back in March we heard of President Davis's need for more men and his request for stronger conscription laws. Before that, worrisome reports had come from Tennessee where some of our German Baptists were held by authorities. But my own testing came, just as I thought, when I met Winfield by chance in Timberville. His reddish hair and large frame were as welcome as a dead carcass on my property.

I had gone to the blacksmith shop to resupply my store of nails. Winfield spoke his fire at me rapidly, as if having saved up for too long. His voice boomed in the cavern of the smithy's shop. "Don't count on that exemption law." Behind him I saw a red glow turning to white hot. "Gonna do away with substitution, too. Mark my words."

"We trust in the Lord," I said. I did not want to sound vain, but I had promised myself to count on being given words.

"Hnnh!" he spewed. "Our Davis, more religious these days. Calls for a fast day late this month. You sniveling—" He glowered at me. "Our Robert E. Lee speaks also of putting the fate of the army in God's hands."

"We are all in God's hands."

"You own no corner."

"That is so."

"Some, like my pious woman, call Lincoln the Antichrist; heading for the End Time."

"I suppose so—s'pose that has been said."

"You smelly ones might not know, hiding the way you do: the North's in disarray. Truth is, we're gaining advantage."

I tried to keep my face blank, inched backward.

"This so-called Emancipation whoop-de-doo! Hypocrisy and desperation."

I pressed my back side into a counter to let him pass, turned and fumbled through nails with clouded eyes, shook to make purchase.

Soon after, the Confederate Congress took further steps. When the weather warmed, army supply officers came to our farms and impressed agricultural products we had grown or bought for our own use. Around the same time Rebel soldiers started helping themselves also; my supply of corn and wheat dwindled. We braced ourselves for more upheaval like last spring. Further into April, Congress passed a new tax law. We farmers had to tithe 10 percent of what we raised, even 10 percent of the hogs we slaughtered. It also became *our* duty to deliver that tenth to the quartermaster general at the local post. No sitting tight, hoping an officer would not find me. I took my fair share, but my lips stayed sealed about my closet.

I sought advice only from J. M. Garber and Brother Kline. My fellow ministers at Flat Rock seemed to prefer handing out rose-tinted encouragement. "We are fortunate, not to be in the thick," Jacob Wine said. "We will prevail by the grace of God," Brother Neff said, "not by giving the querulous undue attention." I did not tell either of my closet.

I asked J. M. if the North was as desperate as it sounded.

He nodded. "Not good. Yanks take off and run at the slightest reverse. They lost thousands at Chancellorsville—not sure exactly—fighting in woods and brambles."

"And the South?" I asked.

"Many shortages, inflation, roads and bridges destroyed; fences burned."

"And the rumor about Stonewall Jackson?"

"Sadly true—mistakenly shot by his own man, unable to make recovery."

"How we despised his men wreaking havoc among us, especially after he had befriended us early on."

"Two sides, that man: piety mixed with valor," J. M. said. "True: he came to accept that our men could not be forced to take correct aim. But now his absence may account for matters being worse. His men, said to be morose."

As for Brother Kline, I traveled with him back in May, following the Lost River to the church at Mathias, one of John's favorite outposts. He had been instrumental earlier in organizing the congregation and overseeing their new building for worship. We thought it safe enough to travel, since most reports of active conflict at the time came from out West. It was very important to John to support the folks at Mathias with their Love Feast.

Like always, my days with him stirred wildly opposite responses. While heading for Mathias on a Friday, riding Nell and Ruby twenty-five miles through mountains, our interactions stayed congenial. Those early May days were still chilly, though, requiring us to wear our great coats with the capes attached.

But my inadequacy grew large, when I heard more of his letter writing and speaking out like a prophet of old on behalf of us German Baptists. He stays involved, too, with projects that benefit the larger community. I learned more of his talks with Sam Cootes, our senator, about building a ford across the North Fork of the Shenandoah River. For years already, public-spirited folks have been raising funds for cutting down the face of Gap Rock and making a new road through the cut.

Once at Mathias, Brother Kline was the presiding elder through the three times of worship from Saturday morning until Sunday evening—a holy time, entirely different from any wild imaginings the world might conjure of a Love Feast. There is always ample time for visiting, whether after the Saturday morning preaching or in local homes overnight. John delights in seeing members inquire as to each other's well being. Even a simple "How are you?" seems to bolster his spirit.

I make no claim to such tender fellow feeling, but a greater weakness struck at me again during the time of self-examination. On Sunday morning, our time of great preaching and joyous singing, my mind was thrown awhirl. Do I hold enmity against any brother or sister? Have I been charitable? Have I attained defenselessness with any who might seek to cause bodily harm? My head dropped as the visage of Winfield intruded.

I knew what was coming: "We are to fear God and Christ, not men." I could not say I had extinguished resentment. I considered again my wiliness in aiding those needing assistance. Then I heard "Exemption does not mean the burden of duty has rolled from our shoulders." I did not want to think of my closet not being enough.

When we rode home again, amidst the beauty of green hills, I told John of my winter's efforts to house vagabonds. He smiled briefly and said, "Honor the Lord your God in all you do." That was all. Later when we stopped to rest at a creek, his words puzzled more. "The poor are more receptive to the Gospel than those who prosper." A woodpecker paused, then resumed its tapping.

Even when home, I stewed. Even when I saw my women had encountered no unwanted visitors in my absence, and my hen with the orange feathers still strutted, I wrestled. What had John meant? "The well-to-do may show an independence and forget God." Why had he said that to me? Brother Kline knows I do not have extra, nor do I plant excess. I have not criticized *him* when it comes to personal money matters. Everyone knows he does exceedingly well, overseeing his farm *and* being a doctor. And yes, he balances his income by extending generosity to all. Why do my efforts always seem insufficient? I will never measure up.

A week later John came to my woods, looking for fresh supplies of ginseng and crowfoot to replenish his store of herbs for medicines. Time had resolved some of my inner torment, but an old thorn came up: his plans to travel to Pennsylvania for our denomination's Annual Meeting, going directly into Northern territory, the same as last year. I was not the only one raising questions, so I said, "You may get there safely through the lines, but you do not know what evil may befall when you come south of the Potomac again." He stayed silent; I pressed on. "You could be arrested, far from home."

At that, he put his hands on the end of the hoe and rested his chin on his hands. "Those days with the brothers and sisters from many locations are of far more blessing than remaining at home because of concern for safety. I cannot compromise because of hostile threats. John Wine has agreed to travel with me again; he understands." Brother Kline looked me in the eye.

I could not detect disgust nor warmth, but I was not deterred. "Your trips north create suspicion. Those who want to discredit you, think you bring back harm to the Southern cause."

He gave careful attention to arranging clumps of wild cherry root in his extra saddlebag.

I plunged ahead. "Is it not enough to labor with your brothers and sisters *here*? We rely on your counsel. Must you seek out trouble elsewhere?"

"It is not a matter of enough or not enough, but of seeking to do the Lord's will." He spoke evenly, swatted at a pesky fly, and turned his back.

I stabbed with my shovel and bent to shake dirt clinging to roots. He *always* has an answer. "I know you take seriously being moderator of the Annual Meeting, giving care to the entire brotherhood. But any decision by consensus only binds for a year. If you deem something unsatisfactory, you can bring it up in another year."

Again I took his silence to be consideration, and I continued. "Brothers from Indiana and Illinois—others already in Pennsylvania—can handle the hard questions. You are not— You have expressed high regard for Brothers Kurtz and Quinter as clerks for the Standing Committee." He lifted his head and I hurried to finish. "Given the circumstances, no one would think a brother from the south shirks, if he does not attend."

"I know the hazards; I have secured passes from both warring parties." He turned fully to me again. "I will be prudent, David; I will ask the brethren not to put forward any question for public discussion that could cause trouble for us southern congregations." He wiped his brow with the back of his hand. "Maintaining unity comes first. We dare not follow other church bodies."

My other line of questions flitted in my head. *Anna? What of her? Her dreams? The weeping. Huge balls of rolling fire. Do you not need to protect your woman? Has she not agonized enough?* But as before, those words never traveled to my vocal cords. I knew what he would say. He had *counted the cost*. In leaving his sickly wife at home, he was reassured by those who would care for her. If I followed with anything about choosing a more reasonable course, he would say: *The gospel is not meant to be reasonable.* Or, *we do not go by what the world views as foolhardy.* His round face would stay serene; I knew him too well.

And now here we are, well into the month of June. All that stayed pent up last month is now a thing of the past. My fears seem as fickle as Abigail's swings with our boys. Brother Kline went as planned near the end of May into the heart of Pennsylvania—the Morrisons Cove area. He and Brother Wine traveled over 300 miles on horseback, much of it mountainous. He remembered the bottle of liniment for Nell and treated her several times for saddle galls. Some of their trip—he actually admitted—took them through sparsely inhabited areas. He knew I knew: they could not always have known where army lines were.

He does not gloat, but he smiles to tell of stopping on the way back— six overnights in the homes of brethren. I know how much that means to him. But I cannot help myself. "Were you and Brother Wine ever detained?"

"I sent word back to Pennsylvania, so those concerned would know of our safe return."

I mull my response to his non-answer.

"Thirty-two questions came before the Committee," he continues.

I give in. "Questions regarding warfare?"

"Yes, it was recommended: All brethren should abstain, as much as possible, from elections right now. Another question centered on members who have gone to the army as soldiers or teamsters—"

I look at him expectantly.

"The delegates supported the Committee when told that churches should seek answers in the Gospel, rather than rely on imprudent discussion at this time."

His trip, accomplished without harm. My fears, petty. My small mind finds satisfaction, though: not nearly as many attended as did last year in Dayton. Many leaders chose wisely in the midst of mounting turmoil.

It is good to have John home again. I do not mean to suggest otherwise. I am relieved. But we do not always see the same. Perhaps that is how it should be. He was here with time to spare for his sixty-sixth birthday. Thirteen years my senior, he is a marvel, even if his legs have not entirely returned to their normal walking gait. Some days, I pray to be as steadfast as he; other times I fall back on contrariness.

Jacob — Iowa, June 1863

My soul is torn apart. Grief, such as I have not known since Barbara was taken from my side. I stumbled to my woodshed, knelt on my worn carriage robe. I could only stomach a few morsels, sips of water. I sent Mary away. Tears—my meat and drink. The one I could not convince, lost to infernal fire. I was not shepherd enough.

Frederick found me in my disordered state. "Father, cease this lament." He pulled on my elbow. "You tried. Emanuel chose the worldly claim."

"Why will the Almighty not hear my plea?" For three days and three nights, no voice from heaven had come with comforting reassurance. "How can I go before others when I have failed? The Lord has turned His face."

Frederick sat himself heavily on the wooden bench; his hand fumbled to reach my shoulder. "We are all humbled, but the young man chose not to be a part."

I flinched.

"We all fail at times. What else could you have done? You spoke. Do not be consumed by the one who chose a different pull."

"A greater grief," I mumbled. "There are others who do not hearken."

"Rubbish," he said and stomped outside, the door left ajar.

I felt like a petulant child, but I could not muster courage to rise. I longed for a tender visage to wipe away Emanuel's mocking grin, John P.'s frown, Susanna's back.

Only on the ocean with my family long ago had I known such desertion. The winds stalled or worked against us. When we had started, of course, we did not know how we might end. May of 1833 it was, delayed in the homeland *Deutscher Bund*, first on the Weser River and then in Bremen. In part, miscalculation. But worse yet, bereft on the ocean. Few ships; surrounded only by water. Water, water on all sides. No headway. No comforting voice. For three months our five youngsters could not run; not till August. Barbara refused to look at me full. Subject to buffeting and often seasick. How low we sank. How low my faith ebbed. Why are some allowed to sail through, whilst others suffer unduly? No promise of safety. No reassurance.

Now here I am, thirty years later, grieving Emanuel's loss. Frederick came again to my shed; he must have consulted with Mary. This time he sat silent. A sunny June day, and I kept him from his work. At last I trembled to rise and buried my face in his shirt. His arms and smell of oats and cow wrapped about me. "Old and spent, my good years past," I said.

He steadied me to walk to the house; he sat with Mary and me. She had put cinnamon in the custard. My stomach rumbled; I ate slowly. After Frederick left, I returned outside and brought up all I had swallowed.

Mary assisted me to the bed from which I have been absent. "Caspar?" I asked.

"I have given care." She patted my arm.

"The custard tasted good." She offered broth, but I lifted a hand and turned my face.

I stared at the ceiling, the uneven beams, their stolidness. I thought on the hands and arms that had lifted them into place. The promise of Iowa. Had it all been for naught?

Already back in May, before Pentecost, we heard Emanuel had been wounded. An awful battle in Mississippi. Vicksburg, it was. My strength, puny from winter sloth, I wielded the scythe to mow winter wheat, only to peter out. I knelt to wash my hands at the stream—my habit to remove caked dirt before going inside to the basin. I turned my hands, rubbing and rubbing. The dinner bell rang; I was late for *Middaagesse*. I struggled to my feet.

Those weeks ago, I rode Caspar to see Henry and Susanna, out planting corn with their boys. Henry's woman walked to a distant row. I have heard she can mow hay as fast as a man. Henry said Emanuel was in an army hospital in Memphis—a wound to his leg. A telegraph had brought word, but no mention of an eye gone bad. Henry had no plans to visit, not with the long trek, not with farm work pressing.

I did not lift my pen to write. Only my supplication doubled, as I entreated the Lord on bended knee. The young man lived two more weeks.

Since then, my grandson Jakob has asked around. This Company G that Emanuel belonged to had moved into Mississippi late in March. They waited a month before called on to accomplish various skirmishes, even capture prisoners. On the morning of the twenty-second of May, General Grant ordered what they call a frontal assault on the Southern fortifications at Vicksburg—thoughts clouded with revenge for a colonel who had been killed. This part of the 22nd Iowa Infantry walked at night—a close bunch, by all counts—and came within twenty yards of the pickets defending a fort called Beauregard. With two other regiments of foot soldiers, they charged up a hill.

As Jakob described it, raising both arms and making a whooshing sound as of an army running, I pictured a flock of geese taking flight. The thought of men, intent on climbing a wall some fifteen feet high, brought the wall of Jericho to mind; the Lord had promised victory to Joshua if he followed the commands. But for Emanuel and these others, they first had to cross a ditch, ten feet wide, past firing guns. Jakob spat with a force. "It hearkens to suicide. Only fifty men made it as far as the ditch; from that point, only fifteen were able to raise each other up to the top of the wall and make it into the fort. What good was that? Nearly dark and no reinforcements. Forced to withdraw under shade of night."

Men blinded by anger! It is thought that Emanuel retreated on one leg, dragging through bloodshed and cursing. Plagued with the need for stealth but, doubtless, wanting to cry out. An army hospital, unable to save him. Jakob says many die *after* battle, what with field operations corrupted by foulness. Might Emanuel have called from his bed—perhaps a chaplain present—seeing at last the error of his ways?

I sometimes get my numbers mixed up, but Jakob said *half* our men were killed or wounded. *Nineteen* captured by the South. The dead left on the field *two* days before enough stoppage for Union troops to bury bodies. One of the expired ones, a Fry boy from Frank Pierce. The only one to survive scaling the wall—a sergeant by the name of Griffith.

Why did I not write to Emanuel? Long before Vicksburg, my excuses piled up. Back in January, according to Peter and Emanuel's father, the young man had sounded boastful, a complainer. If I had encouraged him to desert, he might have been in trouble with the authorities. My letter could have been confiscated. Yet I knew he and his friends courted danger, hunting for Rebs. I could have written.

Instead, I redoubled my efforts for those within my hearing, only to have the one by my side say, "You do not need to preach again, '*He that killeth with the sword, must be killed with the sword.*'"

I looked at Mary in astonishment. "That is God's Word, the book of Revelation. I cannot ignore the truth given us."

Her eyes flashed. "You do not need to employ harshness."

"Your own words are harsh," I replied.

"Harshness begets harshness."

I was dumbfounded. This woman given to me in holy bonds! Her winter chatter and burned meat had turned to back talk. She does not understand. I would be shirking my duty, if I did not continue to give warning against the dangers that can come with involvement in the world's doings. Such appeal comes with cunning: cast a vote here, garner a civic appointment there. All seems easy enough.

But we cannot be too careful, even with people's teeth set on edge. Concern for our Iowa boys—that is good. And wondering if enough others will remain eager, even with Vicksburg, to stop the rebellion—a natural worry. All too soon, a draft could be instituted, livelihoods disturbed. No one stands clear; this war's tentacles reach deep. Its fever—worse than the grippe.

* * *

My days of desolation have passed. Our Lord spent forty days in the wilderness; my time in the woodshed was short by comparison. Now our evenings run long with daylight. Questions and doubts remain, but Mary has turned to offering consolation. She rubs her hand to soothe my bad hip. She no longer calls attention to the cardinal flying at the kitchen window.

We have learned Henry sent two sons, Samuel and John, to Tennessee to accompany the return of Emanuel's body. These young men in their twenties, assured safe passage, joined other sad ones making the somber journey. Word is, our lost one left behind one blanket, a canteen, and $7, along with his personal effects.

I sit with Mary under the large maple that gives shelter from heat, a bucket of pea pods between us. A peaceful Iowa evening, the hills full of calls and swoops. Frederick rolled stumps into a circle for our sitting—the area eaten clean by horses and the goat. I wave a stick at insects set to bite our ankles. "The family did not ask for burial in the Peter B. Miller cemetery."

Mary's opinion comes swiftly. "They may have feared scorn."

I put my head back, look far in the distant sky, gray streaked with pinkish strands, and close my eyes. The pop of pods continues, split open in Mary's fingers. "They buried Emanuel's body on their own farm in a new plot behind the house." Another handful of empty pods lands in the bushel basket. I try again for response. "If they asked one of our ministers to assist, it has not yet come to light."

She refrains from further comment. I follow the flight of swallows amidst the thunk of pods. I hear the shimmer of corn stalks—their whispers—and reach into the bucket to help. My thumb fumbles on the edge of a pod. I am no better with peas than with a tight corn husk. Frederick's big girls would put me to shame.

"Your crop is a nice size," I say.

She murmurs what sounds like assent.

"Should I make another house call?" I ask.

"Let them grieve. Susanna is said to be sore consumed."

"They should grieve *with* us, their brothers and sisters, not keep to themselves."

Mary's fingers stay busy.

Starlings caw in the distance; a breeze refreshes. "Henry shook my hand when I made visit. But they might not have tolerated my prayer at the burial spot."

Mary says nothing.

"Perplexing on many counts."

"You repeat yourself. Loosen your grief, attend to those newly come— their spirit of progress."

She closes her eyes to danger. Too willing to give ear to the contrary winds that blow. Too eager to encourage new voices from Ohio and Indiana. Even Canada. Those who say we must not be backward on the frontier, that we must honor individual understandings.

The cloth that holds our people wears thin. We do not tear each other apart bodily as do warring armies, but we are beset by attempts to undermine established practices. My soul wearies, always needing to keep an eye out. There is no pleasure: the rod of discipline handed to me. Some Sundays, even the harmless young man who sits in church with his mouth half-open—loud, raspy breaths—becomes an irritation.

We had to carry through and silence John P.; his obstinance and dissent continued. What sadness for him, getting on in years. And for me. I cannot say more to Mary, for fear it will travel. He charges me with favoritism, but I should not need to defend reliance on my sons. I will never know the source of his antagonism, but I did not steal Barbara in the night.

If another ministers' conference comes to pass next spring—they say it will be held in Indiana—and if the Lord sees fit to strengthen my body, I may need to take a letter in person. I am keeping notes. Joseph Keim attended the *Dieners-Versammlung* this past spring in Pennsylvania and gave report—barely half as many in attendance as the previous year. Two good things resulted, though: ruling against our Amish men enrolling in the militia or cooperating as teamsters. And second, seeing the dangers of holding office or being involved in any way with how the government determines wrongdoing.

But dispiriting also: the same sore spots of bundling and tobacco. Why can we not purge these two great shames? Some in the East still insist they cannot preach without a chew of tobacco in the mouth. And I do not need to look beyond Iowa for reports of our young men riding home in the light of dawn. What must our neighbors think? Yet when I preach against bed courtship and include the mothers who prepare the beds, some do not think parents should be blamed. Others object to my counsel of how unseemly it is to feast and carry on at weddings when our neighbors may be in mourning. Any rough talk and singing of English songs late at night must stop. This war requires greater uprightness, not less.

I have had to speak about land ownership also. Our people must be more circumspect. I have heard a member, without one blink of the eye, say: "A cow that cost fifteen dollars before the war, now brings sixty." Why does he not see how tainted we have become? Our English neighbor who sends his son to war may scarcely be able to afford *one* cow.

Even among members, our witness to peace goes to shambles with unfair goings on. Hard feelings have cropped up with some of Moses Kauffman's relatives; he has nine siblings living here. They say he took too much land for his own when his father's estate was settled. Locals hear of these disputes and must feel disgust. I have started writing things down: who said what about which parcel of land. It is complicated to sort out what acreage was purchased, what was inherited, or, as some charge—stolen. Moses has always been faithful, sticking with traditional garb, but there is no dispute: he owns very large amounts.

Part of the rub: his father Jacob, a God-fearing man when he died four years ago, did not tell all. I thought his affairs were in order when I signed his will. But I did not know that shortly before his death, Jacob had sold one hundred acres to his daughter Lydia at three dollars an acre. Favoring a daughter! Some say it was poorer land, but there is no question: he sold it for considerably less than the ten-dollar rate he asked the previous year from a son and another daughter for the same amount of land. Shame, shame on us all.

Late last year I began keeping another type of record—there is no injunction against it. Who gave the opening in church, who the sermon, who read what Scripture, where services were held, and on what date. More and more, my memory comes up woefully short; I must be prudent with keeping track. I store my papers in the velvet-covered box that Barbara and I brought with us from the Old Country. The yellow has faded, but the box remains one of my most prized possessions, along with our clock and my Bible.

Yes, more precious than gold and dearer by far to me—my *Biblia Pentapla* already 150 years old. Three volumes to encase the five translations—Roman Catholic, Evangelical Reformed, the official Dutch, the Jewish Old Testament, and Martin Luther's version—side by side on each page. Two volumes for the Old Testament and one for the New. I run my hand over the white leather of sheepskin. Such treasure! And what surcease from sorrow to gain entrance into the mind of God. A balance to my darkening days of men dying on the battlefield, our church loosening its grip on faithful living.

O, Gott, hilf uns.

J. Fretz — Chicago, July 1863

I've argued with myself. Where are we going? I've pounded my words on paper, crossed them out, opened the window wide at night—grateful for any waft of air—looked out on the city. Lincoln's proclamation is needed to release the black man from bondage. But all-out war? Any sense of proportion has been lost. He must have reached desperation—no other way to win control of the South. This phase can't be what he wants. War's benefits don't outweigh the costs. How could Lincoln *not* know that?

After I tire of my torrent of questions and accusations, I look for anything positive. I try to salve a friendship, visiting Joe several times. He's back from Vicksburg, part of his cheek and jaw missing. In their place he spouts hatred. The camps are awful, full of diarrhea, dysentery. The water, foul. After the first visit, I don't know if I can go again; there's no way to cheer him up. Or repair his mangled face.

The next time, I follow the traditions for July 4th in the city—except when I look at my pistol in the morning, I think it's frivolous to practice shooting. Instead, I walk around in the Hyde Park area and take a bath in Lake Michigan. Finally, by afternoon I go again to the Creswell home and listen to Joe's distorted voice rehash vile contempt for the enemy, disillusionment over conduct of the war. We know something's going on at a place called Gettysburg, a small farming village in Pennsylvania, but early reports aren't reliable, so we don't speculate.

He says, though, "Meat on the cutting table."

I swallow hard. "Everyone? What's that like?" I ask. "You never know what's next."

"Waiting's awful. Sometimes another unit hasn't arrived yet with reinforcements. But soon as the shooting starts, you're a target. Someone knows you're near. *Outwit him. Get out alive—one piece.* 'Course, that's his goal, too."

I remember Joe's cunning at the gambling table. "A battle of wits? Nerve?" I ask.

"Mostly strong will and luck."

"You're trained, though, for maneuvers," I say.

"Part of why we have to wait; we're a unit. There's a plan; matching strategy. Can't have one guy go off, break ranks. Can't mess up for your buddies. But when you're in the middle of things, there's little control. Everything inside you says, 'Go!' No hiding."

"But *self*-control?"

He shakes his head. "Near to impossible. Noise, confusion. It's deafening. Horses come at you like a stampede. The raw animal inside breaks through."

I study my fingernails, freshly cut last night.

"If I have to die, let it be in an instant." His face, a darker shade.

I can't respond, can't look away.

"Then you wake up. Terrible pain and retching. Smoke. Coulda been the wheel of a cart, clipped my face. You listen for clues. Men and bodies. Who's where? Awful groaning. You want sleep, safety."

"Scared to look around."

He grunts. "My face hurt like it was on fire. I rolled over. Didn't dare touch my cheek. Afraid to sit up. Couldn't spit." Joe turns the bad side of his face away. "Had to keep myself up enough, though—out of mud and blood."

I can only shake my head. "Andy and Phil— No idea what's—"

"Anyone out there—fodder. Throw enough raw meat to clog up the works. Break up *their* plans. That's the idea. Use *our* smarts. Our *superior* strength. Pfft!"

I don't dare let myself look at the clock on the wall.

"Fresh meat to dead meat. Torched."

I can't argue. I can't agree. I can't change the subject. I leave soon, out of sorts. I spend the evening at home—no desire to make more social calls for the holiday.

Not long after, though, I go back. Disgusted, I hadn't heard him out. This time I will let Joe talk as much as he needs—I can do that much. We sit on the Cresswell front porch. A carriage goes by now and then. Gettysburg never comes up; by then we know too much.

Instead, he describes screams. Still in his head. One friend in particular, legs blasted off. "I couldn't stop the bleeding. Dawson's. A skirmish before Vicksburg. Helpless. If— Can't help a buddy. Life's over. His, mine."

Who am I to tell Joe he still has a future? So what, if he can halfway talk, still see? Anything sounds lame. I reach for his shoulder. "I'm still your friend."

"You've not been there; don't pretend."

I sit back. "You're right."

"You don't know what it's like—starving. Some poor excuse of food they give you. Pale-looking slop with chunks. That's all I'm worth?"

"Limited resources, I suppose."

"Someone else sits down to beef and potatoes. The lieutenant in his cozy tent? I don't know. Now I pick at buttered potatoes Mother offers, knowing— I've hurt her feelings."

"No fairness."

"Damn right. Dawson's a far better man."

"Must be hard to—"

"Hard? You don't know. Hard! Fool chaplain didn't know either. Mealy mouthed. Bass-ackwards. Some of the men still believe his rubbish; hang on to anything."

"Like what?"

"Pfft! Talk about 'rivers of blood.' Or how Dawson's blood 'hallowed' the nation. Bull! Believe crap like that to put up with nightmares."

"Elevate the war, I suppose. Dawson's death—redemption?"

"Some such. Not for me."

I go home, sick at heart again. Not that we've argued. But his contempt! We both know: power tries to sanctify itself. He has a right to yell. Sneering about the right hand not knowing what the left is up to. What could I say? *Be glad you can swallow a little. People won't care—your disfigured face.* I can't offer him a future. He's a noble man without my saying so.

Nor can I tell him about my plans with Salome, my life. Lumber talk seems frivolous.

His last words stay with me. "We're all in this, you know." His brown eyes hold mine for as long as our handshake. "The whole country—no one's hands, lily-white. Me?" He shrugs. "A small part. Everyone's dipped in blood—somewhere on that tarnal chain."

I didn't ask what he meant.

* * *

I've done it. Last fall Dwight said I didn't need the government's permission; I could go ahead, put my beliefs out there, face the consequences.

These nights when the outside air stifles, a moth dances about my lamp. I catch it in my hand and fling it out the window. No sooner done than another takes its place. Who do I think I am? Joe might say—an arrogant elitist, thought to have been given special dispensation. Ross would say—a simple-minded literalist.

I hold up one hand that says: I'm looking to settle with a wife, even father children if the Lord wills. I've purchased $3,000 in life insurance that comes with a hefty yearly premium of $231. So-called protection. I wouldn't have to use this other hand, not remain this divided person. I could set up house with Salome, slip under the covers, not call attention to my heart's distress.

But it's there for all to read: The Sermon on the Mount. That wasn't my doing. But this other part—some days I'm frightened. Sixteen pages, three and a half by almost five inches. Little more than a pamphlet, but out there in the world. I've used my first name, John, reduced Fretz to a middle initial. I can hear people make sport, write my name on the traitor side of the ledger. Beidler has said little since his initial "What in tarnation?" when I carried in box after box. I couldn't store them all at the publisher's place of business, although Mister Hess helped ship copies out. Mary Ann pressed her fingers to her lips, her eyes wide.

After John M.'s visit in May, I returned to the manuscript I'd mentioned. I polished it but set it aside for another month. I've heard nothing further about John's draft of a petition to the president. But Peter Nissley has written about the terrible slaughter at Gettysburg—not far from his place. We're awash in newspaper accounts.

I couldn't keep silent. Too many last straws. I went to Charles Hess, the printer on Randolph Street, and made arrangements to have "Warfare, Its Evils, Our Duty" printed. One thousand copies, coming from long, continuous sheets of paper fed into a steam-powered printing press. Folded and pressed. Phoebe and my carriage lurched from the heavy load. I was still shaking when I walked into the house. I asked Deacon Good to distribute copies in Elkhart County. John M. has been eager to assist in Ohio, although he expressed surprise at my straightforward wording. "Will Chicago people tolerate such difference of opinion?"

It's done, out of my hands, published. I think I've counted the cost, but I can only wait and see. Father might call me as foolish as his church deacons. I gave a copy to Jim, my business partner; he paged through it and thanked me. He's said nothing further. Jim's had his mind on his mother— finally able to bury her body this spring. I picture my booklet tucked at the back of his bottom desk drawer. I see people in Ohio ripping out pages, their hatred against Mennonites redoubled. I chide my inflated self-importance. I don't want to be Harriet Beecher Stowe.

Abe's response makes me nervous. My brother arrived in Chicago when spring suddenly turned to summer, and he's taken lodging with the Moyer family, the same folks Peter Nissley knew. So far, Abe's satisfied working for me—the same menial jobs I did at Beidler's lumber yard when I first came. He'll have to figure out many things on his own, but I'm still the older brother and feel protective. So many things about him remind me of folks back East.

I was showing him around the city a second time, explaining that the original settlers were Algonquian people. Phoebe and my carriage—Abe doesn't think much of my rig—took us from Old Street to the Post Office, then crossed over Clark, up Wells to Chicago Avenue, finally to Reuben Street. I keep my carriage lubricated; it doesn't have to look fancy. Phoebe's what counts.

Abe brought it up. "How can you write these ideas and distribute them?"

"What do you mean? I've come to see what's always been in the Bible."

"Have you sent Father a copy? Plenty of folks would say your pamphlet goes too far."

"It's the meek who are blessed."

Abe scratched his arms. "I'd be run over at work if I didn't stand up for myself."

"Sure. Irish fellows like to poke fun; a couple years ago, they told jokes to my face about Wide-Awakes. Most Irish align with Democrats."

He leaned forward when I suddenly pointed to new wooden sidewalks, but sat back again, tugging on his short-clipped beard. "You put meekness on a pedestal."

"I don't claim to have all the answers. Used to think some amount of force was within the bounds of acceptable. Blinded, I guess." We both half turned to watch a white horse pulling a carriage with gold tassels. "You've probably run into *Peace* Democrats. They'll grab any newcomer and make their credo known: 'The Constitution as it is, the Union as it was, Negroes where they were.' Maybe everyone's blinded over something. Democrats are convinced, Lincoln favors the rights of blacks over whites."

I couldn't interpret the look on Abe's face. Irritated? Bored? I tried again. "I gave myself to abolition awhile. Thought it the end-all."

His reply came swiftly. "Some say abolition *caused* the war."

"Heard that many times—*the cause*," I said. "Others say abolition was the *means* to the war. Complex, for sure. But everyone sees only a part. What they want, I guess. When I open one eye to new truth, maybe I half-close the other. Some part gets dimmer, I suppose."

Abe spat out the carriage. "You think we're all dullards if we don't see things your way. Like we're tricking ourselves? Too stupid to know."

"Really? I sound like that?"

He sat back and folded his arms. When Abe's heavy eyebrows take over his face, he reminds me of Father when we were boys. If he came upon our carelessness, his rebuke left no doubt: we deserved whatever punishment was coming.

"I don't mean to sound smug," I said. "One day I'm certain; the next, not so sure. It's the life I live. Straddling. But I can't be idle anymore. Nor silent. My book's not meek."

"That's just it. You preach meekness, but your book sounds proud."

"Now *you* sound like an Amish bishop! Or some conservative giving Father a hard time about polished woodwork." I snapped the reins, and the carriage jerked forward. "Easy, Girl," I said. That's not who I am, frightening my horse. I took deep breaths. "Back to this city. 'Shikaakwa,' the Algonquian name, means stinky onion."

Abe barely smiled, so I skipped saying that the first permanent resident was a black-skinned man, or telling about the man's log cabin at the mouth of the Chicago River in the 1780s. "The French Jesuits started a mission here in the late 1600s; that lasted a little over twenty years. Abandoned because of Indian raids."

"Hnnh."

"Pushed around, one group or another," I said.

Abe glanced at me but kept his lips tight.

A few days before that buggy ride, I'd shown him articles in the *Times* about draft riots in New York City. He hadn't argued, but maybe I sounded like a know-it-all then, too. I wanted him to understand how this war has spawned other conflicts. I remember saying, "The Democrats may be right about conscription laws making this a rich man's war and a poor man's fight." That time Abe had looked like Jakie back home, barely concealing a sneer.

"Immigrant Irish and Catholics are at the bottom of the heap—seen as foreigners," I had said. "It's true: a man who's *not* a recent immigrant and *not* Catholic can more easily buy his way out of the draft with $300. But here's the thing: the average New York City worker makes eighty-five cents a day. Figure that out—the man has a family to support. See? A set-up for class strife."

Abe had shrugged half-heartedly and I'd put the newspapers away.

As best I could tell from news accounts, rioters had taken out their anger—on hot, muggy days like we've had here—over exemption and substitution rules. They'd been putting up with high inflation and contaminated staples like sugar and coffee. But the draft must have felt like *their* last straw. Mobs of Irish Catholics burned houses of prominent Republicans for four days, threw rocks at draft office windows, lynched innocent Negroes. No thinking man would approve of their behavior—I didn't—but from their perspective, I could see how anyone with dark skin, *if given freedom*, would be competing for a job with a poor white.

Maybe Abe thought I was condoning rioters; they'd burned the building that housed the *New York Tribune,* a Republican newspaper. Of course not. The rioters threw all sense out the window, and President Lincoln had to call in troops. Soldiers who'd survived Gettysburg had to go to New York City and put down riots. But still, Irish men had reason to be upset—stuck at the bottom of the barrel. Their lives viewed as worthless. Joe's "raw meat" to throw at the enemy. More than a hundred died in the riots.

Class strife added to racial conflict, plus the terrible loss of life at Gettysburg. All of it pushed me and led to my trip to the publisher. *Plus,* Peter's letter with word that Mennonite boys in Pennsylvania continued to enlist. I *had* to do more than *not* go to war. Joe's words about our shared "dipped in blood" haunted me, too.

I addressed my pamphlet to Mennonite churches in the United States. It won't start a revolution, but if it gets some Mennonites back on track and reminds ministers of our church's foundation on peace principles, it will be worth whatever personal turmoil comes. I can't take back my words. I don't want to. I'm learning to be brave and scared at the same time.

How can Abe criticize? Didn't we have the same upbringing? War devastates the human spirit; it crushes our sense of being humans together. How can anyone argue that fighting is *not* destroying our country? Or insist, when brother seeks revenge against brother, that we *haven't* strayed from God's desire to bring all people together in harmony? Or claim that our country's *not* gotten off track from our dream of *good*? Maybe it never intended that promise for everyone. We need to *make a new nest, not last year's*—that poem from Henry Wadsworth Longfellow I stumbled on long ago at Freeland. We can make space large enough to contain the black man, the self-righteous Northerner, the defensive Southern white, the Irish immigrant. Everyone who wants in. Pie-in-the-sky, I know, but a worthier goal than destroying the other side.

I'm fairly confident Peter Nissley will approve of my booklet. I still remember how he praised my Sunday school boys in a letter he wrote after he was home. Yes, that modest man offered *praise!* He called it "gusto," the way the boys recited without fear: "*Love your enemies, bless them that curse you, do good to them that hate you . . .*" I had to caution *him* when I wrote back: "They're only boys; they don't know the full import." But I admitted also that they've heard plenty of opposite instruction: Harm your enemies, seek advantage when wronged.

For sure, I need Peter's support. He'll hear whatever aftermath comes from Mennonites regarding my booklet. I don't want him throwing up his hands about educating people, or thinking it goes too far to take up the cause of the poor.

I need whatever encouragement I can get to balance what Chicago folks say about Gettysburg. People here were giddy already when word came that Vicksburg had been taken. And after Gettysburg, folks linked those two battles as the "victories" Lincoln had been waiting for. Now Ross claims we have the South by the neck and Richmond will surrender any time. I don't have the heart to remind him he said the same thing two years ago. The only thing that limits his enthusiasm: General Meade didn't pursue General Lee when he retreated into Virginia. President Lincoln was furious also—another general not chasing Lee far enough.

Joe is the only one I've heard around here, able to talk about heavy Northern losses, or bemoan the conduct of the war. No one else wants to admit that Gettysburg displayed the insanity of otherwise-decent humans.

But Peter's description of hearing the rumble of cannons for three days—"never-ending thunder"—and his writing about the hideous costs, convinced me of the horror. He and his neighbors were left with the stench of 50,000 dead bodies thirty-five miles away from them! How can anyone *not* count the losses on both sides? And why do generals continue to order frontal assaults? This time, it was Lee's disaster to try to account for.

Local Pennsylvania folks had been distraught already for two weeks *before* the fighting. That's when the Confederate Army moved into the state, set up at Chambersburg, and made no secret about their intention to head east. After Chancellorsville, they must have thought they were invincible. But those Rebel moves caused Northern citizens to flee farther north and east, all while the Pennsylvania governor pleaded with folks to join the militia.

Why wouldn't that state's citizens have been alarmed? Already back in June, Early's raiding forces had created chaos. That's when Thaddeus Stevens's Caledonia Iron Works was burned and moveable items confiscated. Some estimates say he lost $90,000 right there. And the magnificent bridge across the Susquehanna River at Wrightsville, only six miles from Peter's place—the North burned *their own* bridge to stymie the South's efforts to get to Lancaster County!

That effort alone: a catastrophe! Lumber like we have stacked at work was piled up at the entrance in order to destroy a beautiful bridge that cost $128,000 to build! How is that not insanity? And that's *before* the loss of *human* life. This bridge, over a mile long and some forty feet wide, with a cartway and two other paths for towing. Railroad tracks, too, all under one roof. Gone!

All Ross said about that conflagration: "It did what the North wanted." He wouldn't hear anything else, even when I told him the same Rebels, angry at being forced back at the destroyed bridge, were the ones who joined other Southern forces that had gotten as far as Gettysburg. One move always invites a counter move. I know that and I'm not close to being a general.

From all accounts, it was a coincidence that Northern forces were at that same innocent location on July 1st. Happenstance or not, two enemies converged, each loaded with harmful intent. A writer for the *Philadelphia Inquirer* called it design and claimed God orchestrated the triumphs at Gettysburg and Vicksburg as a sign that America is His chosen nation. There it is again: warfare and religion, hand in hand. Back home, that's what Jakie and Father read. People all over the North might see it that way.

I can't predict whether my work on the booklet will have value or be a waste of time. But there's one immense drawback I deeply regret. I've had less time to write to Salome. So far, she hasn't said anything negative. She still writes letters, telling about their huge garden and the one ornery cow, Sadie. Sometimes she describes a relative's funeral they went to. She used to apologize for not having more interesting things to write about—her family doesn't leave home much, not even her father or younger brother—but I convinced her: I read and reread her letters, hungry for anything.

When she writes, "I will never forget you, my dear," I'm reassured. And one time she wrote, "If I could talk to you, I could tell you much more than I'm able to write." I wrote back right away that time, saying I knew exactly what she meant. I hold back in letters, too. If only I could tell her all the ways I think of her! Or describe half my fantasies. Oh, no! That might frighten her. But a letter seems too public, even if no one other than Salome ever sees it.

Still, I must find time for all that's important. How could I forgive myself if my business and writing pre-occupations led to cold feet for her? We still have five months to get through before I can see her again. If only I could hold her tenderly right now; it would comfort both of us.

One night, distressed, I came across an old poem by Samuel Taylor Coleridge. I copied it carefully and have sent it to Salome. A gift, or perhaps a repentance of sorts. Certainly, a dream to share. Its simple words may not touch her as they have me, but I dare to hope she'll understand. *"What if you slept / And what if / In your sleep / You dreamed / And what if / In your dream / You went to heaven / And there plucked a strange and beautiful flower / And what if / When you awoke / You had that flower in your hand / Ah, what then?"*

I rub my fingertips, wanting to touch something lovely, something dependable. I don't know half of what I hold already, let alone what I'm reaching for.

ESTHER — Shenandoah Valley, August 1863

I was skimming cream off the clabber several weeks ago, getting ready to churn butter. A sudden voice behind me said, "I can help with that." I turned at once. There was Peter, my absent one, standing straight but holding an arm back. We knew there'd been awful fighting in Pennsylvania last month; Simon thought Virginia men were there.

"Where did you come from?" I asked. A foolish question, akin to my next one: "And how did you get here?"

"Two good legs, Ma. They can't take my legs." His beard as straggly as ever, but his voice softer. He lacked some of the fierce face.

"What happened?" I asked.

"Where do you mean? Ewell led us with a wooden leg—and Rifle, his horse."

"You've been north?"

Mary Grace showed up, fetching another crock from the springhouse and shrieked at the sight of her big brother.

"Call the others," I said. "Hurry!" Peter had stepped toward Jephthah in his basket, but the sudden appearance of a woolly face caused my youngest to cry with a force. Simon and the boys soon crowded around. My eyes blurred. Mary Grace must have picked up Jephthah to hush. The butter came out lumpy.

Through all the jostling, Peter kept his left arm tucked partway under his haversack, the same bag I'd stitched over initials. Not till later, did he show his thin arm, his lame hand, missing a thumb and index finger.

"Gettysburg," he said. "Near to dusk, second day."

We learned more in pieces. Peter's regiment had surrounded Yankees. He motioned with a wide swoop of his right arm. The truth is: I didn't want to know more, not picture men running at each other like crazed warriors. Not hear of wounded ones calling out, bodies reeking of bile and excrement. Horses with legs upended. Whatever Peter had done—taken advantage by surprise, run with a dangling arm, hidden in a cave—he was home now.

Much later, he said what had followed; we sat with our mouths hanging. "After the big battle, told to start walking. If only an arm wound or smaller gash to the leg, such-like, we were to walk beside the wagons. 'Go home and heal. Find a doctor.' Those with severe wounds, given rides by wagon. Those with more severe—" He closed his eyes, his voice tender. "Those with shots to the innards or head, left— That third day—" He squeezed his eyes and lips tight a long while. "Yanks started using canisters, even double-canisters, not just shells." He slowly stretched up his bad arm, propped the elbow with his other hand. "Some friends—Victor, bad luck. Pure random. Nothing like Pickett's men. Third day—" He stopped a long time. "Told to charge into the heart. Lost half. Thousands," he whispered.

"You saw?" I asked.

"Slaughter," Simon said. He started pacing, like Andrew still does at times.

Peter went stony, his head down. I wanted to go to him. I wanted him as a babe again, so as to rock him. How does he sleep at night, troubled by hauntings?

"Gotta go back. Victor would. For me. All of us." Peter paused while Simon stumbled outside. "I forgot how beautiful, this Valley. The whole length. No spoilage. Green by day, this Shenandoah, blue-black by night. Whenever I got lost in trees, I climbed to a ridge and could see afar. The peace of it, no moans or cursing, no running through smoke and fog—no dodging entrails."

"This run of blood must stop," I said.

"A righteous cause, Ma. Always has been. Someone has to do it—preserve the South the way it's meant to be. Hildebrand said losses may be punishment for sin."

"Hildebrand?" Of course, I knew, one or the other.

"The man from Staunton. I told you. After Chancellorsville, he came again. Found Benjamin." Peter looked at the closed door, as if he wanted his father to hear. "All on the up and up, back then. Hildebrand said that about the North—*their* sins. Their punishment. We took 'em by surprise that time."

"Sins enough to go around," I said, wishing at once to take it back.

Peter straightened slowly. "I keep running into strange ones. Two pious ones with big felt hats. The broad brims. John was one." He gingerly pressed on his weak arm. "Doctor fellow."

It was my turn to straighten. "Felt hats?" Simon had come back inside, stood fiddling by the hearth. "What John?"

"Didn't like the look—pus draining. I'd taken a rest coming back—light-headed. Begged and stole my way. Half surprised—made it to the Lost

River. Found a flat rock; legs about to give out. The runs, nothing new. Some miles yet, Broadway."

Mary Grace rested her head on my shoulder.

"Two old men came along on horses. I was too weak to find cover, too tired to care. The one, a doctor, noticed my wound hadn't been dressed. Field doctors only look to the worst ones. This John put a hand to my forehead. 'Fever,' he said, his round face staring. The man carried vials in his saddle-bag. Apologized about no laudanum—too expensive. The other one—thin face, long beard—said little. Looked at me sideways. Took everything in, spit half out."

Peter stood and struggled to slip out of his shirt sleeve, holding his thin arm like a lifeless member. I thought Simon might swoon.

"I told the man, 'You're not taking my arm.'" Peter's eyes had narrowed, his voice as rough as those demanding bread at my door. "'Too many friends died already.' That's what I said. 'Some field doctor, a sawbone, cuts off an arm, a leg. Don't know what for.' I raised up halfway, my good arm the prop. 'Not losing it.' Kept saying that."

I've heard bragging aplenty from Peter, but not such command.

"Might not be good for much, but not going around with a stump. They had Tommy all liquored up. I was right there—a field tent. He screamed under the knife. Those fellows, run short on chloroform, cut straight through bone. I had to go outside—couldn't sit and watch."

I got up to inspect the bandage on Peter's arm. "Someone's household muslin." I put a shaky hand on his good shoulder when he sat again.

"Wet, when the man put it on," Peter explained. "He dug the bullet out—thin one offered whiskey—packed the wound with lint. The round one kept shaking his head. Smell *was* bad—*pus.* 'Not losing my arm,' I kept saying."

Simon sat himself, shaky.

"The doc soaked the bandage good, called it some kind of red-oak bark decoction in the water. A strange one, that doctor. His prayer. Tommy's doctor said pus coming out was a good sign—new tissue in a jiffy. Then they carted Tommy away—hospital somewhere." Peter's face scrunched. "Never saw him . . . No man better'n Tommy. No sin there."

"What'd you pay this doctor fellow?" Simon asked.

What was my man thinking? Peter had to steal his way.

"Wouldn't take anything. I offered a dollar—had three bluebacks left—but this John held up a chubby hand. 'No charge. Go well. If fever persists, make a tea of pleurisy root.' Claimed it works almost as well as calomel."

"We'll get you better," I said. "Rest up and eat some good eats."

First thing the next day, I made dandelion tea and insisted Peter try it. He thought it bitter, but with a drop of honey, better satisfied. He says nothing of pain, so I can't judge severity.

He's stayed these weeks, restless, but at our table. We stretch our supply of beef; no one's complained. When his bad arm hinders, he kicks a post out of spite. He can't hold a handsaw steady but pulls weeds with Mary Grace and puts out feed for cows. Joseph attached a rope to a hook in the shed; Peter pulls the rope with his left arm, back and forth. Says he's gaining strength. I can't wish failure—he looks better in the cheeks—but I fear he'll be gone soon.

Joseph spends the most time with Peter, proud to have overtaken his returned brother in size, tender toward Peter's handicap. It's not uncommon: those two come inside and abruptly end their talk. One time I heard ". . . like pebbles or a sharp *clicking* sound . . . can't hear for all the noise." Another time "bare hands and teeth . . . dirt to the eyes."

We've had flare-ups. Once when we sat to eat, Peter took up his storytelling. They'd come dashing in from thunder and lightning. I hurried to cook up scrawny ears of corn. "Heavy rains after Gettysburg. Those days, followed wagons on foot through the Cumberland Valley a ways. Told to go back the way we'd come, through Pennsylvania and Maryland."

"With Lee?" Simon asked.

"No, he took a shorter route—not sure—those left in his main force, unscathed, probably headed south and west through Monterey Pass. The rest of us—a dreary sight. People sat on their porches; some in their fields stopped work to watch us like a spectacle. I wanted to spit. Our train of wagons went for miles—someone said seventeen. Roads so muddy, the wheels chewed up ground."

"Through Chambersburg?" Andrew dabbed his bread crust in gravy.

"Not right through," Peter replied. "Pine Stump Road. Why?"

"Uncle Matthias lives near." Andrew barely glanced up. "Ma's brother. Somewhere, those parts," he added quickly.

"How—?" Peter stopped. "You all— What?" He looked at each of us. Rain pounded on the porch. "All right then. That first time we went north— Second Corps. That Mennonite meetinghouse at Chambersburg—took it for headquarters. North of town. Our man Ewell. That was before— Never saw much of locals that time; indoors, I guess. When Lee sent us on toward Harrisburg, Longstreet's men took our campsite."

The sky flickered, then thunder crashed.

"What of it?" Peter cut through our quiet.

Slowly, the rattle of spoons on pewter plates began again. Simon grunted and pulled noisily on a piece of gristle. Jephthah pointed to Peter and clapped his hands.

"Yeah, little man," Peter replied.

I reprimanded Jephthah when he gave more shouts. Of all the children, he's the hardest to quiet. Simon says I lack calmness within. My strength has slowly returned from eating my fill of greens and beans, but I often must take Jephthah to the back room during church. Anytime quiet settles, he supplies commotion.

Andrew sat again from getting more water. "Ever steal horses?" he asked quietly.

A sly grin crept on Peter's face. "Not at all. No five-finger requisition. Followed Lee's orders. No looting. This summer, gave bluebacks."

"Last fall?" Andrew asked. "Last year?"

Peter looked long at Andrew. "Chambersburg? That was Stuart's cavalry." Joseph scraped noisily on his plate. "Everyone knew, horses for the taking, that area." Peter looked around the table. "What of it? Always need remounts."

"Yeah, that area," Andrew said. Another roll of thunder rattled the window pane. We waited for the next flash, as if waiting for breath. I held Jephthah's hands tight.

"This year we paid for everything: wagons, horse gear, clothing. Like I said, all supplies, till the middle of June." Peter glared. "'Course, some wouldn't take— Too good for us."

"Worthless," Andrew said, his fist clenched, fork tines upright.

Peter looked like Nimble—nostrils flared, ready to stomp. "We'll make good. Give us time. *Not* over. A man has to eat. Going and coming back. *Am I not right?*" He looked around the table again, as if we all wore blue coats. Even Simon stayed silent. "All of us going through: Early's men, Hill's divisions, Longstreet. All of us needed food. All right? Through Washington County. Whatever it's called."

"Washington County is Maryland; Chambersburg is Franklin County," Andrew said.

"What makes you think you know so much?" Peter asked. Then he laughed that laugh that lacks mirth. "Everybody in the camps heard about plain people nearby. Some old ones met Longstreet and his men. 'So far thou canst go, and no further.'" Peter's eyes, merry. "That's what they said. Quakers, most likely. Or Dunkers. As if they could stop Longstreet. Those men fixed my arm, might be the same. But they didn't *thee* and *thou* me."

I kept my eyes to the window; tree tops whipped back and forth.

Peter said more. "If we needed wooden rails for our fires, helped ourselves. Farmers' fences, right there. Anyone, do the same. North does it, right?" Simon had gone to the window—the fury outdoors. "One old geezer told me he didn't know where the wheels were for his wagon. Bull! His wagon bed sat there, flat to the ground. Pitiful." Peter shook his head. "One thing we didn't touch—hay in barns. Fields? Another story. Ewell kept us under orders. Very strict, that man. Lee, too, this summer. Can't say about everyone. Circumstances dictate."

Andrew's mouth had opened twice, closed again. Simon stomped back and pounded on the table. Empty plates jumped. "No more war talk. Not any of you." It was his turn to stare at each of us. I grabbed Jephthah's hands again.

Since then, Andrew and Peter have kept their separate ways. Enmity hangs in the air like spoiled potatoes in the pantry. Peter may have asked Joseph the lowdown—Andrew's knowing about Chambersburg.

But we've had times of satisfaction, too. Peter's taught Jephthah to bounce on his toes. No one else but Mary Grace takes interest in the boy. I've not said aught, but I suspect another life takes form already. Ever since Simon's time of hiding, he's had more need. I wish for tenderness, but cling for whatever he gives.

One Sunday while others did evening chores, Peter taught Mary Grace the geography of the Great Valley and mentioned one of his favorite spots—same as Simon's. "A magnificent river," Peter said and recited parts of a poem: "*All quiet along the Potomac.*" I hurried to finish tending Jephthah in the back room; I could hear Peter say, "A sad one; can't say all."

"Please, Peter," Mary Grace begged. "A line or two more—"

Peter paused at seeing me but said in his hushed voice—"*All quiet along*"—his eyes shut. "*Except now and then a stray picket / Is shot, as he walks on his beat, to and fro, / By a rifleman hid in the thicket.*"

"Peter," I said.

"No harm, Ma. She—"

"I know," I said.

"People don't think about that." Peter's eyes drooped. "Thousands die at Gettysburg—all the news. But a lone sentry keeping watch— A mere man, not an officer—" I couldn't stop him. "He says a prayer for his children sleeping back home, their mother. Hears a rustle in the leaves. Too late. No one hears him say, '*Ha! Mary, good-by.*' His moans of no count."

"Peter—"

"'*All quiet . . . No sound save the rush of the river . . . The picket's off duty forever.*'"

Mary Grace sat rapt.

"Put out the bowls," I said quietly, and she slowly fell to. I gave Jephthah to Peter to hold, while I set about heating the pot for our Sunday evening fare of popped kernels.

* * *

On yet another rainy day last week—a gentle soaking this time—we were cooped up, our bodies sweaty, the house full of flies. No good air—a portent. Our flax had been spread out thin in long rows for half a month. We waited for Simon to pronounce it leached enough, so we could store in bundles.

Mary Grace was cutting up fallen apples into a dish pan. William asked something about Peter walking from Pennsylvania to our home.

"That's what soldiers do—walk," Peter said. "If I had a dollar for every mile, I'd be a rich man. Even half that would set me up."

"Andrew walked—" Mary Grace stopped herself.

"Not with a bad arm," Andrew said quickly and waved off a fly.

Everyone waited. At last Peter started counting on the fingers of his good hand. "We've been to McDowell, Cross Keys, Seven Days', Second Manassas, Antietam, Chancellorsville. Our 52nd walked—all those places. Gettysburg, of course. Cedar Mountain a year ago. Forgot that. A hundred degrees that day."

"You've done your share," I said. *The longer—, the more chance.*

"Truth is, I didn't walk all the way here," Peter said. "Left the others soon after Oakland; that's Maryland. Wanted a shorter way, so I cut off miles through thick woods. Met a fellow, had four mules pulling his wagon, covered with heavy canvas."

Simon walked around, swatting flies with a sawed-off broom. "You never know, approaching someone in the mountains."

"This one turned out willing. Sometimes a wound catches sympathy. 'Looks like you got yourself a bad one,' the man said. Tight-lipped, but congenial. A peddler, bringing supplies from the North—otherwise, wouldn't get through. Pans, pots, cloth, thread, what have you. I told him I'd been at Gettysburg. Then he said he was a member of the Linville Partisan Rangers. How about that? Rockingham County! Thought I'd hit the jackpot—a ride all the way home. Some say men like that interfere. Not how I see it—a big help. Everybody scared of Mosby's men."

"What did he look like?" I asked. "Strange ones come and go by here all the time."

"Up to no good," Simon said. "Smugglers is what they are. Buy low, sell high. Exceedingly so. Some park their wagon in the mill lot and sell their goods."

"Well, anyway—the man said, 'Call me Sid.' Then he cocked his head and grinned. We got along good. A neat little mustache and chopped-off beard, square at the bottom. Blue eyes. True blue, Ma. Kept pulling a fancy watch out of his pocket. Done himself well, my guess. Carried good drinking water, as much as I wanted. Offered me a chug of mountain stuff. Maybe ten years older'n me. The man, not the moonshine. Couldn't help but think: I could be making good money like that."

Simon shook his head. "Don't you get yourself mixed up. That kind, a tough lot. Word is, they don't get along with each other. Could be spies. Could be working both ways. You never know." He gripped the back of a chair. "Women in the thick around here, too. Never know who might be getting paid. You might *think* a neighbor upstanding. I'm telling you—you don't know."

Mary Grace had stopped stirring apples on the stove, faced us all.

Peter caught a fly in his good hand, ground it between his fingers, and got up to fling it out the half-open window. "This fellow, one of his mules gave trouble—mean old biddy. Sid had to cuss him good. I asked the man where all he goes. He just shrugged. Tight-lipped."

"Dangerous, riding with a stranger—" Simon wiped his brow and rolled up his sleeves another turn. "Men like that— They're why doctors can't get drugs. Nothing costs reasonable these days. Quinine, camphor— things they need most, way high."

Peter smiled. "Yeah, the doctor in the woods apologized. But I could trust this Sid." He watched Andrew's path of pacing, then went on. "Only rode half the night. Of a sudden the wagon stopped. I'd dozed; my neck out of whack, sitting on the wagon floor, back of my head propped against the bench. Maybe not half the night, but pitch black. Only a sliver of moon. This Sid said to get out. I didn't know my whereabouts, what I'd done wrong. 'Service stops here,' he said, looking straight ahead. Didn't sound hateful, but I could see: no arguing. 'Cave back in there a ways.' He jerked his thumb off to the right. 'You'll see better soon; Petersburg up ahead.' I grabbed my haversack and hat, jumped out. Thanked him good. 'Don't ask so many questions,' he said. Next morning, I couldn't tell which tracks were his." Peter shrugged. "Meet all kinds out there."

"Hmpf," Andrew said. "Wonder where—"

"Even the Devil gives rides," Simon said under his breath, sneaking up on another fly.

* * *

Peter hasn't returned. He headed for Staunton with his haversack on Tuesday, same time the cannons started up again. Not a constant racket, but still regular-like. Peter turned fidgety—any loud sounds from the turnpike. His arm on the mend, as good as maybe ever. The last time he took the wrappings off, the red was much reduced. "Only a dead ache," he said, "like toting a brick." He never did heavy work; Simon never ordered him. But Peter hoed with one arm, sometimes bracing with his bad hand. Mary Grace says he was here four weeks and two days. Joseph won't say, when I ask if Peter will be back.

Last Sunday, though, Peter had surprised us and gone along to church. I wonder if he slipped out partway; he stayed to the back so he could have. Bishop Coffman preached the usual: "Pray without ceasing." But Samuel makes distinction: offer petitions for kings and rulers, but don't put yourself at the behest of any government. He mentioned Jeff Davis setting aside this Friday, the 21st—a day of humiliation and prayer. Brother Samuel didn't waver. "We choose our own times to pray and fast, rather than answer to this imposter government." He made a point, too: "We in the Middle District don't bow our heads to the command of President Lincoln either. The only rightful prayer: both sides to cease their killing."

Whatever Peter heard that day, he spoke little all through Monday. He tended Jephthah like always and held the washboard between his knees and good hand, while I scrubbed at clothes. But when the others went out to thresh wheat, he stayed silent. Kept to his thoughts. So far as I know, Simon hadn't asked anything to trigger.

But Tuesday morning right after breakfast, Peter announced he was going to look up Jacob Hildebrand, Benjamin's father. That's all, though later he whispered something to Joseph.

I'd tried to prepare; I knew Peter would leave again. But now a sickness eats my innards. Mama's talk long ago of a beautiful death and a bad one. Like that man walking along the Potomac. Still, Simon's been right about 'most everything: that bird in the house those years ago, turned out harmless. That ball of fire in the sky must have been intended for others. The Lord's been our shield. Over two years now, dodging one trouble or another. Our children spared from diphtheria.

I try to soothe Mary Grace: "We've been given safety," I say. "All those places Peter's been, those thousands killed. Still good legs on him. Even that Sid fellow, could have been a desperate one. All the trips your poppa and Andrew, even Joseph, must make into town. Could have been waylaid."

She keeps her head down, mopes about. We don't know the why or wherefore of mercy. A blessing to have Peter home a month. "My righthand help," I told him, and he didn't mind.

Simon says to stay alert, though, come inside right away when bad men pester. We'll stay watchful, outlive the risks, and outlast these troublemakers.

BETSEY — West Virginia, September 1863

Poppa says we are in the right state now—we are *West* Virginia since summertime—but he does not give much smile. I thought it would make more difference, but we are still in between. We keep watch, like always, and Mother has a bigger cow bell. Tobias claims Poppa warned us: things might not be better.

I asked Tobias also about something-something wild inflation. Twice I had heard it said.

He kept chucking stones down the creek. "A pair of shoes costs $400."

"*Saag mir recht,*" I said. I have watched Poppa cobble a new pair for Tobias; he would not spend that much.

"Poppa said so." The water pooled in circles. "See my side-arm? Like so."

"You have witch eyes!" I said.

"Pfft! If we had to buy flour, a barrel would cost $1,000."

"*Du glenner Keffer!*" I walked away; I was not going to be tricked. All summer Tobias had said the raggedy soldiers were coming. When they did not, he called it a false alarm.

We had to give away bread, though, like before. Union men showed up and settled close by for two days. Mary does not even like bread, but she cried; it was her seventh birthday and Mother had added a pinch of precious cinnamon. The blue men did not come in our house like Lydia wanted. Poppa said they kept their scuffles to themselves. They only wanted food. They did not whisk Poppa away, and I did not have to hide Frank.

But after the soldiers moved away, Poppa and Mother went back and forth about something-something-else taxes.

She said, "We do not have $300. You know that."

Poppa said, "*Mir Kumme aus.* We have each other." Then he spoke as if to Mary: "We are not to make complaint."

"We do not *know* if it will help a brother," Mother said. She splattered batter.

"We help any brother—yours in blood or any others in Somerset County. And they, us." I could not see if Poppa's eyes twitched. "No one is stuck with the full load," he added.

"Are we going to move back?" Lydia asked. They had not seen her tucked in the pantry.

"Now look what you have done," Mother said to Poppa. "Divulging." But to Lydia she said, "*O, nee, mei Kind.*"

Later, Tobias told me the same soldiers who came near our meadow went to the Cheat River; they did not burn the bridge but tore up planking and threw it in the river. He heard menfolks talk when he went with Poppa to David Ridenour's store. Tobias claimed soldiers had also grabbed eats and clothes from right there where he stood. He gets to be with Poppa after church, too, and not be shooed away.

When the womenfolks make ready our food after church, they whisper about babies, but not much about fighting. Sometimes, though, I hear Poppa and Mother talk late at night about captures and cattle.

One time Poppa said with a whisper that floated up, "We should not have proceeded to church. But Daniel kept saying, 'It is appointed unto me.'" He meant the time of the hats, when the soldier man tried to get Brother Daniel to switch on the wrong side.

But Mother said, "That is no way to do. Elizabeth and hers, left with babes. Soldiers all day, in and out of their stable."

I had to ask Sarah the next time I saw her. No one else was around, but she covered her mouth to say, "Momma sent Jonas and Jacob out to tie the best horses deep in the forest. Jacob still shouts out at night."

"Where we found the turtle?" I asked.

"No, deeper yet; past the cemetery. It was near to dark when Momma went with them, each towing a cow and bucket. She feared harm for them to stay in the milk shed."

"But you stayed safe?"

"I had to help inside with the little ones. All day Momma was shaking like she was cold. One soldier came with a bad horse and took our better one. He garnered forage, too. Then twice more, a different soldier left a worse horse than the bad horse before. The last could barely wobble. Only Baldy walks able now."

"Did they take of your bread?"

"No, but the big boys slithered away to stow hams in the cave. My sister and I wrapped our best plates in blankets to hide, too. When at last Poppa stepped on the porch and dropped his saddle—the owls *schpuckich*—Momma went all *verhuddelt* and could not think straight. The big boys had to budge the chest by themselves to unbar the door."

I am glad we live up high, so not as many soldiers come our way. And with our cold nights now, they may stay low to huddle, not trudge extra to bother us. Already Tobias and I have to wear coats when Poppa takes us to the woods to pick the last of the blackberries. I love my berries; they are precious with bread and milk. But it is spooky when light starts to fall from the sky, and we have to watch for bear scat, too. I show Poppa my full bucket, but he always wants to reach in farther. "But a few more," he says. Sometimes he snags his jacket on thorns.

* * *

Now we know of another bad result. We still have corn to husk, but we have lost our Jakie Swartzendruber and his bride. Nothing is *gwehnlich*. Last Sunday we had to give them goodbye because they are moving back north. We had already given them wool coverlets when the soldiers took their bedding last spring, but even that did not stay them. We never had church at Jakie's all summer, all because of that Oakland Road. I want everyone to be safe and not have to move. I would not know where to look for Jakie and Elizabeth in Somerset County, for I do not remember my home-home.

That same Sunday of goodbye, Brother Daniel read from a Bible book called Lamentations. That was not the usual either; he wiped his nose and said, "*Gfaerlich, gfaerlich.*"

He also read about an unforgiving servant, for we had extra need. Daniel said we must not err like the servant. That man was forgiven a great big debt by the king but did not forgive a tiny debt another servant owed him. Instead, the first servant put the second in prison, like a capture. What did the king do but change his mind about the big debt! Daniel made what he called application: we are to forgive soldiers their transgressions. And we are to be at peace in our homes, not distraught, one to another.

"Dry your tears, girls," Mother said at home. "Jakie and his Elizabeth, sore distressed."

"We are not to blame them," Poppa said, "or think ill." He looked right at me.

"Losing two precious babies in two years' time," Mother said.

I gave a start; I had not seen any signs in Elizabeth.

"Not in that woman's constitution," Poppa said.

Mother gave Poppa a look. That was the same word Poppa used about our new state—radify new Virginia something-something constitution.

I tried not to be sour—only disheartened—when we milked cows the next morning. I like our milk shed with the low ceiling; I can loosen my head scarf and stay warm when we huddle with the cows. I get to take Goldie far to the back, away from the doorway and the cold.

Sometimes it is hard to hear others, though, when the milk cows turn restless. But I sat extra still when Tobias asked Poppa, "Is it true, soldiers killed one of Jakie's cows and roasted it outside his barn?"

"Who said thus?" Poppa's voice came loud like a roar over our new cow's rump. We have not named her, but I want to call her Bethie for something new.

Tobias answered very quietly, "Jonas."

Poppa kept silent a long time. Finally, he said, "Soldiers last spring were very hungry—Jones's starving men. They took all Jakie's eatables, all that was left from Elizabeth's labor the summer before. Not once, mind you, but several times. Elizabeth never made recovery." Mother would not approve of Poppa divulging. "Different soldiers, different times, made raids. *Hungrichi Mannsleit zelle sich bicke.*"

Goldie stepped jittery, sideways and back; all unawares I had stopped pulling on teats. I had to hum and talk low for her, not think about hungry men.

When the squirts came again, Poppa said, fast but quiet, "The first time, soldiers marched right inside. They ate buckwheat cakes faster than Elizabeth could make them. Some ate dough from the tray. She never could get over. Other hungry ones yelled and slapped at her to hurry."

No wonder Elizabeth's hair had gone astray. Sometimes only Jakie came to church.

Tobias piped up. "Soldiers grabbed a setting hen from her nest and ate raw eggs—unhatched chicks and all."

Poppa came close to yelling, "*Schtopp grad nau!* Were you there? Idle talk, the Devil's workplace."

But the next day when Tobias and I dug potatoes, he could not keep still. "Know what else?"

I did not say one way or the other but kept groveling for spuds.

He leaned down. "When the soldiers left, they drove off Jakie's cattle and horses as if they owned the right. Jonas said so."

I stayed hunched. Jonas would not make things up. I want him to like me—not be a fraidy girl—for he is thirteen and has the good looks.

"They drank from Jakie's swill barrel, too."

I jerked up to see; Tobias stood rooted, as if he heard Poppa coming. He talked garbly. "Not swill for animals, but the grown-ups' barrel." He jabbed the fork into a fat potato. "They fought amongst themselves and whisked Jakie's watch."

It was worse than I thought. All of this happened last spring, and I did not know. If soldiers drank bad at our place, Poppa might send me outside with Frank—more reckless than he thinks. Lydia would have a time inside with Gideon. He is as big as Levi and would run to the window and pound. Then Levi would commence jumping and hollering, and Noah would follow.

Nor do I want church folks to talk more about Iowa. Auntie Mommie whispered to Mother that Peter Schrock's sister Lydia went there with her man, only to take sick and die.

That started another back-and-forth at home; that is not how things are to be between them. Poppa said, "People die when the Lord calls them home." But Mother scootched a kettle loud on the hearth and said Lydia was too young, only thirty-six. That is one year older than my momma ever got to be.

I want everything to be settled right again; I will have to grow up faster and not ever be in a huff with Tobias.

J. FRETZ — Chicago, November 1863

Will it never end? Less than two months until marriage and all should be smooth. Is it *only* two more months, or is it two *long* months yet? Salome remains steadfast; she's not the problem. Her letters show no faltering about her move to Chicago. She only writes of eagerness to be one in heart, mind, and body.

When I'm prone to dwell on uncertainties, Salome reminds me of her daily prayers that I will know direction. When I fret over my neglect, she writes of joy at having time yet to help her sister, Annie, set up the big loom again. She tells also about her best friend, Ann Lib Bryan at Nace's Corner, and how they walk back and forth between their homes to admire each other's spinning and needlework.

I'm at a crossroads. *Again.* Salome doesn't fully know. Nothing is as I expected. All year I've waited for *next* year, when I'll board the train for Pennsylvania. *The best will come soon,* if I can only be patient. But *best* by what measure? Now *this other* intrudes. Do I ever get to choose? This urgent need in unstable times. What lot has the Lord cast for me? I've resisted the idea of God *conducting* a war or *directing* a child's death. For years already, I've balked at the thought of a human playing only an assigned part in the drama of a predestined life. But now circumstances—*"a divinity shapes our end"*—starting a religious newspaper!

Already three times this month, I've decided to give up my Sunday school work. As soon as I do so, I'm sick with a fever. Restlessness seizes. How can I let my boys and girls down? I go back on my resolve; *I can't give up teaching.* I remember last spring when I was out walking in our mission district, trees unfurling their light green leaves, and two little girls from our school saw me and ran to walk along, holding my hand on either side. I still feel joy whenever I think of making their day brighter! The father of one stepped from his house and expressed appreciation for me as their teacher. I acknowledged we care for the little ones on Sundays but, of course, we can't reach them the other six days. He protested: "Your influence lasts all week." I was surprised and humbled.

But this other—it's been building, ever since I published my pamphlet against warfare. If I started a newspaper, free of all party spirit, Republican or Democrat, I could remind Mennonites of our heritage as peacemakers. I've given license to wild imaginings—my own printing press some day! There's no argument: if we want to grow as a church, we must have our own literature. Have I become sucked in by self-importance, as my brother Abe suggests?

All through the war I've read sermons by Henry Ward Beecher and Horace Bushnell. Increasingly, I want to counter their voices. Salome says she'll support whatever I'm being called to. She doesn't know. I'm sickened by references to martyrdom on the altars of the country, connections drawn between shed blood and religious atonement. At first, I thought it was only a few of the clergy. Now I've concluded it's a widespread belief. Joe heard the same from an army chaplain: the American nation and Christian church as one. Humans only need to pray and fight; right will be vindicated. And if, along the way, deaths happen all out of proportion to the hoped-for result, that human price must be paid. Astonishing, how many believe this.

Ross likes nothing better than to toss a copy of the *New York Times* on my desk—his favorite way to live under my skin. He knows I'll read it. The *Times* has joined the religious chorus. A special correspondent, reporting from the headquarters of the Army of the Potomac, apparently has a direct line to heavenly thought. I took the copy home to show Abe when he came for a meal. Written back in July, the man's words stick like a thorn:

> Oh, you dead, who at Gettysburgh have baptized with your blood the second birth of Freedom in America, how you are envied! I rise from a grave whose wet clay I have passionately kissed, and I look up and see Christ spanning this battle-field . . . His right hand opens the gates of paradise—with his left he beckons these mutilated, bloody, swollen corpses to ascend.

I gulp water, take deep breaths. I'm not privy to the spiritual state of war dead, and I would never deprive a man of eternal rest. But the glorification! Someone has to counter these sentiments; they're reprinted in nearly every household's secular or political paper. Adults *and* children, subjected to this kind of persuasive writing. I've read my fill.

Killing, whether from a minnie ball or hand-to-hand combat, can't be the means to a righteous end. This war has *never* been God's purpose. Yes, I sound dogmatic. But from my view, God has *allowed* humans to carry out their foolish wills, even fight and kill. A year ago when Lincoln decided to make this a war to free the slaves—even said both sides *may* be wrong—I thought him back on track. But instead, he's broadened the war to affect civilians, saying escalation is the only way to emancipate the black man. Sometimes he's dragged a leg, but he's never looked seriously at any peaceful option, other than shipping Negroes *out of the way*. Where is this going to take us? It's frightening.

The idea for a religious newspaper became stronger when John M. showed up with his manuscript. No, not his petition to President Lincoln; he's never said another word about that. He brought what he called his written contribution to the cause of nonresistance. I was honored to edit and see to the publication of "Christianity and War" last month—twice as many copies as my own booklet. I would have chosen different wording at times, but I didn't want to discourage his efforts. John's more convinced than I: being involved in any part of government, voting or serving on a jury, can embroil one in a state's questionable ways of doing.

Back in the summer, I never expected to maintain regular correspondence with John. I'm too young; I dress too well. But our snags came over much more substance. He accepted some of my suggestions but refused to allow his name to be attached to his booklet.

I kept my voice calm. "An authorless booklet loses some of its power to convict."

John met my steadiness, his nose like a fortress. "Then it shall not be published." He gathered the loose pages, his eyes watery.

I stared back, speechless. The man was a fool!

His eyes receded further under heavy eyebrows. "Some folks hold exceeding prejudice against Mennonites because we don't participate in war." His hands shook on scrawled pages. "The vocal ones, all too eager to latch onto printed evidence, especially against a minister. Endless accusations and consequences—" He fumbled for a handkerchief. "I can do no other." He didn't apologize; nor did he make any attempt to conceal the magnitude.

I said I would sleep on it. How could he say God's people are to be a suffering people, not shy away from tribulation? But then, not want his name included? I'm not easily convinced to go against my better judgment; I felt caught between indignation—such inconsistency—and sorrow.

In the morning, though, I knew it had to be John M.'s decision. It was *his* name. *His* life. I couldn't be the one, instrumental if calamity came to him. He handed over his manuscript again. I took charge of printing arrangements with Charles Hess.

Another difference disturbed also; John refused a written statement as to my intent. We shook hands instead. My only recourse regarding authorship: I noted it in my diary. Likely of no use, but I wanted to eliminate any possible uncertainty in years hence.

His booklet is three times as long as mine, and he uses more Scriptures to support our position of defenselessness. He knows better than I what will convince Mennonites. His greatest revulsion: the thought of a church member from the North facing a Mennonite brother from the South on the battlefield. At that, his eyes get watery again. His voice sounds weak, far from his rallying cry: "Stand aloof!"

But to his credit, in our work together I've never heard him condemn anyone of another denomination who believes differently from him. I was far less generous in my booklet. I don't see what can be any clearer than Jesus overturning the Old Covenant with his command to love our enemies: "*A new commandment I give unto you.*" How does anyone argue that away?

But on yet another point I strongly objected. John seemed to accept *our own people's* support for Clement Vallandigham. He stayed even-tempered when telling about Ohio's rabid element. "The eastern parts of Holmes County voted heavily for Vallandigham for governor; Mennonites and Amish make up most of that population."

Without hesitation I said, "Hoodwinked by the *Peace* Democrat label! They vote to let the South go its way with no restrictions on owning slaves."

"Some of our people think Lincoln unfair, banishing Vallandigham to Ontario."

"The man made treasonous statements." I had to lower my voice, not get riled like I do with Ross. "Didn't that cause alarm?"

"Not everyone admires our president. Some think he only cares that Vallandigham not become a political martyr."

I wanted to say how naïve that is. I've heard Peace Democrats here in Chicago applaud the man's boldness in campaigning from across the border. In truth, it's their way to criticize the war effort without clearly standing up against fighting. But it undermines Lincoln. They want to further the interests of white people, but they won't say that. Nor can I say that to John.

His silence remained unbroken. I asked, "Do you mean Mennonite ministers in Ohio look the other way at this kind of injustice toward people with dark skin?"

"We're told not to judge."

"We're also told to discern between right and wrong." At that, I had to clamp my mouth. But I stew inside. Why couldn't John see that people twist things around in order to think unfair rights are appropriate? He should know, it's been a trademark from the beginning of our country. White men have established their own privilege, starting with citizenship. Already in my school days at Freeland Seminary, we discussed that. Sure, some dis-agreed, but it was clear: our race defends advantage while calling it the natural order.

"The western part of Holmes County has been no calmer," John M. droned on. "Conscription, the bugaboo there. Already back in June some-one threw a stone at a draft enroller; a riot took off."

"People need to read more than the *Holmes County Farmer*. How can they look the other way when wrongs are committed?"

John smiled and said, "That's what I've been telling you."

Oooff! He's been my biggest support for starting a newspaper. *Do I want this or not? Do I have a choice?* His encouragement has gone beyond idle talk; he'll submit frequent articles if I go ahead. His main caution: Chicago's a dangerous place for me to live. At that, I laugh and point out *he's* the one in the middle of a hornet's nest. This fall they drafted seventy to eighty men in Columbiana County, Ohio.

And yet, despite our differences, I end up listening to John M. like a dutiful son. *Work together; don't let differences separate or stall the cause.* Last month I attended the conference at the Yellow Creek Meetinghouse, exactly one year after my first encounter with Indiana Mennonites. This time again, *getting there* was unpleasant. Not mud, but the Elkhart Hotel was full on Thursday night. I slept on a sofa under a damp buffalo robe.

But once I got to the conference, I had no regrets. Worthwhile meet-ings from sermons to the Communion service and baptisms. The singing reduced me to tears again. A year later, after terrible loss of life and un-certain futures, these folks still sounded angelic—their simple tunes came without ornamentation.

But the biggest surprise: how many folks knew my name. "That young man from Chicago"—yes, my booklet! By the end of four days, I no long-er flinched when called John. I wouldn't have one foot in the Mennonite world—so many names and faces to remember—if John M. and Peter hadn't spread the word about my pamphlet. And now, they have people for me to meet on my way back East! Have they forgotten I'm going there to get married?

But Abe's words hit like a thud: *"Pride will get you."*

Am I letting friendliness and support blind me? John F.—is that who I want to be?

I try to be realistic. Many Mennonites oppose any organized effort to educate young people. My future father-in-law isn't the only skeptical one. A printed periodical?—*oh, the horror*! A Sunday school?—*worldly*; parents can teach all that's needed. Yes, I exaggerate, but some of them sound like missionary work would carry more danger than enlistment. As closed as some can be to innovation, it's preposterous to think they'd support a Men-nonite newspaper.

But maybe I'm too harsh. Am I looking for an excuse? I swing back and argue the other side. Maybe I can convince—at least some. It's *my* decision. Am I afraid of failure? I shouldn't stop before I start. *Be bold.* Don't succumb to people's worst impulses.

My teeth take up the battle—countless trips to the dentist. First Dr. Cushing, now Dr. White. Grinding, grinding, both men say. Well, yes, there's stress. Is it seeing my name? I can't admit that. Wondering if enough folks will read on a regular basis? Giving my soul to the cause of Mennonite understandings? *My time!* Why walk uphill with a chain and ball around my ankle?

Abe might be right: I've abandoned all sense and don't know my true motives. I told him, though, I had asked John M. directly, "Is there no one else?" I waited for his deliberate head shake to change. I stalled over his knitted brow, watched the slight tremor of his hands with their dark spots.

All John said: "You're young. We need your courage." He didn't embellish. He didn't use glowing language or repeat endlessly. Only straightforward need, a dearth of options.

I plotted once more. I would manage all three: keep up with lumber, handle Sunday school tasks, start a newspaper. I could get up earlier—four in the morning. Add more work hours to my day.

Another time, I showed Abe more of the report Professor Fowler had written of my phrenological character. Yes, it's been a year since he studied me, and yes, his is a secular voice. But an outsider's opinion can be useful. I'd never voiced serious doubt to Abe about my work in lumber, but the more he read, the more he scratched his arms. "What's this? '. . . may venture to change your business if needs be, for your talents are adapted to a variety of avocations.'" Abe didn't wait for my answer. "What does he mean? A strength?"

"Complimentary, right?" I pointed to the professor's list of my personal traits: "'. . . a practical available cast of mind, fond of knowledge.'"

Abe stayed silent; he grinned only when he read, "'Too modest, so cultivate brass . . . not quite patient enough towards little children.'"

Our laughter relieved some of the tension. "That was before Augustus," I said. Abe knows the new boy's cries still come upstairs and wake me at night. I thumbed to the last page of Fowler's report. "Look at this. 'Could make a good writer, but not cool enough for a Speaker.'" Abe raised his eyebrows. "The man doesn't think I have the proper temperament for direct interaction with the public," I explained. "Never mind his poor use of capital letters."

"'Not cool enough,' the man says, but you sure like to talk."

I might have looked miffed—doesn't he know I can be moody, too?

Abe looked away when our eyes met. Then he shrugged. "You're asking me?" He ignored the other pages and said, "I don't know as how I'd put much stock in this." He stared at me like he was meeting a new person. Finally, he quoted idly, "'. . . your mother's son in every respect—'"

It's probably good Abe slows me down. I need to stay in the lumber business—a wife to support! Salome could make it easier, if she said she made promise to someone secure in the lumber business who holds his Sunday school work dear. I know all too well, if I start a newspaper, I'll want to publish in German *and* English, so both young and old can be informed. That means more time translating, more cost to print twice as many pages. Doubly frightening! I'm not assured of enough time or money. When I look seriously at numbers, publishing for a year would cost around $500. If there aren't enough subscribers, I'd have to make up the difference. That's another reason to stay in the lumber business: use regular income to supplement.

This infernal internal battle! Part of me says: *try it for a year*. If you fail, you won't have lost that much. But then John M. suggests starting right away: January 1st! "People need a call to peace *now*, not in five years."

My teeth shoot pain. Tossed about again: *let go your Sunday school boys*. No other way. One sacrifice for another. *There are other teachers. You can't do everything.* But my boys' fertile minds! Not be a part? How can I let them down?

One night a darker voice stepped in: *you've hurdled the insanity threshold*. I sat up like a bolt had struck in bed. I thought someone else was in the room. *You're getting married in January! Ten months ago, Salome was all you could think about. Now you want to add a second new enterprise for the same time?* I waited for a cackle, some shadowy figure to emerge from behind the large wardrobe. Have it out with me.

Other developments have added more confusion. Last summer, John G. Stauffer from Bucks County—a Mennonite about my age—showed up unsolicited. Abe didn't know the fellow either. It turned out John Oberholtzer had told the Stauffer man about me and our similar concerns—nonresistance and publishing! He'd been working in the office of *Das Christliche Volksblatt* but took a seven-month travel break in the West. I didn't want to think he'd timed his departure from the East as a casual escape from war's pressures.

His experiences in publishing excited me, but his words gave me pause. "Never-ending," he said. I can see him tap each fingertip: "Composing, editing, overseeing hired help, keeping the books." Then he wiggled his thumb. "The actual printing."

Of course, that took me back to thinking of Salome. Am I ignoring her wishes? Her needs? If she knew how consumed I am—how others are planning my life. My heart drops. If she knew everything, she couldn't ask playfully, "Have you put up a hand to stop Chicago's fierce wind yet?"

As for others back home, it takes little imagination to hear some of them saying: *Off the deep end! Does he think we need another Pope?* My cousins—bless them—offer no uniform opinion about my booklet. Every Mennonite family is likely divided by the same rifts. One cousin wrote, "Exactly right," but another admitted to being "more of the fighting order." Yet another one said she wouldn't respond about politics, because she'd be at odds and didn't want to mar our personal correspondence. My goodness! Can't we discuss disagreements? And then there's the cousin who made his own statement by enlisting.

Father hasn't responded to my booklet at all, but I've excused him because of his poor eyesight. Jakie spared little, though. "I can't believe I'm reading my own brother's words." He doesn't understand how much my thinking's changed. Even a year ago I might have given mixed signals and said I wanted the North to whip the South.

Jakie wrote pointed statements—somehow directed to me—about his own decision regarding President Lincoln's call last month for 300,000 more volunteers. If Jakie were drafted, he would need to pay another $300 to be exempt. Without batting an eye, apparently—or giving evidence of genuine religious sentiment—he had joined the Mennonite church so he could rightfully claim conscientious objection. "Not giving up my life!" he wrote, explaining that the option to hire a substitute still runs to $1,000 in Pennsylvania, especially if a broker is involved. "Not living with guilt, if my substitute dies."

His letter drifted off to describe the draft method in Doylestown. Officials oversee the process, starting with someone putting tightly folded scraps of paper, each with a man's name on it, inside a tin wheel. Another person spins the wheel. Then a blindfolded man pulls out enough names to fill the quota. A clerk fills out draft notices for the unlucky ones, and messengers—the most to be pitied—carry out the last step, taking the sad news to the homes of draftees. *Lives changed by chance.*

I've come too far; I can't rely on war developments to settle my indecision. I have to choose, based on my own beliefs. How I wish I could talk with Salome; it would take much too long to write out all the dilemmas. How many forks are there in this road of my life?

Two weeks ago I tried another test: I rose early and wrote the first article for a newspaper. The ideas came easily, and I thought I had my answer. But shortly after, I fell ill with another fever and dreamed about my teeth. A filling had fallen out and the tooth gave much pain. In its center a speck remained, surrounded by pearly grains. What sense was I to make of that? A mote in my tooth?

Mary Ann says I'm prickly, but it's hard to communicate with her. When I questioned Lincoln's proclamation for all citizens to set apart the last Thursday of November—coming up on the 26th—as a day of Thanksgiving and Praise, she asked, "Doesn't God bring you comfort?"

How was I to explain? We start at such different points. Lincoln's advice hit me wrong when he said we're to be thankful not only for fruitful fields and beautiful skies, but also for peace with other nations and order and harmony at home. *What?* He acknowledged the military conflict but asked us to confess our perverseness and disobedience and pray that the Almighty would heal our wounds and restore us *as soon as fits with the Divine purpose.*

Shades of Shakespeare again! I couldn't voice my doubts to Mary Ann. If she wants to understand my discomfort, she can read my booklet for once. How often must I remind her, Jesus's new commandment to love stands above any other purpose?

Surprisingly, Walt Whitman's words and actions provided a better model than Lincoln's. I've always liked poetry for its cadence and rhyme, but when Whitman improvises, it throws me off. Yet his thoughts while tending the needs of soldiers convey much beyond words:

> I do not ask the wounded person how he feels
> I myself become the wounded person
> My hurts turn livid upon me as I lean on a cane and observe.

Day after day Whitman exposes himself to war's grief and devastation! So much so, he's had to go home to Brooklyn to rest.

His words made me realize I hadn't visited Joe in over four months. When have I taken on the lives of others to the extent they've become my own? I knew Joe would appreciate Whitman's lack of sentimentality in describing war as "nine hundred and ninety-nine parts diarrhea to one part glory."

So I went once more to the Cresswell home. I don't remember much of our initial comments. But Joe dismissed with a wave my apology for having been too busy. "You don't owe me anything." I thought that reply rather strange but told him I was glad to see him looking better. Partly, he's grown more facial hair to cover some of his disfigurement. But his eyes were brighter, his body, alert. I soon found his mind, sharp and caustic; his tone, rough.

"You still think war can be fought to make opportunity more equal for coloreds?"

I wasn't sure he was asking a question, but I tried to give a neutral answer. "Achieving equality may necessitate some loss of life, but how these huge numbers today can be just—"

"What's in it for you?" he interrupted. "You talk a lot about a *just* war."

"What's in— I, well, I think we're to look out for those who have less."

"Look out?" he asked.

I smiled uneasily; I hadn't expected to be grilled. "Stand with. Not be self-satisfied, I guess; not count my fortune, a white man, as a right."

"You are a white man, you know." He slumped to one side, grinned slyly. "So you're still, uh, still getting yours? A little carrying on perhaps."

"Getting—?" I saw a glint in his eye, an undercurrent of ugliness.

"Come on, Fretz," he said, "we're friends. Our good times—I haven't forgotten. Is it some little sweetie of the other race now? Your *helping*? Your little adventuress?"

I gulped and stared. My carefree past. My dreams, desires. "No, no. Not that, Joe."

"Right." His upper lip curled.

I wanted to tell him of Salome, of my plans to bring her here in two months. I couldn't get it out. He might laugh aloud at the idea of my life with a plain Pennsylvania girl.

"You always were a shyster. Backing out."

"Yeah, well, I suppose so. Some truth there, but—trying . . . straight-forward living now." I looked around the parlor, found nothing to say about the greenish-brown settee, the ornate clock's minute-hand, resolute in its ticking movement. "Guess I'd best be going." I shook my head and stood, halting. "Wanted to make sure you were doing all right."

Joe might have laughed. I only remember sticking out my hand like a pistol. He hesitated. Our hands met like two limp rags.

"So then—" he said.

"Be going on," I said again and waved slightly from the front door, not calling a goodbye as I usually would to Mrs. Cresswell.

I grabbed the steps' handrail, as if unsure, paused down one step. *What if Salome heard something or suspected?* She's never asked regarding past dalliance. I never meant— Never meant to own. Nor use a woman. No, not malign.

I continued quickly before anyone could call me back.

* * *

A week has passed. I'm not the same, but I've gone through the motions of work. I say little to Ross or Abe, keep my distance from extended interaction with Jacob or Mary Ann at home. I try to put Joe out of my thinking—the death of another friendship.

I've forced myself to look to practical matters—a list of topics I must write about, if I start a newspaper. *If . . .* woodenish words to blot out pain.

Mutual aid is one topic. If each church member would give *"according to that a man hath"* as Scripture teaches, we wouldn't find ourselves in dire straits when an honest believer gets drafted and suddenly needs to pay an exemption fee of $300. John M. tried to organize people in Ohio to be prepared like this, saying the burden of commutation should be borne equally by the rich and the poor. He was making progress, until a few of the men who had the most wealth—and no draft-age sons!—balked. The whole thing fell through.

Money. Sometimes I despise it! I can't resolve the chasm: lack of money among immigrants in New York City, abundance of money in the church. Outsiders have noticed how Mennonite noncombatants are acquiring great wealth because of high grain prices. John M. says it's happening to farmers here in Illinois; people in states back East are desperate for grain and meat. Where are church folks on this? Where are brave voices, helping each other live what we believe, sacrificing our standing and financial stability? Where's my voice? Does everything come down to integrity? Nobility?

I appease myself; it's not only Mennonite farmers. There's terrible poverty in Chicago but also excessive wealth. Not only in trades and manufacturing like Mr. McCormick's mechanical reaper factory, but also in new business buildings going up—stone, brick, marble—in addition to huge residences.

My struggle, too. I came here to make money! *My* expediency. *My camel*, trying to slip through the eye of the needle. Beidler might be right: wealth isn't necessarily wrong. But the fact is, I'm making good money, while Joe . . . He and his family have a right to be bitter. Sometimes my good prospects shame me.

I ran into Dwight Moody last Sunday—another person I had little interest in talking with. But he didn't seem to notice; he was eager to tell me how he's changing his goals. For years he'd been successful, selling shoes in Boston and again when he first came to Chicago. He saved $7,000 in four years; money came that easily. But his cheeks got flushed when he admitted his goal had been to reach a personal fortune of $100,000. Then he relaxed and smiled, telling about going to Cyrus McCormick and getting support for his projects with the United States Christian Commission of the YMCA. They've been bold, providing food for Scandinavian immigrants, evangelizing Union troops. And yet one thing hasn't changed for Dwight. He's still adamant about not going to war. But he's refusing to stay at home and build up riches.

I'm thrown back—Whitman with his cane. Am I strong enough to do what's in front of me? If so, what am I leaning on? Salome's steadfastness means the most, but she doesn't truly understand how dangerous it could be to write about putting up the sword and giving Negroes equal rights. The truth is: I don't fully know either.

Sometimes an image quiets my restless mind. In the last stanza of a hymn I wrote—yes, I put it at the end of my booklet—I entreated our God of Love to send forth *"another dove to bear another olive branch."* I don't know what that means—so certain a few months ago—but it will take more than human determination to rebuild a climate of peace. I cling to the thought: others walk with heavy hearts also, burdened with their own quandaries and failures. Struggling to avoid our divided country's abyss. We still want to extend a twig of peace—literal or not—to the fellow about to fire another cannon ball, the slave hunter who thinks he rights wrongs, the politicians and preachers hopelessly wrapped up with each other.

Jacob — Iowa, December 1863

The full load has fallen. Not the loss of a life companion, but a heaviness like unto Barbara's departure. Not the responsibility for an unchurched young man. No, this new load comes from self-inflicted wounds.

Last Sunday I made confession, although not on bended knee as one seeking reinstatement. No, I was not put out. Only bruised and smitten. I have been part of the difficulties with Joseph Keim. The transgressions of one, visited upon another. If I were not a minister, I could be at peace with others, tend my water wheel and be content.

The four who came from afar only asked that I confess to being party to the disputes. Chastised for all to see and in need of forgiveness. I take small comfort: those who went before me back East, Benedict Miller and Jonas Bitsche, also knew criticism. Not formal proceedings, but they also suffered regrets.

The trouble came to a head this fall when Keim invited John Mishler, a deacon, to join him in meeting separately on a Sunday morning—October 25th it was—with their followers. Most of those in opposition have come here in recent years. I told both men to take their families and leave our settlement. But four weeks later, defiant, they met at the Mishler home. Ever since Keim attended the meetings in Pennsylvania last May, he has been more set in his ways—very strict on some matters, while pounding for change on others. Consistency has been sorely missing. But I did not realize how much ill will had flourished so quickly.

Four ministers from out of state—one each from Ohio and Indiana and two from Canada—were called to settle our disputes. I never thought to be the object of censure. But inasmuch as I am bishop, final responsibility must rest with me. These men stayed one week plus four days, seeking first to gather understanding before bringing reconciliation. "Mend what has been broken," they said. They were fortunate to complete their work before heavy snows and fierce winds set in.

No one claimed my preaching had drifted from my days in the East or from my beginnings in the Old Country. My ministry was not removed from me. But I am to proceed with fear and trembling, rightly dividing the Word. *Ja, a part of the difficulties.*

Some things I do not remember ever having said. "Take your poison that spreads discord." Or, "Get out! You are not worthy to be entrusted with a child." But when others attested to harshness, it became harder to dispute. I am to use a more tender voice when warning of fiery battles and the final Day of Reckoning. I am to listen to the counsel of others before proceeding over thorny ground. Not become testy when questioned.

For Keim and Mishler, there are to be no more separate meetings. Rather, we are to build each other up, not concern ourselves with who is right and who is wrong.

Brother Miller from Holmes County looked right at me. "Do you ever think you are blamed for someone else's problems?"

I could not help but nod. "Much ill has been unjustly spoken."

"Well, then," he said—he was not puffed up, though he spoke with half-closed eyes—"is it not possible you have erred in the same way and blamed someone else for *your* failings?"

Sobering indeed, those days of rebuke. But in the end I could say without reservation: "I desire to be at peace with all men. Just as the apostle Paul taught, we are to cleanse ourselves of any warring spirit, not arm ourselves with words as weapons."

At home I asked Mary, "Why has the right spirit not been given me?" I never know if she will extend mercy or heap condemnation.

"You were not brought up with the proper disposition." She spoke softly and leaned a shoulder into me. "You are unbending, like a straight pine tree, not a willow. But your innards are soft; therein lies the tenderness."

"I am bereft," I blurted, "exposed. Outside forces have encouraged a spirit of dissension."

Her voice turned brisk. "The men did not take everything. I am here." She thrust her arm about to take in our four walls. "We have our home."

"I never meant to cause harm. Only, encourage faithfulness."

She settled her hand on the coarse cloth covering my thigh. "Of course, Jacob. Surely, God weeps with you."

I trembled before her. "The men suggested I preach again about the Good Shepherd. I reminded them, I have covered all those stories: the lost sheep, the lost coin, the prodigal. But Brother Miller repeated: 'Beckon with more loving-kindness toward those listening.'"

"Yes, with mercy, Jacob, not reproof, so people can hear. Is that not so?" she added with a squeeze of my hand.

I sighed. "Yes. I will try again. Less harsh. With another year upon us, we will begin another round of the prescribed Scriptures."

"Think how to soothe, Jacob. Like you do with Caspar." She kissed my cheek ever so tenderly. "People are frightened."

"One thing I confessed to: my record keeping. But they found no fault therein. You know, do you not, Mary? The wrongdoing was not all mine." I grabbed her arm; I did not want her to get up. "Nor did they criticize my plea that there be no feasting at weddings."

She nodded. "You have said."

"The men abhorred all manner of merrymaking—kissing games! That should not be among us when we have neighbors, crushed with sadness from the consequences of warfare. Nor did they dispute: we cannot serve Communion if we do not have harmony."

"Yes, Jacob. It is not what, but how."

I fumbled for my handkerchief, wiped my runny nose. "There is a *what,* though—a sore item that festers. They cautioned in the same vein: I am to give myself to diligent study of Scriptures regarding our practice of buying substitutes."

"That *is* the custom."

"*Ja.*" I raised an open palm. "Refuse to kill." I lifted the other hand. "Turn around and pay someone else to do the deed—?"

With barely a pause she said, "Inconsistent also, to overturn established practice."

Her eyes showed no perverse flashing, so I said, "*Ja.* A dilemma—the wineskin of precious truth. My sole intention is to follow the Lord's precepts."

"And to do so peacefully."

"But the bursting—one Scripture over against another—may bring dissension." I could not quell the rise in my voice.

We arrived at no complete conclusion. She went about her work, busying herself, stirring milk into cooked turnips.

Abraham Lincoln must know weariness also. Even here in the North, people do not agree about whether to abolish slavery or let it die slowly. My soul shudders when our president professes conviction about the necessity of bullets. Yet his inner being must bleed—how could it not?—at the count. Bodies pitched in graves.

My legs quiver, not only from worn-out bones but also from known snares. I see faces ready to pounce. Mary admits that some women still murmur. They sit with heads lowered, as if determined to flash decorative combs and hair pins. How is that not defiance?

In the past I have prayed for an extended length of days to complete my calling. Now I long to turn the task over to younger ones. "Finish the work," I want to say to Frederick. So much up in the air, even the acceptable tasks of a full deacon.

I rise slowly, seeking solace in my woodshed. I run my bare hand cautiously over the yoke once placed on our oxen—no man could lift alone—meant to keep beasts of burden intent on the task of uprooting prairie grasses with four-foot roots. So it is, I walk bowed down—my own mantle of leadership. But walk I must; the Lord it is, numbers my days.

DAVID — Shenandoah Valley, January 1864

The beginning of a new year should herald promise. We close our church records and business dealings for the past year and begin with a clean slate. We are to open the door—a time to start again, much like the promise of seed time. But how can we start afresh when men have not cast aside their stale grievances? They wait for the bugle to sound, so they may spring with the same fierce hatred. The air stays cold; the sky over the mountains is a dark blue-gray. The only green, dark almost to black, found in my pine grove and shading the faraway ridge.

Three years ago in January, we feared a vote on secession; Brother Kline warned of sadness and destruction. One year later, we waited to hear regarding exemption. Last year we started the new year giving God thanks and praise, but unease sat among us. Today I shiver in my winter coat. Confederate officials, set to track down anyone who deviates. My closet remains my heart's thump. I go to church; I ride to Timberville on occasional business. Beyond that, I ventured out last fall only to Johnny's or J. M.'s farm. So much turmoil swirls, I have needed their assessments of developments.

Johnny tells of his travels last year: over 4,000 miles by horseback. And that included his restraint in the fall! Many of his earlier trips had pertained to funerals from diphtheria's grip. He came to Flat Rock for the four children under the age of five we had to part with. Counting all German Baptist churches throughout the Valley, he helped conduct fourteen other funerals for that same age last year. Besides that, another fourteen youngsters between the ages of five and twenty were lost to us, including John's married niece. So few friends our daughter's age survive at Flat Rock; two more expired recently. No young men to be found!

Johnny intends comfort when he breaks into song: *"Hide me, O my Savior hide / 'Neath the shadow of thy wing."* My heart wants to dispute. Does he mean a *hen's* wing? *"Cover my defenseless head / With the shadow of thy wing."* The Lord's wing is mighty, but I am sore afraid. The promises do not cover me as they do John. I always come up short.

Already after the terrible battles at Gettysburg—could Elijah have been among the 3,000 dead horses?—I pulled inward. We had thought the madness at Antietam bad—corn husks as bandages for wounds—but even that did not prepare us for reports of Gettysburg. Citizens asked to help bury the dead. Unnamed bodies rupturing in summer's heat; maggots eating flesh. What kind of nation produces such carnage? On its own people?

Some say there will be *corporeal* reunion in heaven: bodies purified, mothers reunited with sons. I take little interest in such miracles. But Delilah maintains awe at what cannot be fully understood. One night she read aloud from John, chapter 9, and asked, "Why was that man born blind?"

I responded dully. "Why ask questions that have no answer?"

"Think of it," she said, "Jesus healed on the Sabbath and surprised folks. More so, some were *offended* at the miracle of clay to the eyes."

"They wanted a known sinner," Abigail said. "The man born blind or his parents."

"Some named *Jesus*," Delilah said, "at fault for *working* on the Sabbath."

"Or the *parents*," Abigail repeated.

"The blind one became a believer," I said. "That is all we need to know."

"But others could not hear or see," Delilah said.

"No explanation," I said. "Why pretend to make sense?"

"They *thought* they saw, but they did not truly recognize Jesus," Delilah said.

"Confusing, when rules are broken." I stood to make ready for bed.

Abigail looked at me cross-eyed. "Delilah said *not* seeing. Where is your noggin?"

"We are to believe," Delilah said. "Not only look to Moses."

"As disturbing as this war," I said. "Where to pinpoint blame; where to find hope."

Delilah's voice stayed calm. "God can do what we do not expect. We are to look for the Almighty's hand. The man in the story did what Jesus told him to do."

I drained my bedtime cup of milk. "What difference for us?"

"Sit down, Father; be not so hasty. Things inside out. *I am come into this world that* they which see not *might see; and that* they which see *might be made blind.*'"

Abigail clapped her hands.

I shook my head. "Upheaval! Bafflement! And you clap! Our sons are still gone. Am I not right?"

"No, no, you misunderstand. We are *not* to find fault, nor claim better sight. Nor give up, Father. Look beyond the sin that surrounds." Delilah nodded as if fully satisfied.

I sniffed. I do what I see to do, but I do not warble about clear sight.

Last summer Brother Kline commended the Mennonites; they gave eleven barrels of flour and a significant amount of bacon to poor families of Confederate soldiers living in the Brocks Gap area. I felt pained to have erred. Those of us at Flat Rock are closer and should have been the ones to give of our surplus. But I had grown weary with lawlessness prevailing. How was I to know? Only in hindsight I could see it would have been better to have given to the poor, than to have surplus on hand for repeated raids by either army in the fall.

All of summer's disarray wore me down. Lee's men on the highway, enroute to secure Richmond after the disaster at Gettysburg. Imboden and his men, attempting again to drive Federal forces back north. Mosby's men, too, made effort again to break the North's supply lines here. Always this or that movement. How was I to know? What was I to think? Endless caravans of wagons and cattle, trampling.

Adding to the confusion, Brother Kline and Jacob Wine were arrested in August. I did not have to say to Abigail: that could have been me. Our men had gone to the churches in Pendleton and Hardy Counties—usual places for visiting and giving counsel. But unwise. Those parts are now West Virginia and part of the North. *They* could have known . . .

On their return, Jacob stopped at Johnny's house; I never heard why, for it was out of his way. But finishing the travel to his own house never happened as planned, for both men were taken before authorities. They had nothing to hide, of course. Their purpose was to carry out an annual visit of oversight, so they were released without further ado.

But then—there is always more! Six days later Johnny was taken in again for questioning. About this he has said little—tight lips and eyes. But from that point on, he traveled less. Was he issued a threat? A stay of some kind? I do not know. Did he decide on his own to limit his travel north? He said nothing to me. As usual, my concern for his Anna went unasked. How much had she comprehended?

John would rather talk about trees. Yes, trees. He makes comparison to building up the young when he points to my walnut grove near the creek. "Trees that grow in a sheltered place never develop the deep roots of a tree that finds itself bent back and forth in a stormy location." For the latter, he points to my large white oak that sits opposite the pine grove at the entrance to my lane. He looks pleased, as if he has explained all.

Even after we heard in September of the death of a German Baptist— a Bowman!—in Washington County, Tennessee, John preferred to make application to the youth in our church, saying, "They will develop strong muscles from the toil of making hard decisions." I wanted to stop my ears.

As if our youngsters draw strength from going to sleep, knowing one army or another travels somewhere in our Valley. Has John forgotten that the psalmist talks of *green* pastures?

I do not mean to suggest he took lightly the reports of terrible happenings in the eastern part of Tennessee where our daughter lives. We all were sadly touched, and John continued writing letters on our behalf. But he refused to dwell on the negative, commenting instead on the learning someone gained, somewhere.

This Bowman's story distressed me terribly, although I doubt that we are kin. It begins as do so many others: Confederate soldiers came to a man's barn, looking for horses. Even if only *one* soldier was involved, as some say, Bowman's favorite saddle horse was the object of theft. He tried to reason with the intruder, stating the importance of this horse. Our brother is said to have been an outstanding speaker—sixteen years younger than John—and would have doubtless made numerous trips of mercy by horseback.

But here is the part: This Elder Bowman stretched out his hand to touch his horse's mane. Who would not want to extend one last, loving touch? My *Elijah!* But at that movement, the soldier, who had ordered him not to approach, drew his gun and shot our brother dead through the abdomen. Then—here I warn my women to cover their ears. The man struck our brother's skull with the butt of his pistol. All for reaching to offer a tender goodbye. I was heartsick. I looked at Ruby and gave her an extra scoop. I touched my forehead to hers; she nuzzled back.

The lawlessness that pervades around here has been limited to petty theft like what we experienced in the spring of 1862: nuisance-taking of grain, snatching a harness left at the ready. There is no way to know who writes crude sayings on my barn. These annoyances I can overlook. *Take a hen, if you must. But do not harm my women.*

But others, overwrought, have set up elaborate schemes to catch the man who comes a second day to take another half sack of ground corn. Why spend hours seeking to ensnare a thief? He might have great hunger in his family. Or far worse, he might be part of the Linville Partisan Rangers. I do not want to come up against a local! What would I do if later, I found myself face-to-face with the same man, reselling my grain for his profit? That is not for me. I have heard enough heckling from Winfield.

The smugglers continue unabated, too, wreaking havoc while taking great risk. Long into cold winter, they carried heavy loads while traversing mountain terrain, often made slippery by rain or snow, eager to sell musket and pistol caps at a high price. Or they toted this new Yankee rifle, a Spencer carbine that needs far less reloading. Enough desperate citizens have given incentive to these seedy merchants by paying large sums. How foolish to think they are safer with more ammunition! The prices should be sufficient to scare anyone away from purchase. Even a harmless spool of thread fetches outlandish profit. At the start of the war, I could purchase one for five cents in Harrisonburg; a year ago already, that same item sold for five dollars.

If someone is caught peddling such Northern goods, he is to be arrested on the spot. Yet some think it patriotic for men to ensure these goods get through. The inequities abound! These smugglers become wealthy, while underlings in the army are paid ten dollars a month.

But that was not the worst news for me. Late last year, the *Rockingham Register* reported that a William E. Coffman had been court-martialed at Harrisonburg; he was to be hanged exactly one week before Christmas Day, between the hours of nine a.m. and four p.m. His offense? Being a pilot. Yes, helping deserters from the Confederate Army escape to the enemy. He is a married man with children, but the newspaper described him in the vilest of terms: betrayer, depraved, unfit to live, deserving of his fate.

When I first heard that this Coffman had been captured by soldiers under the authority of John Imboden from our Shenandoah Valley, I went at once to see J. M. He knows of my closet set-up and keeps his ear to the ground. He was glad to rest, while his young boys continued sawing firewood. How well I remember those days when Amos and Joel helped me with the same. We would pause to marvel at yellow-to-lavender shades of grain inside split poplar.

"Coffman faces trial in Imboden's camp," J. M. said. "Charged with giving information and intelligence to enemies of the Confederacy—a violation of the 57th Article of War."

"And he will be hanged?"

"Yes, but for a glitch." J. M.'s thatch of straw hair stuck out crosswise under his work hat. "He was found guilty in a military court, but Coffman is a civilian, not a soldier. He was smart to make petition on his own behalf, insisting he had been detained unlawfully." J. M. propped his foot on a felled log and tugged aimlessly on his beard. "Something to remember, I suppose. A new trial set for this month."

I pulled my coat tighter and backed up against a young maple. "I am not well versed in the law. I know, of course, not to testify under oath. That would suggest I might be dishonest other times."

"True enough," J. M. said. "This Coffman made request for a writ of habeas corpus, and two days before he was to be hanged, a judge in the Rockingham County Circuit Court—last name of Allen—awarded him the writ. Suspended his detention and execution."

"I do not—habeas corpus?"

"He asked to be released from unlawful restraint."

"Of course," I said, my boots scuffling at loose brush underfoot.

"As you can imagine, Imboden was furious. Called the writ a technicality and made a dreadful scene, swearing he could have hanged Coffman immediately. Angry at having applied due caution, at the man being given a new trial." J. M. brushed sawdust from one pants leg, then the other. "If it happens again—my guess—Imboden would execute on the spot. He could claim some degree of official authority."

"I have heard tell—the man's temper. I would be a poor one—"

"Yes, incensed that his view was ignored. Felt certain a military court's decision could apply to a civilian. Wanted his brigade present to watch Coffman be hanged."

I took a seat on a large stump, gripped my knees to steady and scrunched my body forward. In my travels with Brother Kline, I have never communicated with the North. Nor have we ever led anyone across mountains. But there is no denying: I knowingly give shelter to men seeking escape from army duty. I could be viewed as an accomplice of sorts, although without monetary benefit. Even today I willingly feed a man wanting freedom—possibly from this very Imboden's command. I shelter a woman, fleeing some owner's strap. Yes, I do that. I will not flinch.

"Not one you want to run into," J. M. said, "this Imboden."

Ever since, I see a hangman's noose dangling at night from the rafters. I close my eyes tighter. When I open again, the image sways.

What choices do I have? Those who escape servitude face far greater risk. So, too, those who desert. *Die in battle or die seeking to escape death in battle.* Before Stonewall Jackson's untimely death, he had ordered two soldiers from Rockingham County shot for their escape from the army. Since then, as more men see the folly of the Southern cause, the numbers on the run have increased. Desperate men turn to desperate means, attempting to cross lines.

Word gets around as to where the safe houses are. Some would call my barn a depot; Winfield would call it a Union rat hole. Yes, I do that much—my defenseless head, offering some *small benefit to a few.* Sometimes I am unaware a desperate one has spent the night; the next morning, Delilah and I see straw matted in a manner different than we left it. I no longer tell Abigail of every vagabond or every missing ham. This war compels secrecy on many counts. She does not need to know about the broken padlock.

But one of the men we harbored was a Dietz by name. He turned out to be a peaceful one, caught in the web of a past conscription obligation. We took him inside. *A little aid.* Tall, with a face full of pockmarks, he did not mind being scrunched in the closet with the sweet potatoes. After he ate his fair share for two weeks and our relations became familiar, Abigail remarked, "You have eaten enough to clear a larger space for your pallet."

He stayed in good humor and wanted to help with harvest. But it became a nuisance; he had to rush inside at every sound of hoofbeats. Delilah and I became as skittish as he, to the point that we both preferred he stay inside and help Abigail with kneading dough or peeling apples. Before it turned too cold, the two of them sat on milk stools in the barn and plucked feathers from our small flock of ducks. Abigail insisted we needed a better pillow for Dietz or the next traveler who might sleep in the closet. Dietz had a quick jerk of the wrist that removed feathers faster than I ever could. I do not like to hurt any of my fowl friends.

At night, I watched him play checkers with Delilah and thought a spark might grow. I determined to overlook his being a Mennonite. How we wish she might find a companion! Sometimes they sang a line or two together: *"I'm but a stranger here, Heav'n is my home . . ."* She usually was the one, kept him in tune better, but he also taught her a new chorus he learned when with soldiers a month. We all learned it; the two of them sang it so much.

> *Weeping, sad and lonely*
> *Hopes and fears, how vain . . . praying*
> *When this cruel war is over,*
> *Praying! That we meet again.*

Delilah asked one time, "Are there verses?"

But he snapped his head like he was plucking a feather. "Each side sings different words."

I never heard more than the chorus.

In the end, Dietz secured a pass from a Union official near New Market and set off down the Valley to Winchester. Young men have more pressing matters to think on these days than burdening themselves with the duties of a new household. He spoke warmly of an uncle in Maryland, but his eyes stayed on Delilah. We could only offer blessing. We watched him out the lane.

Now he is on our list of those we pray for daily: our boys, Lila, other Visitors. That is how we refer to the travelers who come inside and go again. The Visitor who had red scabs and stubby fingernails. The Visitor who would not eat eggs. Dietz always stayed Dietz. *A little aid freely given.* Along the lines of *aiding and abetting,* whether or not—

After receiving two letters from our boys last spring, we have heard nothing more from Joel and Amos. *Oh, my boys!* What have they been put through? Have they had to stoop? I would not care at all, if they cut off their long beards to better disguise. How many nights have they gone hungry?

Delilah sent several letters again in the fall, but to no avail. Abigail has ceased her wailing; I am the one who lets slip exasperation, even despair.

Conditions for all our men have darkened with conscription laws tightening. Already back in September, officers threatened to extend the noose of military service to all males, ages *sixteen* through *sixty*. That proposal met with strong opposition, but last month Jefferson Davis took up the drumbeat again. Finally, on the next-to-last day of 1863, they annulled the law that allowed for the use of substitutes. Just as Winfield had warned! Those who had paid for a substitute were subject to the draft again. There is no doubt: the system has been abused. A wicked one may serve a short time, only to desert and move to another area where someone else hires the same man. Brokers have added to the inequities also. J. M., not one to exaggerate, knows of a wealthy man who had to pay $3,000 for a substitute last year.

In December, our Brothers Moomaw and Beyerly went before legislators in Richmond again to keep our position clear. Few civil service positions remain; only one postmaster is needed per area. Some of our men have been detailed to haul iron and ore for Senator Lewis's Furnace in Rockingham County. But what good can be said for work as teamsters? Whether furnishing niter to the Confederate government or making shoes for soldiers, our men are forced to contribute to the war effort. I will not be surprised if our few spry ones who remain will have to flee again before crops can be planted. Next thing we know, authorities could remove the exemption for ministers! *Nothing is impossible.* Not for those who want to put a crimp on our faithfulness.

Can anyone blame me, shivering in this cold hood of winter? What good, a new year?

What will *we* do—my women and I? If forced to depart this beloved Valley, *where* would we go? Only a fool would seek permission to take a boat back to the Old Country. It would not be safe with our daughter in Tennessee. Go to Maryland? But where? Pointless to set out for Iowa when we hear nothing. I will *not* flee alone, not abandon Abigail and Delilah. One night I dreamed we sought escape together, all dressed in my clothes, made smaller for Abigail, larger for Delilah.

My daughter remains my anchor, though bereft of companionship and attracted to baffling questions. She does better than I, holding on to hope. Sometimes I hear *"Weeping, sad and lonely . . . Praying."*

And last week she surprised me. I first noticed a different odor when she brought the hot loaves in from the oven, but she said nothing. When Abigail cut slices, no mention was made. I held up a piece, though, and sniffed at flecks. Still, neither woman showed a hint of interest.

But when I tasted, Abigail says I broke into a smile the length of our lane. I have never tasted such little bits of bitter with the sweet. "Ohh," I said. "Where did you ever—?"

"Delilah thought to try dill seed," Abigail said, slabbing butter on her slice.

"A little onion added also," Delilah said.

"And curd." Abigail smiled and clapped her hands.

I stood at once and gave her a hug and a kiss upon the cheek. I nuzzled Delilah on the forehead, more tenderly, even, than is my custom with Ruby.

Author's Note - Spring 2020

Historical fiction is a strange blend. The extremes of each, history as sacred truth and novels as dangerous fabrications, would seem to make the two incompatible in any satisfying way. Of course, neither view is accurate in its overgeneralized assessment. Historical accounts vary, whether from two onlookers describing an accident scene a week ago, or two historians writing about what happened in the American Civil War. As with any topic, perspective and vantage point are crucial.

When I first started meshing history and imagination, I read and made notes about the basic factually-substantiated events of the Civil War. From this work I identified happenings and people who interested me most, including where Anabaptist civilians lived at the time and faced the most personal turmoil or consequential impact from national events. I made subjective choices of focus, avoiding overlapping stories and finding geographical locations that could broaden readers' awareness of the war's reach.

From there, I determined what characters would best carry the stories that haunted or intrigued me. As you may know from my Book I notes, some of my characters are based on historical people; others come from my fictional musings, knowing of actual experiences. Characterizations developed through research and imagination, showing up in physical appearance, quirky habits, and distinctive voices. What developed became the building blocks of my writing knowledge.

As a historian, I interpret as I write. As a fiction writer, I want history to be appealing in the storytelling; I invent scenes and dialogue to show personalities and conflicts. I want characters to act and sound like people the reader knows and may have read about in the past, complete with laudable qualities and flaws. Careful readers determine whether fact and fiction are served in the combination of all these elements.

Another fascinating aspect of these three books in a series comes from how they are constructed individually. Book I, *Shadows*, uses a more traditional structure with conflict building near the end. The historical record provides this naturally with heightened interactions between Anabaptist civilians in the Shenandoah Valley and soldiers who camped nearby. By May 1862, army units had moved elsewhere and conflict tapered off in the Valley. But characters elsewhere felt increasing pressure that spring, realizing that the war wasn't going to be over as quickly as they had once expected. By the end of the first book in the trilogy, some conflicts have moved toward resolution in the overall story, but far more counter-movements unsettle the reader.

The pattern of increasing and decreasing angst occurs repeatedly in Book II, *Loyalties*, with mini-high points of tension at one location, followed by some leveling off of stress for a particular character. At the same time, fear builds for a character elsewhere, because of increasing draft calls. This zigzag pattern of conflict in individual lives and at separate locations takes place against the larger backdrop of three main battles affecting Anabaptist civilians and developing from the fall of 1862 through 1863: Antietam, Vicksburg, and Gettysburg. As the national furor of war and loss of life threatens to overwhelm, civilians face greater uncertainty and distress. Any sense of *final* resolution is impossible at the end of Book II, even though there's a wintertime lull and major battles have favored the North in terms of "victory." Instead, the accumulation of pressure still builds: How will this war ever cease?

Even if the reader knows what's going to happen in the historical framework, the fictional suspense stays high. What will happen to characters who have been woven into the story? What parts of human nature will prevail? Who might lose the fight, while others survive? And what will those general terms of winning and losing mean in this story? The fiction has become wrapped in realistic life.

Finally, I want to comment on my choice of a poem from Emily Dickinson for the epigraph of this book. Her written expressions from the standpoint of a civilian during the American Civil War have been widely overlooked. Of course, she has been recognized for writing about death, but not specifically about death during wartime, even though nearly half of her poems were written from 1861–1865. Historically, her father was an abolitionist; her brother Austin paid $500 for a substitute. She was not at all removed as a recluse from the Civil War, but rather, her poems weren't printed until in the 1890s. Indeed, in her "Autumn" poem she tells the truth "slant" and doesn't romanticize what happens in war. Her lines move far beyond describing a season; they are filled with metaphoric images from the war and its human costs. She read and knew; she too, imagined.

Acknowledgments

Writing a book is far from a solitary process. Of course, there are days of work where no outside influences interfere with my stream of writing, thinking, and revising. But whether I turn to the dictionary or internet, to a current bestseller about race in America or parts of Frederick Douglass's *Narrative of a Slave*, I'm always working among sources that require interpretation and that find new life in the pages of this book.

My debt to many institutions grows from receiving small grants at UW-Whitewater to accessing library holdings that feature Anabaptist history on the campuses of Goshen College and Eastern Mennonite University. Elsewhere, I recall walking through a display of American Civil War guns at a museum in Virginia, of spending a morning at a history museum in Chicago and understanding better the lumberyard and warehouse areas along the Chicago River.

Many people assisted me during times of research: Lois B. Bowman, Denise Ehlen, Lois Gugel, John Roth, and Joe Sprunger, along with unnamed library assistants who helped me find material in the library stacks or in file boxes at church archives. People gave generously of their time and wisdom from their own research and stories: Christopher and Marti Eads, James Lehman, Steve Nolt, Paul Roth, Marie and Paul E. Yoder. Countless people offered their own favorite story from the American Civil War or church history. Curiosity and exploration became part of an expanding circle, from eastern Pennsylvania with Mary and Merlin Grieser, to the Shenandoah Valley with Sarah Piper and family, to my multiple trips at different times of the year along today's Rt. 50 in West Virginia. Whether investigating the Harriet Beecher Stowe museum in Cincinnati with Carol Lehman, visiting a horse farm in Indiana with Joanne Yoder, or exploring southeastern Iowa cemeteries, I've become more educated about the richness of experience in the American Civil War.

No thanks could be stronger than my gratitude for questions, comments, and encouragement by early readers of the long manuscript: Marilyn Durham, Alex Hancock, Carol Lehman, and Andrea Wallpe. Later, Firman

Gingerich, Brenda Smith White, and Wesley White added their responses from reading other drafts. Influence on the shape of the manuscript also came from Lisa Weaver and the UW-Madison Writers' Institute (2019). I'm indebted to Susanne Gubanc for further development of my website, new videotaping, and publicity ideas. I also remember fondly the inspiration among fellow writers and artists at the 2016 Glen Workshop, Santa Fe, New Mexico, especially from fiction workshop leader Suzanne Wolfe. I hold much appreciation also for others who have assisted with formatting and miscellaneous computer help: Jodi Brown, Alice Schermerhorn, and Steve Tomasko, as well as Hannah Sandvold for creating charts and Jeanie Tomasko for designing maps. Joanie Eppinga ably handled the copy editing of these chapters, and Mark Louden again supplied Pennsylvania Dutch words and their spellings. Many professionals at Wipf and Stock Publishers added their expertise in moving the manuscript through various stages to publication.

As always, for the errors that have survived, I remain fully responsible.

CREDITS

(first words of quoted material and sources, if not identified in the text)

"All quiet along" begins the song first published as, "The Picket Guard," and written by Ethel Lynn Eliot Beers. Available under Creative Commons Attribution-ShareAlike License.

"Children, Go Where" and the word pattern of "two by two," come from an African-American slave song by an unknown writer.

"A divinity shapes our end" is from William Shakespeare's *Hamlet*.

"Hide me, O my Savior" are words in Charles Wesley's hymn, "Jesus, Lover of My Soul," as found in *Papers from the Elder John Kline Bicentennial Celebration*.

"How firm a foundation," words written by George Keith in his hymn "Protection," are found in the Mennonite *Church Hymnal*.

"I do not ask the wounded person" is in section 33 of Walt Whitman's "Song of Myself."

"I'm but a stranger here" comes from Thomas Rawson Taylor's hymn by that title.

"Like a motherless child" are words in an African-American spiritual known by the title, "Sometimes I feel like a Motherless Child."

"O, for a closer walk with God" are words of William Cowper's in the hymn by that name in the Mennonite *Church Hymnal*.

"Oh, you dead . . ." comes from S. Wilkeson's report from Headquarters Army of the Potomac on July 4, 1863, as found in *The New York Times Complete Civil War, 1861–1865*, edited by Harold Holzer & Craig L. Symonds, published by Black Dog & Leventhal, New York, 2010.

"On Jordan's stormy banks" begins the African-American spiritual written by Samuel Stennett that includes the refrain words "Bound for the promised land."

"Sure he'll come again," "cheer my weeping eye," and "Yo! ho! Yo! ho!" are in the song "Southern Soldier Boy" written by Captain G. W. Alexander.

"We Are Coming, Father Abra'am" is the title that uses the same words by James S. Gibbons. Available under Creative Commons Attribution-Share-Alike License.

"Weeping, Sad and Lonely," the well-known title used by the North side, compares with the slightly different words found in the South side's version, "When this Cruel War is Over," written by Charles Carroll Sawyer and licensed by Creative Commons Attribution-ShareAlike.

"What if you slept . . ." are the first words in Samuel Taylor Coleridge's poem, commonly known by the same name.

"(What like a bullet can undeceive!)," found in Herman Melville's poem *"Shiloh: A Requiem."*

(first words of Scripture references, KJV, if not identified in the text)

Gen 9:6 – "Whoso sheddeth man's blood"

Exod 20:13 – "Thou shalt not kill."

Matt 5:38 – "an eye for an eye"

Matt 5:44 – "Love your enemies"

Matt 6:9 – "Unser Vater, der du bist in Himmel"

Matt 10:11, 16 – "Into whatsoever city" and "Behold, I send you forth"

John 9:39 – "I am come . . . that *they* which *see* not"

John 13:34 – "A new commandment I give"

2 Cor 8:12 – "according to that a man hath"

1 John 4:18 – "Perfect love casteth out fear"

Rev 13:10 – "He that killeth with the sword"

Glossary of Pennsylvania Dutch and German

Ach, du Kind! – Oh, my child!

Befreiung – deliverance

Biblia Pentapla – five Bible translations

Brockelsupp – bread soup

Das Christliche Volksblatt – title of newspaper: *The Christian People's Paper*

der alter Henner – the older Henry

Der Paep is fatt! – Poppa is gone!

Der Paep is widder do! – Poppa is back again!

Deutscher Bund – German Confederation

Dieners-Versammlung – ministers' meeting

Du hast Stolz! – You have pride!

Du glenner Keffer! – You little bug!

en dunkler, finschderer Weg – a dark, darksome road

Fernweh – longing for far-off places

Ferwas hoscht net? – Why did you not?

Gemüths-Gespräch – Mennonite catechism

gfaehrlich – perilous

Gott is gut. – God is good.

Hungrichi Mannsleit zelle sich bicke. – Hungry men will stoop.

Ich vergeb dich, mei Kind. – I forgive you, my child.

Ja – yah

Middaagesse – noon meal

Mir kumme aus. – We will make do.

Nimmand dutt was gwhenlich is! – Nobody does what is normal/usual!

O, Gott, hilf uns. – Oh, God, help us.

O, nee, mei Kind. – Oh, no, my child.

Saag mir recht. – Tell me true.

schpuckich – spooky

Schtopp grad nau! – Stop at once!

schtruwwelich – stringy or disheveled hair

Sell is en Sege! – That is a blessing!

Unser Vater, der du bist in Himmel – Our Father who art in heaven

verhuddelt – confused

Verschtehscht? – Understand?

Wehrlosigkeit – defenselessness

Wer wees devun? – Who knows of this (careless behavior)?

CPSIA information can be obtained
at www.ICGtesting.com
Printed in the USA
BVHW041916100921
616557BV00018B/336